Praise for

BRIGHT LIGHTS, BIG CITY

"Exuberantly comic."
—NEWSWEEK

"One of the biggest surprise best sellers in years."
—THE SATURDAY REVIEW

"Remarkable. . . . McInerney has an incredible ability to pack more substance into one sentence than most writers are able to convey in ten. . . . He is, in short, a born novelist from whom, I hope, we'll be hearing more and more."
—MADEMOISELLE

"Engagingly modest, funny, perfectly balanced."
—THE NEW YORK REVIEW OF BOOKS

"Short, sleek and very funny. . . . Beneath its surface, though, a heart's cry for a saner, sweeter, more thoughtful and restrained existence."
—RICHARD FORD,
THE CHICAGO TRIBUNE BOOK WORLD

"Hilarious."
—THE WALL STREET JOURNAL

"A rambunctious, deadly funny novel that goes right for the mark—the human heart."
—RAYMOND CARVER

"Smart, economical, beautiful. . . . Think of it as a *Catcher in the Rye* for the M.B.A. set."
—PLAYBOY

"A dazzling debut, smart, heartfelt, and very, very funny . . . calls to mind such classics of knight-errantry as *The Ginger Man* and *The Bushwhacked Piano*."
—TOBIAS WOLFF

JAY McINERNEY'S
RANSOM

ALSO AVAILABLE IN VINTAGE CONTEMPORARIES

Airships *by Barry Hannah*

Bright Lights, Big City *by Jay McInerney*

The Bushwhacked Piano *by Thomas McGuane*

Cathedral *by Raymond Carver*

The Chosen Place, the Timeless People *by Paule Marshall*

Dancing Bear *by James Crumley*

Dancing in the Dark *by Janet Hobhouse*

The Debut *by Anita Brookner*

A Fan's Notes *by Frederick Exley*

Far Tortuga *by Peter Matthiessen*

A Handbook for Visitors from Outer Space *by Kathryn Kramer*

Norwood *by Charles Portis*

A Piece of My Heart *by Richard Ford*

Something to Be Desired *by Thomas McGuane*

Taking Care *by Joy Williams*

The Wrong Case *by James Crumley*

RANSOM

A NOVEL BY

Jay McInerney

Vintage Contemporaries

VINTAGE BOOKS · A DIVISION OF RANDOM HOUSE · NEW YORK

*I am grateful to Syracuse University,
its English Department and the Trustees of
the Cornelia Carhart Ward Fellowship
in Creative Writing for their
generous support.*

A Vintage Original, September 1985
First Edition
Copyright © 1985 by Jay McInerney
Library of Congress in Publication Data
McInerney, Jay.
Ransom.
(Vintage contemporaries)
"A Vintage original."
I. Title
PS3563.C3694R3 1985   813'.54   85-40151
ISBN 0-394-54995-3
ISBN 0-394-74118-8 (pbk.)
Manufactured in the United States of America
Author photo
copyright © 1985 by Marion Ettlinger
Courtesy *Esquire*

FOR MERRY

RANSOM

1

When Christopher Ransom opened his eyes he was on his back, looking up into a huddle of Japanese faces shimmering in a pool of artificial light. Who were these people? Then he placed them. These were his fellow karate-ka, members of his dojo. And there stood the sensei, broad nose skewed to the left side of his face, broken in the finals of the Junior All-Japan Karate Tournament fifteen years ago. Ransom was pleased that he could recall this detail. Collect enough of the details and the larger picture might take care of itself.

The sensei asked if he was okay. Ransom lifted his head. Turquoise and magenta disks played at the edge of his vision. He was hoisted to his feet; suddenly the landscape looked as if it was flipped on its side, the surface of the parking lot standing vertical like a wall and the façade of the gym lying flat where the ground should be. Then the scene righted itself, as if on hinges.

The sensei asked him what day it was. The surrounding darkness indicated night, but which night? Ransom thought it was Friday, and said so. The narrowness of the sensei's eyes and mouth Ransom took to signal annoyance, although it was hard to tell. He had less range of expression than the average household pet. Ransom looked away. Obviously he had fucked up. He had been knocked down, and one did not get knocked down except through an abdication of vigilance. It was axiomatic that you got what you deserved. Ransom tried to remember how he'd gotten his. His left temple throbbed painfully. He recalled that he had been sparring with Ito. Despite the ache in his temple, he experienced a warm sense of relief that the match was over and the results no worse than this. The pain was fading and he was relatively intact.

"Mawashi geri," the sensei said, specifying the gambit to which Ransom had proved susceptible—a reverse roundhouse kick. The sensei mimed Ransom's last moments of consciousness, dangling his arms beside his hips and rolling his head idiotwise. He told Ransom his guard was low and that Ito had faked with a left. Ransom nodded. Divided between chagrin and relief, he hoped only the chagrin was showing. The last time he sparred with Ito he'd been kicked in the balls and was sick for three days.

The others stood around him, absorbing the lesson of his failure. Ito stood with his hands folded across his crotch, distant and innocent. Ransom wanted to remove his front teeth with extreme prejudice. At the same time he felt humble, contrite. He wanted to be as good as Ito. Going up against him was a way of learning quickly. Ransom reminded himself that there was nothing personal in Ito's violence. He was a pure instrument of the discipline, a regular martial arts batting machine.

The arrival of Yamada was a merciful diversion. Yamada's Nissan 240Z squealed around the corner and stopped sharply just short of Ransom's motorcycle. Yamada jumped out and stripped off his shirt, bowing repeatedly and begging the sensei's pardon as he approached the group. He quickly donned his gi, then dropped to his knees on the asphalt in preparatory meditation. The sensei narrowed his eyes still further. A general restlessness spread while everyone watched Yamada and waited for the sensei's next command. Ransom tried to regain bearing and dignity with a few high kicks. The others stretched and shadow-boxed. The spotlights from the gym cast their elongated forms against the wall of the adjoining building. Ito alone stood perfectly still, his eyes barely open.

The sensei would sometimes pause like this for minutes. At first Ransom suspected absentmindedness, but by now he realized that the sensei was managing the tension and energy of his students. The present caesura seemed directed toward Yamada, whose nearly consistent tardiness, Ransom thought, was beginning to erode the sensei's patience.

When Yamada finished stretching, the sensei called his name and Ito's. Two points, no restrictions—no restrictions meaning that the head as well as the body was a target, although you were supposed to pull your hits short of the face. The others formed a circle some ten feet in diameter around them, and the younger boys were visibly excited

5

by the prospect. For his part, Ransom was glad to see Ito fight somebody besides himself.

They faced off. Ito crouched low in a cat-leg stance, his weight all back on the right leg, the left leg cocked in front of him, toes pointed for the kick. There seemed to be no straight lines or acute angles in his posture, his limbs tracing a series of S-curves. Almost six feet, and thin, he had the build of a basketball player and the flexibility of a gymnast. In his current posture he looked weightless, as if the breeze might waft him away at any moment. Yamada, on the other hand, had the aspect of a Patton tank. He held his arms nearly straight out from the turret of his massive shoulders. He looked martial, whereas Ito appeared serene, almost sleepy. Both held the same rank, but they appeared to be practicing distinct, incompatible disciplines.

Yamada had done most of his training at another dojo, a Shotokan school, and had joined here only two years ago, shortly before Ransom did. Shotokan was a hard school, and Yamada's karate was based on straight thrusts and relentless attack. By comparison Ito's karate, the sensei's karate, was circular and fluid. The school was Goju: hard-soft, based on a notion of alternating tension and relaxation, systole and diastole. The style combined hard Okinawan techniques and the more flexible Chinese kempo. At least so Ransom, with his imperfect Japanese, had gathered. Whatever it was, Ito had it down, with an emphasis on the soft techniques. He turned his opponents back on themselves. It was always hard to remember how he had gotten you. The last thing you remembered was thinking you had him.

The difference was also a matter of temperaments. Yamada was rough and garrulous; Ito had the demeanor of a monk on Quaaludes. Ransom thought of him as the Monk.

When he had begun, trying to learn the basics while keeping his face intact, Ransom used what he had—his relative size and strength. In this he was like Yamada, who was built like a weightlifter. The sensei was always shouting at both of them to stop *boxing*. Ransom found Yamada and his karate to be congenial, more accessible; but Ito, in his foreignness, came to be his model. The Monk embodied something Ransom did not understand: a larger set of possibilities than the pursuit of, say, football or golf. Ransom knew that eventually, with practice, he could do what Yamada did, which was a sophisticated form of kick-boxing. But he aspired to that which he did not know he could do. He didn't just want to be good. He wanted to be transformed.

This ambition did not necessarily make facing the Monk in combat any easier.

Yamada feinted with a jab to the face. Testing the waters. The Monk didn't move. Yamada launched a barrage of front kicks, the Monk retreating and sweeping the kicks away with rhythmic forearm strokes. The kicks had enough force to break an arm, but Ito finessed the contact, making it sound like distant clapping. Yamada followed with a combination of front jabs. The canvas sleeves of his gi snapped crisply on the rebound. Then they were both still, holding their original stances, the distance between them just longer than a kick. Yamada attacked again. Ransom didn't see the opening until the Monk had already filled it. When Yamada reached on a jab, bending forward from the waist, Ito snapped a kick into his gut.

The sensei called the point. They faced off again. Yamada noisily drew breath, and then, grunting, expelled it. For some minutes they stood perfectly still, watching each other's eyes. Yamada was going to try to wait Ito out. The Monk made waiting seem like the smart strategy. He seldom initiated attack. Now, though, he threw a kick. Yamada smashed it down and followed with two front kicks and a roundhouse, all of which the Monk slipped away from. Yamada's was basically a machine-gun strategy: spray the target area. The Monk was a marksman who fired few rounds.

Yamada's arms had dropped during his barrage. The Monk aimed a front jab at Yamada's face, but was knocked backwards by a kick to the chest before he could deliver it. Propelled back into the spectators, the Monk quickly resumed his fighting stance.

The winning point was so quick Ransom wasn't sure he had seen it. He heard the snap of the Monk's sleeve, saw Yamada's head jerk back. They exchanged bows.

Ransom was anticipating final calisthenics and a shower when the sensei called his name. He felt a sudden terrible plummet of spirit, an ominous premonition of vacancy in the bowels.

Sparring, one point, the sensei said. *Ito and Ransom.*

Ransom smiled inquisitively as if he had not comprehended the announcement or else expected revision. He then bowed to the sensei and took his place opposite Ito in the circle. He bowed to his opponent, keeping his eyes

8

fixed on Ito's, because you should never drop your guard, and because the fight was often determined, before the blows were struck, by the eyes; then slowly lowered himself into a ready stance, wishing to prolong the process indefinitely with meticulous adjustments of posture, weight, balance, stance; noting the smell of pork and garlic from the noodle shop across the street and hearing the metronomic progress of a Ping-Pong game from a room within the gym. The same breeze that chilled the sweat inside Ransom's gi lifted Ito's cowlick aloft. Ransom inhaled deeply and expelled the air in forced bursts from his diaphragm. He inhaled again and told himself that his fear was right there, balled in his lungs. He blew it out with the bad air. Then it was time to fight.

Ransom bent down in order to get his head under the jet of the shower. The cold water focused the ache in his forehead and numbed his scalp. Someone banged on the wooden door of the stall for him to hurry up.

He was changing into his street clothes when the Monk approached and asked if he was all right. During practice any gesture of concern would have been irrelevant and insulting, but now it was okay. Ransom assured the Monk that he was fine and that it was his own fault anyway.

You're improving, Ito said. *The second bout you almost scored with that mawashi geri. Soon you'll be defeating me.*

Ransom protested that he was a rank beginner, although he was in fact rather proud of his second bout. What he told Ito, however, was something to the effect that he was no good and never would be. The Monk disagreed. He was already good enough for a kuro obi, the black belt.

Oh, no, not at all, Ransom protested.

This was all terribly Japanese.

The Monk bowed and said goodbye. Yamada was towelling off beside the door of the gym, telling the high school boys about a cabaret he had been to the night before. The sensei approached from behind, smoking a cigarette. With his free hand he grabbed one of Yamada's arms and twisted it until he went down, his cheek almost flush against the asphalt.

He let go and said, *Don't leave your back exposed like that.* He asked Yamada why he was late for practice and Yamada muttered something about his job.

The sensei turned to Ransom. *You wanted to talk?*

Beg your pardon?

The sensei said, *Before practice you said you wanted to talk.*

Ransom remembered, sickly, that he had wanted to ask about the kuro obi. This was an unfortunate time to raise the subject. For months his confidence had been accruing. He was staying on his feet, staying on his toes, mastering through rote repetition the kata and the kumite—the forms and the fighting—until they began to seem instinctive reflexes of the blood. He was the best in the dojo—after the sensei, the Monk and Yamada—and in any other dojo he'd be a second-dan at least. The sensei did not put much stock in belts. Ransom understood the principle, but he wanted some verification of his progress. Somewhere along the line, the Monk had gotten his black belt and added three grades to it. Yamada had gotten his elsewhere. Everyone else had white belts, Ransom included.

The sensei was waiting, so Ransom asked if his front

kick needed work. The sensei said his everything needed work.

Excuse me for asking, sensei, but, unworthy as I am, do you think that it is possible that in the near future, at some time, I might receive the kuro obi? Or not?

The sensei reached under Ransom's arm and tugged at the obi wrapped around the bundle of his gi, both white. He said something Ransom couldn't make out, and slowly repeated himself. The sensei said, *If you get this obi dirty enough, I'm sure it will turn black.*

I'm serious, Ransom said.

What difference does it make, he asked. *When you're good enough, you won't care what color your belt is. As long as you want it, you're not ready for it.* The sensei lit a cigarette. *If I were you, I'd concentrate on not getting knocked down.*

Ransom bowed. *Thank you, sensei.*

The sensei nodded.

Ransom thanked him again, walked over to his bike and tied his gi on the back. Yamada hailed him from the other side of the lot. Though Ransom liked Yamada more than anyone else in the dojo, tonight he needed quiet and expiation, feeling on the verge of some incremental addition to his knowledge of himself.

Yamada slapped Ransom's shoulder and lit a fresh cigarette from the end of a butt. They chatted for a few minutes, replaying the practice, then walked across the street to the noodle shop. The toothless old sobaya-san bowed as they came in and called out a welcome. The warm interior reeked of pork broth, garlic and tobacco. The sensei sat with some of the others at a corner table. On the walls were photographs of him—holding trophies, shaking hands with the mayor, smashing a stack of pine boards with his fist. Kojak was on the television set over the counter, speaking perfect, lip-synched Japanese. You can run, Ransom thought, but you can't hide. You don't even have to go home again. His father was one of those listed in the credits. After his first karate practice, Ransom had come here with his new comrades, suffused with the glow of initiation into a foreign sect; following his introduction to the aged, somewhat shabby proprietor, he had glanced up and seen his father's name on the television screen.

Ransom sat down next to the sensei. The Japanese-speaking Kojak screamed something that translated, "Get in here, Crocker." Yamada went behind the counter and changed channels. He called for quiet. The face of a game-show MC filled the screen.

Hope you enjoyed our fat girl contest last week, the MC said. *Our winner, Miti Keiko of Hyogo Prefecture, has received a lot of mail since the show, including an invitation to participate in the summer sumo tournament.*

The sensei offered that the champion fat girl looked like Yamada's sister.

Tonight, the MC said, *we have something really special for you.* Ransom didn't catch what came next.

What did he say?

Farting contest, Yamada said.

The four men in director's chairs on the stage introduced themselves: a Keio University student who said his main interest was video games; an office worker from Nagoya who clearly had second thoughts about the whole thing, since he would not look at the camera; a tongue-tied fat man whom the MC finally identified as a Tokyo subway motorman; and a sushi-shop apprentice who kept waving at the camera. Standing beside the fat man, the MC suddenly pinched his nostrils and shouted, *False start.* The fat man squirmed in his chair. *One more and you're disqualified.* The MC flourished an aerosol air freshener.

The fat man took the prize: ten cases of canned sweet beans and a life-sized poster of Olivia Hussey as Juliet. Microphones and matches had helped to determine the outcome. All very tasteful. Coming up next was a man who swallowed live gerbils. Somebody, Ransom thought, ought to save Japan from the Japanese. He hated to admit it, but the crap his father turned out was better than this.

He left at ten and rode home along the river, which rippled with moonlight like the slow bulk of a sleeping reptile. The river looked much better at night, when you couldn't see the submarine garbage and the water's dubious tint. He stopped beside the Imadegawa Bridge and shut down the bike, an aging Honda 350 Scrambler that fashion-conscious Japanese bikers wouldn't be seen dead on. The air coming off the river was cool and rank with effluvia. The moving water made him restless. It was April and he could feel the ferment of soil and flora around him. He was twenty-six years old and he had been in this country almost two years. He felt a keen pang of nostalgia, but he didn't know for what. Maybe for the time before he had realized that good intentions don't make you innocent, for the time when he had less to regret. Ransom wasn't sure if he was waiting for something to happen, or hoping that nothing would. Sometimes he felt he was preparing for some sort of confrontation, and at other times he believed that he had seen enough trouble already.

Ransom kick-started the bike and turned around, retracing part of the route he had just taken, giving in to an urge he had been resisting—for easy company and conversation in his native tongue.

2

Buffalo Rome was the place to go if you hankered to see someone you'd met in Katmandu or Chiang Mai. The Asia pilgrims were a different type from the less druggy Japan hands, professorial students of Muromachi period temple architecture, acolytes of Zen and tea ceremony. The Dharma Bums washed up here after bleary months on the subcontinent, travelling high and dry—ahead of the monsoon rains, behind the cannabis harvest—arriving at this terminus trailing strange stories and doctrines. The Japanese patrons, mostly students whose costumes ranged from beatnik to proto-punk, were here to cop some cool from the various gaijin.

The first person Ransom picked out of the crowd was the narc sitting near the door. Shades, Berkeley sweatshirt and beads. The obvious wig. He smiled when he saw Ransom and snapped his fingers. "Be crazy," he said.

"Rock out, baby," Ransom said.

"Right on." The narc held out his palm and Ransom slapped him five, wondering if there were a special school where these cops were trained, and if so who were the teachers. Buffalo Rome had yet to host a single bust, not that it lacked for drugs; only the mentally impaired could mistake a Kyoto narc for a real person. All this was amusing until you considered the fate of someone busted by sheer luck. The Japanese took dope very seriously, reportedly to the point of beating prisoners on the feet, withholding food for days, interrogating round the clock. Ransom had avoided drugs for some time, so it didn't much concern him now, although thinking about it always made him nervous, reminded him of casualties.

Ransom generally felt slightly tainted after a night at Buffalo Rome. He stayed away for weeks at a time, then went in three or four nights running. That his friend Miles Ryder was co-owner was among the reasons he found for squandering his time and money there. He saw Miles's Stetson above the heads at the bar. As always, returning after a fair absence, Ransom had the impression of great space; the bar was huge by Japanese standards—nearly the size of an indoor tennis court, with a high cathedral ceiling. Before Ryder and his silent partner had turned it into an absurdly profitable watering hole, this had been a sake warehouse. They had set up a bar at one end, a stage at the other and wire spool tables in between.

Miles was talking to a blonde in a white dhoti, and made an elaborate show of greeting Ransom.

"Sensei. We are honored to have you with us. What news from the front?"

"Are you a teacher," the girl asked. A gold ring decorated one side of her nose. "*Sensei* is teacher, right? I did a little studying on the boat from Pusan."

"Right you are," Miles said, "but that's just the beginning. It's a high honorific for which we English speakers have no true equivalent. It means master, doctor, honcho. I bestow it on our friend Ransom, because he is an inspiration to us all, gaijin and Japanese alike."

The girl studied Ransom with interest. "What are you doing here," she asked.

"I hope to slake a mild thirst and an inexplicable urge for company."

"I mean in Japan."

"Ransom is in training for the afterlife," Ryder said. "He is a nonviolent samurai warrior who hopes to qualify as a bodhisattva."

"My boyfriend's back from the bathroom," she said. "I guess I better go see if he's okay. He's had amoebic dysentery ever since Lahore. See you guys later."

"What are you drinking," Miles asked, bowing extravagantly to Ransom.

"Tea."

"On the wagon?"

"Neither on nor off a wagon," Ransom said, irritated. "I just don't drink anymore."

"The people who saw you last Saturday night will be relieved to hear it."

Ransom had quit tobacco and alcohol when he took up karate, with only occasional backsliding in both departments, Saturday night, for instance, involving two Aussie merchant marines and one bottle of absinthe. Some of his most precipitous backsliding involved absinthe. He had thought this beverage the casualty of changing tastes and law, the downfall of French Symbolist poets as well as the source of their twisted visions; but in Japan it was still legal. Naturally, he investigated.

As Miles ducked behind the bar, strains of amplified guitar began to rise through the crowd noise. On the stage, Kano was hunched over the neck of his Gibson, fingering the tuning posts. Ransom smiled. Mitsuhashi thumped the pedal of the bass drum, which bore the roman letters MOJO DOMO. Up front, people were making encouraging noises in English, broken English and rehearsed black dialect. *Play those blues. Get funky. Get down.* The band had a hard-core following, both gaijin and Japanese, and regarded the blues as a spiritual orientation—for them the spirit born in red delta clay out of the souls of black ex-slaves was universal and redemptive. Their Mecca was Chicago. Mojo Domo hoped someday to make a pilgrimage in veneration of the masters—Muddy Waters, Howlin' Wolf, Willie Dixon, Elmore James. Meanwhile, they were fiendish collectors of old Chess and Vee Jay recordings and devoted servants of Muddy Waters, for whom the band had once opened a set in Osaka during his last Japanese tour. Kano breathed his name with a mixture of reverence and chumminess, although Ransom felt that Kano disapproved of Muddy's longevity; Sonny Boy Williamson and Robert Johnson were, in dying young, perfectly immortal. Mojo Domo had been offered recording contracts backing up Japanese pop stars but they refused. They only played blues. Ransom thought them admirable, if faintly comic.

He took a seat at the bar and ordered a cup of tea. A tall, ethereal-looking American he knew only as Eric appeared beside him.

"How's the karate?"

Ransom shrugged.

"You really ought to try aikido," he said. "No offense, but I mean, karate is so violent. In aikido you learn how to overcome through yielding. It's like that game kids do, what do they call it, Paper, Scissors, Rock. Rock dulls the scissors, but paper covers rock."

"You left out the part about the scissors cutting the paper," Ransom said.

Eric assumed an expression at once indulgent and triumphant. "Even in conversation you're aggressive, combative, unyielding."

"You should hear me talk to myself. It's brutal."

Eric ordered a beer and attempted to explain how Ransom could get in touch with his *ki*, the life force, the whole ball of wax. Listening to Eric, Ransom decided that one of the things he liked about the Japanese was their distrust of loquaciousness, their suspicion of language itself, although he wasn't sure what was left if you dispensed with it.

Eric buzzed on and Ransom considered the hollowness of expatriate communities. The individuals might be interesting enough, but they had in common only what they had already left behind. Having exhausted the subject of ki, Eric said goodbye and shuffled off when Miles drifted back.

"DeVito's acting up tonight," Miles said. Ransom followed his gaze to a table where two gaijin were arm wrestling, one of them sporting a samurai haircut. This was DeVito. "I may need you to help me beat him senseless."

"DeVito's already senseless."

"You think you could take him?"

Ransom shrugged. "It's not something I've given any thought to. I don't fight outside the dojo."

"What good are fighting skills if you can't thrash scum like DeVito? What are you supposed to do if someone picks a fight with you?"

"The sensei says the best defense is two feet."

"Kicking ass, right and left. I rest my case."

"Not quite. You run away."

"This took you two years to learn?" Ryder's eyes registered a new point of interest. Ransom turned to look. Marilyn was just inside the door, looking around.

"What's she waiting for?" Ransom said. "A drum roll?"

Ryder waved her over. She didn't move in the tentative and pigeon-toed manner of Japanese women. It seemed to Ransom that she didn't walk like any Asian women he had ever seen. He supposed that she had adopted this bold Western stride in her native Saigon, back when it was an American outpost. Ransom had met her here last Saturday. Ryder, who had met her at the same time, was already infatuated. She was a refugee from Vietnam, she explained, and her real name was Mey-Van. She was a singer in a Kyoto nightclub, where her manager billed her as Marilyn, which, although virtually unpronounceable for the Japanese, had a shamanistic power because of its former attachment to Monroe-san. Marilyn herself much preferred it to Mey-Van.

She and Miles kissed. Ransom stood up.

"Hello, Ransom-san." She looked him over and turned to Ryder. "His breeding is wonderful. It wouldn't occur to you to stand up when a woman enters the room, but Ransom does it in a bar for a woman he doesn't even like."

Ransom was surprised all over again by the quality of her English. Certainly none of his Japanese students could rival Marilyn, even if he worked with them for years. To him her slight accent seemed vaguely French.

"Ransom likes you just fine," Miles said. "Don't you?"

"Who could resist Marilyn's charm?"

The bartender called Miles to the phone. "Keep an eye on my baby," he said to Ransom. Marilyn pulled a cigarette from her purse and hunted for a light. "The only defect in your manners, Ransom, is that you never light a girl's cigarette. But you don't approve of smoking, do you?"

"I gave it up myself."

"And you don't drink?"

"Not much anymore."

"Bit of a bore, aren't you?" She took his hand and fingered the callused knuckles. "Karate." She flipped the hand over and spread the palm open on her knee, as if to read his fortune. "*Kara*—empty. *Te*—hand. Empty-handed Ransom. Is that it? You give up everything for your quest." She leaned close and whispered, "How about girls? Have you given up girls, too?"

"Some girls I have given up in advance," Ransom said.

Marilyn finally produced a lighter and lit her cigarette.

"You know, I asked Miles if you were running from some terrible secret. He's says there is no warrant for your arrest he knows about, no pregnant girlfriend. What is this mysterious problem. You can tell Marilyn." She smiled coquettishly.

"Original sin. I'm Catholic—born and raised guilty."

"I was raised Catholic, too."

"In Vietnam?"

"Yes. Where else."

"That would make you French Catholic, basically. French Catholicism is different. The French are only in it for the art. Cathedrals, paintings, gold chalices. Pomp plus bread and wine. It's a wonder they haven't added cheese to the service. Nothing like the Irish or the Spaniards, who are in it strictly for the self-abuse."

"Which are you?"

"My mother was Irish Catholic."

"Is she religious?"

"She's dead."

"I'm sorry."

"Happened quite a while ago," Ransom said.

"And you? Still a Catholic?"

"Not practicing. But it's not necessarily something you can shake."

Miles reappeared. "What can't you shake?"

"Those old lonesome blues," Ransom said. "Who was on the phone—your wife?"

"What are you, my mother?"

"That's what you have against me, isn't it?" Marilyn said.

Frank DeVito strutted up to the bar, pointedly leering at Marilyn, bringing eyebrows and tongue into play. She stared back belligerently and Miles glowered. Something ugly verged on happening until DeVito turned slowly away and moved to an opening several stools down.

Frank DeVito, ex-Marine and current Bruce Lee clone. Enlisting with the fervent desire to see combat, he got out of basic after they stopped sending Marines to Vietnam. Posted to Okinawa, he acquired a taste for the martial arts and, eventually, a dishonorable discharge, the cause of which was variously attributed to drug trafficking, assault on an officer, assault on an Okinawan schoolgirl. From what he knew of DeVito, Ransom thought assault more likely than drugs, and the schoolgirl more likely than the officer. The rumor was that, despite the discharge, DeVito had wangled a disability pension for an alleged back injury and was thus able to devote his time solely to training. Shortly before Ransom landed, DeVito had come to Kyoto to study at the dojo of a maverick sensei of dubious standing in the karate world who made movies starring himself and who demonstrated his skills by killing oxen barehanded. His disciples, among whom DeVito was prominent, were required to take a blood oath of allegiance and secrecy. DeVito, who modelled his appearance on the old samurai, was embarrassingly eager to please Ransom whenever he didn't choose instead to insult him, his dojo, his sensei and his mother. Ransom was consistent in his dislike of DeVito, who reminded him of grade school misfits who gave you all their toys one day and beat you up the next. His only achievement, in Ransom's view, was his exceptionally fluent Japanese.

"I'm going to boot him out of here," Ryder said, after he had walked away.

"Don't," Ransom said. "It will be a mess if you do. He just wants the attention."

"I hate that fucking Okie."

"He's not worth getting upset about," Marilyn said.

Ransom turned toward the stage. Kano was still tuning his guitar with the intense concentration of a man wiring a bomb. Sato, on rhythm, watched and tuned with him. Bubba, the bass man, née Satoichi Yasuhiro, was rocking back and forth on his heels, ready and waiting. Finally Kano stepped up to the mike and said, "Let's get down and dirty." The gaijin up front hooted and clapped, while the Japanese looked on politely. Kano counted out the beat—"Ichi, ni, san, shi"—and they started into "Got My Mojo Workin'."

Kano had once asked Ransom how he would define *Mojo*, leaving Ransom very much at a loss. When Kano had tried to enlist the guidance of the only black patron of Buffalo Rome, an aikido student from Oakland, he had been told that the blues were strictly Uncle Tom and very uncool. He was shaken, but he kept the faith.

Ransom observed the crowd and half listened to the set. Miles and Marilyn fondled each other's limbs. Ransom couldn't help but feel sorry for Miles's wife, Akiko. On the only occasion when Miles had felt obliged to explain his womanizing, he invoked the when-in-Rome theory, claiming that Japanese women expected no more fidelity than Japanese men delivered. Ransom thought this extremely swinish. He was also suspicious of this Marilyn. He had no reason to doubt she was a Vietnamese refugee, nor that she was a singer in a downtown bar. But he wondered if she didn't do a little after-hours work as well.

When the set was over, Ryder seemed wistful. "If only

I could find a Japanese band that played Hank Williams."

"You've got everything he ever recorded on the juke-box," Ransom said.

"I know. But I'd love to hear that high, lonesome twang in Japanese."

Miles was taking another call in the office, and Marilyn was in the Ladies', when Frank DeVito returned with an empty glass.

"Ransom, you scumbag. I thought it was you. Old handsome Ransom."

Ransom glanced briefly at his fellow American, tonsured in the fashion of a sixteenth-century samurai, the front and sides of his scalp shaved, a long lock of hair doubled over and tied along the ridge of his skull. "Hello, Frank."

DeVito pulled a long face. "*Hello, Frank.* What kind of greeting is that?"

"Sufficient, I'd call it."

"I'd call it unfriendly. What's with the chill here? Fellow karate-ka ought to get along. Are you still hanging out at that wimpy dojo?"

Ransom looked into DeVito's dark eyes but he didn't say anything.

"What do you call that brand of dancing they teach you there? Go-go?"

"Goju."

"Tofu?"

"It's called Goju," Ransom said. "Hard-soft."

"Hard-soft? What's that? Soft guys with hard-ons, or what?"

"The principle works many ways. Like, you apply a hard weapon—say, fist—to a soft area—say, belly."

"Think you're pretty good, don't you?"

"I'm just a student," Ransom said.

"Don't hand me that humility shit. Show me your stuff."

"I've got nothing to show," Ransom said.

DeVito called for a beer. Miles came up behind the bar, watching DeVito intently, and set a bottle on the counter. DeVito lifted his beer and drank off half of it.

Marilyn returned, nodded at the seat beside Ransom and looked at DeVito. "Do you mind?"

"Yeah," DeVito said, still facing Ransom. "You can just wait a minute. There aren't five men in Japan fast enough to knock the neck off of a standing beer bottle."

"There aren't two," Ransom said, "who could care less."

"You think you can do it," DeVito asked.

Ransom raised his hands and flopped them down on the bar. DeVito was the sort who made a personal contest out of a coin toss, invested a game of checkers with the aspect of an epic struggle for survival. A few weeks back he had taken bets and broken one of the spool tables in half. Miles threatened to call the cops, but DeVito had contemptuously turned over his winnings to pay for the table. Because he would stake everything on nothing, DeVito would have been dangerous even if he was weak.

"Let's just see," DeVito said, stepping away from the bar and drawing a deep breath. He closed his eyes and drew his hands up to his chin. Opening his eyes, he swung his right hand, palm open and rigid, in a slow arc that ended at the neck of the beer bottle. Behind him, the onlookers were divided—one could judge from the expressions—between those who admired DeVito's strength and audacity and those who hoped he would slice his arteries and die. People cleared away from the bar. DeVito practiced the move several times, closed his eyes again, and gathered himself up from the shoulders, inhaling violently.

The bottle skidded along the bar, spouting foam, and disappeared over the edge. Miles retrieved it and held it up, intact.

"Great trick," Marilyn said.

DeVito examined his right hand, sorting out his failure, and looked up at Ransom. "Your turn, handsome." He called for another beer. "I want it tonight, not tomorrow afternoon"—drumming his hands on the bar as the bartender reached into the cooler.

DeVito lifted his head back and held the bottle high as he swallowed, then slammed it down in front of Ransom. By this time he was surrounded by spectators, some explaining to others the nature of the challenge.

"Go ahead," he demanded.

"I need a reason," Ransom said. "Even if I could do it, why should I?"

"The thrill of victory. Because it's there. But mostly, because I say you can't do it."

"You're probably right."

DeVito seemed at a loss. "You think you could land a hit on me?"

"I don't think about it at all. I don't spar outside the dojo."

"Try it."

"Not interested."

"How about if I start things off. Is that what it takes?"

Ransom turned away and took a sip of his tea. At the edge of his vision he saw Miles winding through the crowd behind DeVito, then he registered DeVito's move. He dodged quickly enough so that the blow glanced off his shoulder instead of his temple, and saw Miles bring something down on DeVito's head. The impact sounded like a bat connecting with a ball. DeVito slumped to the floor as the bar gradually went quiet. Miles was radiant.

"I didn't want you to break your priestly vow of non-violence," he said to Ransom, ax handle in hand, "so I had to drygulch the fucker. It's my prerogative as owner and proprietor."

Ransom nodded—the brief surge of adrenaline beginning to subside. He knelt down and checked DeVito's scalp and topknot with immense distaste. No blood.

"Last of the Mohicans," Miles said, and laughed.

Together they carried DeVito, now starting to moan, out into the street, depositing him on the sidewalk, followed closely by the two women he'd been sitting with. One of the women cradled DeVito's head in her lap while the other massaged his shoulders.

Inside, the music resumed. The Japanese were still stunned by this American display of violence.

The band started into "Stormy Monday," one of Ransom's favorite songs, and did a creditable cover, but there was always a little trouble with the vocals. Kano's face was red and slick with sweat.

> *They call it stormy Monday, but Tuesday's just as bad.*
> *They call it stormy Monday, but Tuesday's just as bad.*
> *Wednesday's worse, and Thursday's oh so sad.*

Kano plucked his Gibson and winced as if he were tearing the notes out of his chest. He made it through Friday and Saturday admirably the first time, then fumbled the repetition:

The eagle fries on Flyday, Sa'day I go out to pray. Sunday morning, he was playing where he should have been praying.

3

If you were a tourist coming in from the train station en route from Tokyo, you would be prepared for the winged rooflines of ancient temples and the crabbed enigma of ideographic signs. You would have found Tokyo disappointingly modern, but this is Kyoto, the ancient capital, founded in the eighth century, spared the American bombing. From the taxi window, rolling along broad boulevards laid out a thousand years ago, you would see castles and palaces, temples and shrines. But if your hotel were in the southeastern section of the city, you might be brought up short by the prospect of a billboard almost two stories high: a desert landscape in garish oranges and yellows, cacti and cowskulls, presided over by a mounted, golden-maned cowboy with psychedelic eyes, under the legend:

HORMONE DERANGE
Western Goods and Sundries
Hats, Boots and Everything Between
Miles Ryder, Owner and Proprietor

Hormone Derange, sole distributors for Tony Lama boots on the Japanese archipelago, had first opened for business under a more conventional, phonetically similar name. Miles Ryder explained to his friends that he had changed the name to conform with standard Japanese pronunciation. Ryder was the model for the cowboy on the huge billboard atop the storefront, and himself appeared to be based on photographs of Wild Bill Hickok. There was drama in the sweep of his blond hair around his shoulders and in the droop of his mustache on either side of his chin. The black Stetson was habitual. He was something of a legend in Kyoto; besides running two businesses he occasionally appeared on television talk shows and currently was the star of a commercial in which he bellied up to the bar of a saloon and called out for his sake of choice: *Even cowboys like it.* Either out of loyalty to American engineering or concern that a six-foot-two blond gaijin in cowboy togs was not conspicuous enough in Kyoto, Ryder drove a full-dress 1962 Harley-Davidson Electra Glide complete with buckskin saddle bags which he had imported at great expense.

Even before the Friday night in the spring of 1977 when he poleaxed Frank DeVito in Buffalo Rome, Ryder had experience coming upside people's heads with hardwood. In May of 1971—shortly before receiving notice that he had flunked out of the University of Texas, Austin—he had opened a man's skull with a two-by-four in the parking lot of a vast honky-tonk called the Armadillo World Headquarters. The man had inquired of Ryder's date whether she would like to perform a certain sexual act upon him. The sexual act was one which happened to be illegal in the state of Texas. The two-by-four was lying in the bed of a pickup in the parking lot. The man turned out to be a heavily connected dope dealer and sent word from the hospital that Miles Ryder's ass was grass. Miles considered taking his chances with the drug dealer, but the farewell card from the university seemed another good reason to push on.

An additional problem was the draft and his sudden eligibility. Ryder's old man was career Army, and Miles had more than enough military discipline at home. Ryder *père* was then in Vietnam, safely behind the lines, whence he'd sent a snapshot of himself and several buddies with half-a-dozen Saigon whores. Ryder's mother was too numbed by this time to be appalled. Miles had no desire to join his father. With the help of an Eastern Religions prof from whom he had taken a survey, about the only course he enjoyed, he managed to get himself enrolled in a dubious program run out of L.A. that sent people abroad for college credit. He was presently in Japan, at a Zen monastery in the mountains north of Kyoto, sweeping cobblestones, washing dishes and sitting lotus-posture on the floor until his knees screamed with pain. After a month he decided he did not have the patience to wait for satori, quit the monastery, moved to Kyoto and supported himself, like all the other gaijin, by teaching English. The Japanese, he discovered, had a kind of mania for learning English. Businessmen, high school girls—they came after English conversation like it was a drug. Ryder set himself the task of learning Japanese, and his crash program of acculturation culminated in marriage to one of his students, Akiko, who seemed to him to embody all of the traditional virtues of Japanese womanhood. When her parents disowned her for marrying a gaijin, Ryder understood that no matter how good his command of Japanese verbs and their tenses, he would always be one.

His mother, living with a new husband in El Paso, wrote to wish him happiness in his marriage, which was more than she had learned to expect. Wedding presents from friends in Austin included a pair of handmade ostrich-skin boots and a black Stetson with silver and turquoise band. Ryder wore both to the ceremony, and continued to wear them. A year after his marriage he opened the first cowboy supply store in Japan.

The location he found for the store was nearly ideal, on the street car route a few blocks from a major intersection. Rent was reasonable; in fact, it seemed like a steal. Then Akiko told him that the oyabun—literally, father; colloquially, godfather—of the largest yakuza syndicate in Kyoto lived practically next door, in a walled compound guarded by a large detachment of foot soldiers, latter-day would-be samurai, who lounged around the gate comparing shoe shines and fingering dice. They were under strict orders not to harass the local citizenry, on the principle of not fouling the nest. But so much coiled menace was not easily contained. There were incidents. People got pushed around. Missing finger joints testified to the occasional breaches of discipline. Those who called unnecessary attention to the organization atoned by severing one of their own fingers with a sword in the presence of the aggrieved superior, and presenting it, wrapped in silk, with humble apologies. Starting with the little fingers, violent or very stupid subordinates would lose half a hand learning about discipline.

The sentries didn't know what to do when a cowboy appeared at the gate of the compound one day asking to see the boss. Protocol was unclear. There ensued a conference at the gate. Ryder waited, a large gift-wrapped package under his arm. After fifteen minutes he was admitted, and passed through a courtyard of immaculate raked gravel, the kind you saw in the gardens of Zen temples. The house was elegant and austere. Ryder was disappointed, having expected something spectacularly tacky— statues of nude women, pink flamingos. A brawny thug with a marbled face escorted him along the stone walk. The door was opened by an even larger man, who was alarmed when he saw the package. At his command Ryder opened it, taking care not to tear the wrapping paper. He had been in the country long enough to know that the presentation was as important as the present itself.

He was shown to a room at the back of the house, where the man told him to wait, closing the sliding screens behind him. Ryder seated himself on the tatami floor. The room was bare except for a scroll, a pen-and-ink landscape, enshrined in the corner alcove. The sliding glass windows on the south wall overlooked a garden with a fish pond. Orange and white carp cruised the murk beneath a canopy of lily pads.

An hour later the door opened again, and Ryder rose. The man bowed; Miles bowed lower, uncertain if this was the big guy, the oyabun, or just a subordinate. He had a mild, chubby face, wore a dark dress kimono, and looked like someone whose spare time was devoted to calligraphy or stamp collecting. This, Ryder decided, had to be the honcho. An underling would flaunt his authority. They exchanged traditional greetings, Ryder outdoing himself in his employment of polite verb endings and honorifics. His host matched him to a point, finally conceding to Ryder the humbler rung of address. His name was Koyama, Big Mountain. He complimented Miles on his mastery of the language. Ryder protested that he was a rank beginner. He commented on the beauty of the house and garden. Koyama said that the gardener had been sick and apologized for the scruffiness of the grounds. On the contrary, Ryder said, they were immaculate. Koyama took a gold cigarette case from the sleeve of his kimono and offered Ryder a smoke. He accepted. The lighter was also gold, the cigarettes English.

They were still standing and there was some question as to who would sit down first. Koyama asked if Ryder-san would like a chair brought in. No chair necessary, he was assured. Koyama's gestures—lifting the skirts of the kimono as he sat down, tapping the ash from his cigarette into a tiny earthenware ashtray—were almost feminine. Although he was probably a killer, his face bore no indication of his vocation. Ryder felt warm and lazy in the yellow afternoon light. He spoke of the beauties of Kyoto and the graciousness of its inhabitants. Koyama spoke warmly about the American people. He was a great admirer of the

American cinema, especially Westerns. He had a screening room in the house, and prints of *Stagecoach, Red River, High Noon* and *Shane,* among others. Perhaps Ryder-san would be so kind as to view a movie with him someday. Ryder considered telling Koyama how much he liked Japanese gangster flicks, but thought better of it.

After fifteen minutes of chat Ryder said that, sadly, he had to be leaving. Koyama asked him if he couldn't possibly stay longer. Ryder answered that he could not conceivably impose even further. As he stood up, Ryder mentioned that he planned to open a business establishment in the neighborhood and that he hoped to have the good will of his neighbors. He then looked down at the box in his hands, which he had held throughout the interview, as if noticing it for the first time and uncertain of its exact nature. He presented Koyama with the box, along with the ritual incantation that it was a trifle unworthy of his attention. A quick study, Ryder had learned that the smallest gift put an obligation on the receiver; a ploy so simple it was hard to believe it worked so well.

Negotiations for the lease on the store, which had been dragging for weeks, were concluded the next day. The owner of the property fell all over himself when Ryder appeared at his office and enthusiastically conceded on each of the terms that had previously been in dispute.

Ryder's operation was in the black within a year, and he branched out into the drinking business—what the Japanese called the water trade. The demand for Western paraphernalia was greater than even he had anticipated, though he often wondered what happened to all of those Tony

Lama boots, all of those Stetsons. Not once in two years had he seen any of the merchandise on the street, except for the odd piece of Navaho silver and turquoise jewelry which he imported from Afghanistan. Sometimes he imagined Koyama in his screening room, watching *Rio Bravo,* aiming his fingers and making shooting noises, his feet kicked up to reveal beneath the kimono his Dan Post lizard-and-antelope hand-tooled cowboy boots, compliments of Hormone Derange.

Saturday morning, Miles woke up wondering if *he* had been hit from behind. After he closed up at Buffalo Rome, he and Marilyn went dancing and he got home sometime after four. Akiko was chilly as she served his coffee. He was dimly aware of having behaved badly, stepping out on a seven-months-pregnant wife, but in his present state much of his sympathy was reserved for himself. He wished she would fling out an accusation, just to clear the air. But *no,* she wasn't going to dirty herself by naming the stink. Duck-walking around with her pregnancy.

Finally she said, "Isn't today your rally?"

At first he couldn't make sense of the word *rally,* which refused to connect with anything out there in the world. Then he remembered. Ryder was a member in good standing of the All-Japan Harley-Davidson Motorcycle Club, composed of some thousand bikers, most of them pillars of the community throughout the working week, who on Saturday mornings dressed up in Los Angeles Police Department uniforms to ride their Harleys en masse. Once a year the local chapters gathered for the annual spring rally, which this year was convening in Kyoto. Even now they would be assembling in the parking lot at the Holiday Inn. The thought of all that two-cylinder racket was painful. On the other hand, the weird celebrity he enjoyed in the organization was gratifying. Also, the carburetor trouble he'd been having would quickly be diagnosed and corrected by a fellow member. Then he realized that he would have to ask Akiko to watch the shop, which, after last night, seemed too much. Miles Ryder was not entirely shameless.

"I should mind the store."

"I will take care of the store," Akiko said, and he loved her for not saying it in a bitchy way, and for her precise, uncontracted English.

"I'll be back by supper," he said. "We can go out for dinner and then catch a movie. I'll leave the bar to Sato."

"On Saturday?" she said. "It will be very busy."

"We'll have dinner, anyway."

If she was skeptical, she didn't say anything. Serving up a plate of scrambled eggs and rice, she demonstrated the calm resignation that was the heritage of her race and sex and that had sustained her once she realized her husband had no desire to return to the United States of America, as she had once hoped.

Because the house they rented in this quiet residential block had no garage, Miles parked his bike in a shed adjoining the store, which was a short walk from the house. Akiko handed him a box lunch and said she would be down shortly to open the shop.

When he saw the door of the shed lying flat in the small lot behind the store he thought it was strange. He tried to remember if last night was especially windy. Then, as he came closer, he saw the chrome pipes, twisted into shapes which made them difficult to recognize at first, and after that, the handlebars. His first thought was, Who threw the junk into my lot. Catching sight of the saddlebags, slashed into rawhide strips, he stopped. Then he began to run.

4

When the water boiled, Ransom removed the kettle from the gas and filled his teapot, pouring the rest into the tin basin in the sink. Made of soapstone, the sink tended to turn green around the edges in summer. He topped the basin with cold water from the tap, then lathered up his shaving brush. With a clean bathtowel he wiped the mirror over the sink. He shaved his upper lip first and poured a cup of tea. When he was done, he rinsed out the basin and hung it on the nail over the sink, then poured out another cup of tea. He went into the other room, folded up his futon and stashed it in the closet, from which he took a broom. He opened the sliding doors onto the terrace and swept the tatami, which glowed yellow in the patch of sun. Dust teemed in the light. The sweeping didn't take long. That was one of the advantages of small quarters.

As he was donning his gi, Ransom heard the drone of the monks from Daitokuji, a nearby temple. He searched the pockets of his jeans and found a couple of coins. Downstairs, he opened the gate and stepped out into the narrow, unpaved and unnamed lane. Several houses up, the monks were waiting beside an open gate. Presently, Mrs. Miti came out and gave them something. They bowed, thanked her and proceeded, picking up their chant, their broad, squashed-cone coolie hats rocking from side to side. Ransom threw the coins in the wooden bowl the lead man held against his chest. The man bowed. After they had passed, Ransom began his run.

The packed dirt of the back streets was dark and damp where housewives had sprinkled it to keep the dust down in front of their doors. Moving between sunlight and the shadowed cool of the narrower lanes, he passed women with babies and the tofu man on his three-wheeled cart. At the Karasuma intersection he waited for the light. A cop with a cauliflower ear, probably from judo, looked him over. On his rusty three-speed bicycle he looked quaint enough, but he could break your arm for you. Ransom gave him a nod, which was returned almost imperceptibly.

The sky opened up as he approached the Kamo river, the swampy smell reaching him before he could see it. Kites hung in the sky over the trees along the outer levee. He jumped the first levee and ran across the broad, grassy flood plain. The kite flyers were scattered along the river bank, facing north. In the keen light the strings were invisible; it appeared that some cult had gathered to worship, hands clasped as if in prayer, eyes raised to the northern sky. To the northeast was Mt. Hiei, the highest in the horseshoe-shaped ridge of peaks that nearly enclosed the city. In the ninth century, to protect the new capital, the Emperor Kwannon sponsored a monastery on the peak, with monks on duty twenty-four hours a day to watch for evil spirits coming down from the northeast, the sector from which evil spirits were known to descend. They were to ring a large gong if they spotted anything suspicious. Ransom wasn't sure what was supposed to happen next. The monks eventually tired of the vigil and began periodically descending the mountain to rape, pillage and burn, incidentally confirming Kwannon's conviction about the direction from which trouble comes. Today a thin banner of cloud flew from the southern face, like a shred from a passing spirit's robe. Ransom thought it fortunate that from here you could not see the fantasy-amusement park which had been built beside the temple grounds.

He picked up the hundred-yard cinder track along the river's edge and ran downstream. Standing on the bank, two fishermen were trying to conjure something out of the water with long bamboo wands. Ransom always wondered if these anglers ate their catch, a thought that made him queasy. From its source the river drained fields and paddies heavily fertilized with petrochemicals and manure. Closer in, the Kyoto silk dyers dumped their rinse tanks. The white herons that fished the shallows had purple plumage one day, green the next—weeks in advance of the women who bought the kimono silk in the shops downtown.

The cinders from the track pricked his insteps. He came up on a volleyball game—schoolgirls in uniform gym suits. The team facing him dissolved in giggles as he passed, trading the word *gaijin* among themselves like a dirty joke.

One of them, a girl in yellow sweats with a thin, aristocratic face, definitely sparked his interest. He thought of the seduction line one of his students had taught him recently: *Asita asa, kohi nomimasu-ka?* Will you have coffee with me in the morning? This one, though, was about thirteen years old, and would be until she suddenly turned thirty.

He crossed the river at the Imadegawa Bridge and started up the other side, running in the shade of the trees along the levee. The cherry trees were budded and ready to blossom; in Tokyo they had already come and gone. Ransom passed two men in kendo helmets and breast plates, dueling with bamboo staves. Fellow budo-ka, followers of the Martial Way. He had thought about studying kendo, but he didn't like the idea of all that equipment. Further on, a young man in a beret was blowing an alto sax out over the river, eyes closed, head thrown back. Certainly he was very far away, Ransom imagined, from the three-room apartment he shared with his parents and sister, dreaming of Greenwich Village.

As the notes of "Take the A Train" faded behind him, Ransom heard a high whine that sounded like cicadas. A radio-operated model airplane appeared above the trees upriver, banked and then dove at him, pulling up sharply just as he was about to bat it away. The plane swept out over the river and came back around, buzzing him and again pulling away just short of his reach, then cruised north before disappearing over the treetops.

He scanned the riverbanks and then ran to the spot where the plane had gone over the trees, but there was no sign of the operator. He went through the trees and, at the top of the levee, startled a young couple in matching running suits holding hands on a bench. When he asked them if they had seen an airplane, they looked at him fearfully, as if he himself had just fallen out of the sky.

"How is your head," the girl asked DeVito when he opened his eyes.

"Shut your face," he said softly.

She didn't understand. Lying on the futon beside him, she had been watching him sleep, wondering if he *was* asleep. The tight set of his eyes and mouth made him appear to be lying in wait, ready at the slightest sound to leap up and strike out.

Last night, after he was carried out of the bar, she and her friend had walked him through the streets. He wanted to go back in and fight, but she lied and said that the police were on their way. DeVito took her back here to his rooms on the motorcycle, went out again, and returned near dawn, slipping into the futon beside her. She pretended she was asleep.

"What time is it?" he said now.

She told him it was almost noon.

"Make some breakfast," he said. With one motion he was on his feet, standing nude beside the futon, looking around the room as though he expected to encounter an intruder.

While she cooked the rice, he put on karate gi and went outside. Taped on the mirror over the sink was a quotation typed on a sheet of rice paper: "It is necessary to maintain the combat stance in everyday life and to make your everyday stance your combat stance."

When he came back half an hour later, breakfast was

ready. After she cleared away the breakfast things, he drew a pitcher of water at the sink and told her to come outside.

The temple grounds were deserted. Beyond the wall, over toward the main temple, she heard the sound of someone raking gravel. She did not understand why he lived in the temple compound. He was very strange, this gaijin.

In the courtyard next to a sawhorse was a case of empty beer bottles. Placing one of the bottles on top of the sawhorse, he half-filled it from the pitcher. "Hold this," he said, handing her the pitcher. As he stood in front of the sawhorse, drawing deep breaths, the distant sound of traffic from Nishi-oji Dori gradually seemed to underline the silence of the temple grounds. The raking had stopped. She felt sleepy. Several minutes later, a limping pigeon on the roof of the Hon-do caught her attention, and she didn't see him strike, though she heard the unbroken bottle hit the sand.

After his third attempt, he stormed behind the house and came back with an armful of bricks. "Get a towel from the house," he said. When she returned he had arranged the bricks in two stacks. He laid the towel on top of the first, knelt down in the sand and placed his right hand on the bricks, raising and lowering it slowly.

DeVito shouted as he smashed the bricks. He held up the broken pieces for her inspection. The second stack he broke with his head. When he turned to look at her, his forehead was cut and bleeding. He smiled.

"You're hurt," she said.

He said, "But we're having fun, aren't we?"

He allowed her to wipe the cut with the towel and then told her to set a bottle on the sawhorse. This time, he knocked the neck off without spilling a drop.

When Ransom finished his run, Kaji, the landlord, was waiting for him in front of the house. Kaji lived downstairs, and at first he had been reluctant to rent to a gaijin, having no experience of them and speaking no English. Now he was almost too enthusiastic a neighbor. He frequently came up to apologize for obscure nuisances or oversights he imagined Ransom to have taken to heart, and his wife was always sending up food. They had two preschool children, boy and girl, who rolled around in the dirt of the street and ate sweets all day.

Konichiwa, Kaji-san.

Konichiwa, Ransom-san. After two years of practice Kaji had mastered a fair imitation of his tenant's name.

Ransom said it was a fine day and Kaji agreed. He looked pleased with himself and clearly had more to say. Ransom asked after the kids—they were fine—and then Kaji said he had a little surprise. Not really a surprise; in fact, it was nothing at all, barely worth mentioning.

What is it? Ransom could see that he was excited.

Slowly and with much gesticulation, Kaji explained that a friend of his could get him a very good deal on a hot water heater for Ransom's apartment. It was just a kitchen model, of course; Ransom would still have to use the public bath.

Ransom didn't want to hurt Kaji's feelings; neither did he want Kaji to spend money unnecessarily. He thanked

Kaji for thinking of him, but the apartment was just fine the way it was.

Was Ransom-san worried about the rent, Kaji asked. *Not to worry. There would be no additional rent.*

Ransom-san said that Kaji surely had more important things to spend his money on. He himself wanted for nothing, and his teaching salary was if anything generous.

Think of the winter, Kaji said. *Think of the cold.*

It keeps me moving, Ransom said.

Kaji withdrew inside like a man defeated. Among the many reasons he had worried about renting to a gaijin was the primitive state of the family property. His old, prewar house was made of mud and lime, had tatami floors and minimal plumbing, and Americans, he knew, were used to all the latest of the modern conveniences. The newer homes and apartments in the city had these things. He tried to discourage his prospective gaijin tenant. Later, when Kaji had come to know him, he offered Ransom the black-and-white television when they had purchased a new color set. Kaji had feared the offer of the old set was a terrible insult to Ransom, and Ransom, knowing that his refusal of the gift would be taken as a rejection of an unworthy object, had thanked Kaji profusely. Later, under cover of night, he carried the set down to Buffalo Rome and gave it to an English friend, who would enjoy watching sumo wrestling on television.

Ransom had not come to Japan to watch television. He knew when he arrived that American shows were among the staples of the local airwaves, but was surprised to discover that the local product was even trashier. Ransom had strong opinions on the American medium, his father being a director and producer. He started out as a playwright, and although Ransom was only three years old when his father's last play was produced, he never quite forgave him for abandoning that vocation. A year ago, on Ransom's twenty-fifth birthday, his father sent him the manuscript of that play, still revived from time to time, a tragedy about a New England family with skeletons in their closets; the play's excellence had long been a matter of faith with Ransom, who used it as a point of reference against which to judge the situation comedies which had occupied his father since. Though a critical success, the play was commercially as modest as its predecessors, and Ransom's father turned increasingly to script writing and doctoring. He began to direct commercials. When Ransom was five the family had moved from New York to Los Angeles, and for reasons having nothing to do with art or geography that relocation had come to symbolize for young Ransom a fall from grace. He started school, and hated it. His mother opposed the move. She liked New York, her family was in New England. And she wanted her husband to write plays, not television scripts. Ransom's parents seldom fought, but he began seeing less and less of his father, who worked progressively later into the evening. His father stopped going to church— he had converted to Catholicism to marry Ransom's mother. Materially, things got better and better, yet the widening gap between the family's prosperity and its happiness made Ransom loathe his father's success, even as he rode the minibikes and watched the newest features in the screening room and swam in the pool and smoked cigarettes with the sons of movie stars.

Then, when he was fourteen, his mother died of cancer. Ransom knew the marriage would have ended even if his mother hadn't gotten sick. His father quit the series he was working on, becoming a model husband at the end; his son irrationally blamed him, his girlfriends and his career for his mother's death. She was sick for eighteen months, during which time she tried to prepare her son for her passing.

When it was over Ransom went back to Beverly Hills High. After his sophomore year his father sent him East to prep school, a move they both wanted, although both acted reluctant to the very moment when they stood outside the white clapboard dorm, Ransom, Sr., standing beside the rental car with his hands on his son's shoulders, telling him to call if he wanted anything and, after an awkward embrace, handing him ten twenties. Ransom was furious with impatience, just wanting the old man to be gone. He stayed East for college, despite his father's half-hearted lobbying for Stanford.

In the meantime, Ransom, Sr., had given up writing almost entirely for directing and producing. Ransom came home summers, and spent one as an assistant grip at one of the studios. His father made sure that Christopher knew the times and the networks of the shows he had a hand in, and Ransom watched more than he would care to admit, though without much pleasure. His father's greatest success, a family sit-com which started running when Ransom was seven and had its last season when he was thirteen, featured a successful Hollywood-scriptwriter father, wholesome mother-who-knew-best and mischievous son. Over the years Ransom heard his own words come back at him from the screen, things he'd said and done as a child, the kind of things that other children heard repeated about themselves at family reunions. At home, a cold war set in; the television family remained wacky; not rich, but happy.

Upstairs in his room, Ransom picked up some student essays for grading, then headed off to Kitaoji Street. En route he passed the cardboard man, ancient and hunched, who collected discarded boxes from the sidewalk, crushed them under his feet, and piled them on the tall stack on the back of his fantastic homemade tricycle, while his dog, an obese pit bull chained to the vehicle, waited patiently in the gutter.

Ransom bought an English language *Japan Times* at the newsstand and took it to the coffee shop on the corner, where he spent part of every morning. The telephone in the coffee shop was Ransom's major electronic interface with the rest of the world. Following the practice of Japanese college students, he gave the phone number of the shop to his friends. In exchange for regular patronage, the coffee-shop owner, Otani-san, took messages for him. Anyone who called for Ransom was told he was usually in between nine and ten.

Otani welcomed him with a hot towel when he sat down at the counter. Ransom wiped down his face, still sweaty from jogging, and browsed through the newspaper while Otani prepared his coffee. Vietnamese refugees were floating into Malaysia and Hong Kong in leaky boats; leftists in Tokyo had beaten an ideologically suspect comrade to death; Sadaharu Oh was on the verge of breaking Hank Aaron's home-run record.

At a table in the back sat two young women, and propped beside them on the floor was a tumescent shopping bag with copy printed to resemble an English dictionary definition.

> FUNKY BABE: Let's call a funky girl "Funky Babe."
> Girls, open-minded, know how to swing.
> Love to feel everything rather than think.
> They must all be nice girls.

The women did not look very funky themselves.

Otani placed Ransom's coffee in front of him. Ransom asked when he thought Oh would break the record. Otani, a Hanshin Tigers fan who hated the Tokyo Giants, didn't want to hear about it. Ransom pursued the conversation eagerly, dreading the stack of student papers in the envelope at his feet. According to the lesson plan of the A-OK English Language Program, the topic was "Business Etiquette." But since Ransom knew nothing about business and his students knew little about English, that subject was likely to be a standoff, and he had substituted the topic, "My Personal Goals," *goal* being one of the vocabulary words of the week. He nevertheless doubted that the essays would be much different from those written on business etiquette.

The alternative to this drab semi-employment was to accept the money his father continued to offer, and this was what kept Ransom going in the teaching business. He didn't want the old man's baksheesh. From time to time he still sent checks, which Ransom kept in an unread book in the bottom of a drawer.

Among the disadvantages of small quarters was not having room to work out. Saturday was officially a day of rest for the dojo, but in order to be merely competent Ransom had to be fanatic. After an hour of essays, he changed into sweats and rode the Honda down to the gym, an ugly prewar box with a peeling concrete skin. The smell inside was forty years of sweat and ammonia. Ransom greeted acquaintances as he walked among the scattered barbells and dumbbells. The gym had one Universal; otherwise it was just a matter of finding a bar and slapping on the weight.

He took a jump rope out back to the parking lot. After half an hour of cals and stretching he went over to the punching post—a four-by-four wrapped in hemp at fist level. He did fifty and fifty. After two years of this, the skin splitting and scarring over again and again, the right hand was tough enough that he barely felt the impact. The more sensitive left still bled every time.

He went back inside to bench press, beginning at sixty kilos and working up to a hundred. He had started toward the Universal when someone threw an arm around his neck and pulled him back hard.

You're dead.

Ransom planted a foot behind him, struggling for leverage, but the arm tightened and drew him farther back, off-balance. He was fighting in earnest for air, couldn't move, then was released.

You never know, the sensei said, *when I'll be behind you. Coming out of your house in the morning, rounding a corner downtown. I might be waiting underwater in the bath.*

Ransom bowed and nodded, trying to catch his breath.

What are you doing lifting weights, the sensei asked. *Too much weight-lifting will stiffen you up and slow you down. I told you this. You're stiff and slow already.*

Excuse me, sensei.

Do you have your gi, the sensei asked.

When Ransom said he did, the sensei told him to put it on, he would show him some moves. But he couldn't, he said, show Ransom how to see.

5

When Ransom showed up at Buffalo Rome on Saturday night, Miles Ryder was waiting for him. They retreated into the office.

"I want to rearrange his face," Ryder said. "I am going to make a study of methods of inflicting pain and suffering."

"How do you know DeVito did it?"

"Get serious. Who the fuck else is going to trash my bike? Okies love to beat on things."

"Did you file a report?"

"I told 'em. Not that it'll make a difference."

"What do you propose to do if he shows up?"

"Eventually call an ambulance."

Ransom hoped DeVito wouldn't show, since nothing good came of Texas–Oklahoma blood feuds. From his seat at the bar he kept an eye on the door. Possibly he could head DeVito off before Ryder spotted him. But Miles was also watching the door as he talked to a few friends at a table, and Ransom suspected that DeVito had devolved some blame for last night's disgrace onto him as well.

Dana the Potter joined Ransom briefly. He had been snowbound for most of the winter at a kiln town in the mountains, making the same tea bowl over and over. Laboring over the wheel, referring to a model shaped by his sensei, Dana regularly presented a new bowl to the sensei, who examined each one briefly before ordering him to squash it down to clay and start afresh. Ever since the roads opened Dana had been bingeing in Kyoto. In a few weeks Dana would go back to the kiln and beg his sensei's pardon and then they would not see him again for several months; meanwhile he would talk to anyone who listened. What Ransom thought remarkable was that, after two years in a small village where no one spoke English, Dana did not speak Japanese. Talking to Ransom, he made large, pot-shaping gestures with his hands, as if unaccustomed to having his words understood. Ransom wondered what he was doing up in those hills besides learning how to make a tea bowl, suspecting that Dana's program was not so different from his own.

Mojo Domo was onstage. Kano was singing about a woman who had done him wrong, his face sweaty and twisted with apparent pain. The worst blues, Ransom thought, was the hurt you carried after you did someone wrong.

A man standing near Ransom in puffy Chiang Mai hill tribe pants kept looking him over. When the set ended and Dana cleared out, he took the vacant stool. "What's happening," he said, then pointed at Ransom's callused hand. "Karate, am I right?"

Ransom said, "India, am I right?"

The man smiled like an aspiring saint and said, yes, he'd been there. He had that look of curiosity which has been sated, a long-distance gaze which had stretched so far it finally snapped and turned back on itself. Either drugs or religion. Asia burn. He had seen things, and he would tell you all about them while leaving the impression that he was holding back something larger and more profound. *And I only am escaped alone to tell thee.* Sufic mysteries, corpses burning on the ghats of Benares, eternity in a grain of Thai heroin.

"Just arrive?" Ransom said. Feeling he'd heard it all before, he was hoping to keep it short.

"Three days. Flew into Tokyo and I mean I couldn't get out of there fast enough. It reminded me of this dream I had in Lahore. I was inside this beehive—terrified, right? All around me these giant bees with like TV antennas on their heads. But I kept moving deeper and deeper into the beehive 'cause I was looking for something. Then it comes to me, right? That there's no honey in the hive. *I* know it but the bees *don't*. They kept building these wax things— *cells*, fucking *cells*, right? Think about *that* for a minute. But they'd forgotten the original purpose. That's what was frightening. That's what Tokyo was like."

The movement of his face and his body seemed weirdly out of sync. His hands were in constant motion and his shoulders jumped at odd intervals, but the face remained sleepy and serene. The smoke from his Indonesian clove cigarette was beginning to irritate Ransom's eyes.

56

"We've forgotten the original purpose," he said. "We've forgotten the honey."

"What honey?"

"*That's* the question, isn't it?" He smiled at Ransom as if they were co-conspirators. "From the Zen point of view, it has no name. The Hindus have exactly one thousand names for it. In Hebrew the name is a secret that can't be spoken and that's only known to a few initiates at any one time. But it's within us all."

"Right." Ransom had heard enough.

"Hey, have you ever hung out in Goa? I feel like I've seen you."

Ransom shook his head.

"Sri Lanka?"

"Nope."

"I have this like image of you on a beach."

"I'm not really the beach type."

"I'm a writer," he said. "I try to observe everything wherever I am."

"What do you write?"

"Apocrypha. The unauthorized version. You've probably seen some of my stuff here and there. Carl Digger's the byline."

Ransom shrugged.

"You're thinking, what about *Rolling Stone,* right? In your view a hip mag, a forum for the unexpurgated stuff. Forget it. They're government-CIA operated. Why do *you* think they do all those pieces on celeb interior designers and four-star restaurants? *Hey,* General Westmoreland doesn't want you thinking about what he's up to."

"I don't think you're going to like Japan," Ransom said.

"Why not?"

"Lacks the landscape of Nepal and the epic spectacle of India. It's a small-screen culture. You've got to be a miniaturist to appreciate it."

"There's a story here," Digger said. "A big story." He paused. "You're not a writer are you?"

"Don't even write letters home," Ransom said.

Carl Digger nodded. He looked around with an air of suspicion, then leaned closer. "I was in Thailand when I heard about this monster strain of Vietnamese clap. You've heard about this, right? Gonzo gonorrhea. A clap that eats penicillin for breakfast. These U.S. Army doctors hit it with everything they had and it just kept on coming. So, what to do? Send the boys back home to infect our daughters and sisters? Not fucking likely. So what are the options? You could kill them. Killed, missing in action, that's what the letters home would say. Hey, the U.S. military's done worse things. Anyway, there were rumors to that effect. The *Barb* ran a piece in seventy-two, interview with a GI who said his buddy vanished from the infirmary. *They* said he was transferred to a hospital stateside. A week later, word comes down he's officially missing in action. Like, what action? Vicious sponge bath from one of the nurses? This was *not* an isolated case."

He pulled a small vial from one of his large pockets and shook out a pill. "Lomotil," he said. "When you do India you sacrifice your lower intestine to the gods in the water."

And some, Ransom thought, sacrifice their gray matter to the gods in the hash pipe. "I don't see what your story has to do with Japan."

"Hey, how could you? They don't *want* you to see.

When I started checking into this thing, there were no end of leads, rumors, whispers, but one kept coming up. The specificity of place, the fact that unconnected people had the same story—this was something." He leaned still closer; Ransom could feel his breath. "An island in the Inland Sea, somewhere off the coast of Shikoku. That's where they're keeping the boys. The island's patrolled by U.S. Navy gunboats disguised as trawlers, no communications links with the outside world. I've talked to people who have talked to Japanese fishermen. Some fishing boat picked up an American in those waters, one of the clap carriers, and he's hiding out on a farm in Shikoku." He sat back and took a drag of clove. "I'm going to find him."

"Good luck," Ransom said, holding out his hand to shake by way of ending the conversation.

Digger shook the proffered hand as if he were out of practice. "You haven't heard anything about this?"

"Only rumors."

"Nothing specific?"

"No. But I'll tell you this much. One of the great things about Japan is that nobody can use that excuse about catching it from a toilet seat."

"Why not?"

"No seats."

"Oh, right." Digger wasn't sure whether to laugh or not.

Ransom excused himself for purposes of using a standard international urinal. He stood up and shook Digger's hand one last time. "Have you ever run across a guy named Ian," Ransom asked. "Ian Haxton. Tall guy with red hair?"

Digger repeated the name several times, nodding his head gravely.

"In Goa, maybe, or Katmandu?" Ransom said.

"Hold on. Red hair, plays the sitar. Great sitar player. Scottish, right? Real heavy accent?"

Ransom shook his head.

"Pretty heavy accent. Maybe not so noticeable."

"See you around," Ransom said. He knew it was a long shot, but he always asked.

When he was halfway down the bar, Digger called out after him: "Kuta Beach, Bali?"

"What?"

"Did I see you there?"

"Not in this life," Ransom said.

When Ransom returned, Digger was gone. Kano was sitting in Ransom's seat, looking as if he had just run a marathon.

"My man," Kano said.

Ransom slapped him five.

"How was the set," Kano asked.

"Bad sounds, Kano."

"Bad?"

"Bad as in *badass*. It means good."

Kano asked the bartender for a pencil. He scrawled a note, then looked up. "What does *good* mean?"

"I don't know. I really couldn't tell you."

"But *bad* means good?"

"Sometimes it does."

"Another question, please. We're working up a new tune. What do you think it means. 'Tired of Fattening Frogs for Snakes.' "

"That's the name of the song?"

Kano nodded.

"Sounds to me like his woman has been stepping out and he's sick of it."

"She's got a back-door man?"

"I'd say."

"Like, another mule's been kicking in his stall?"

"Same idea."

Kano made another note.

"How's it shaking in general?" Ransom said.

"No fucking bread, man. My lady lost her job. She was, what do you say, a waitress. Person who waits out front in office."

"Receptionist."

"Right. Some asshole from office comes here one night, sees her with me and the guys. Goes back to office and says, this don't be the kind of bitch we want working in our nice office. So that's all she wrote."

"They can't do that," Ransom said.

" 'Course they do that. This is Japan. That's how it works."

"She should get a lawyer," Ransom said.

"This ain't America, man." Ransom knew what he meant. "What are you drinking?"

Ransom said he was drinking tea.

"You on the wagon train?"

"I'm not on anything," Ransom said.

"Okay, sorry."

A schoolgirl wearing a *Playboy* sweatshirt approached Kano and whispered in his ear. "She wants your autograph," Kano said, as the girl held out a small spiral-bound book. She kept her eyes fastened to her feet. The book, presumably a diary, had bunny rabbits on the cover and except for short handwritten entries was blank inside.

Ransom signed with bold indecipherable strokes. The girl took the notebook and bobbed up and down in thanks, excusing herself over and over. From a nearby table her friends watched and giggled, covering their mouths with their hands.

"Who am I supposed to be?" Ransom asked.

"Keith Richards."

"Not bad. A few days ago I was Michael Landon—you know, Little Joe—and that really pissed me off."

"You gaijin all look the same, man. Have something to drink."

"Can't do it."

"Karate?"

"Four hours tomorrow. If I'm lucky I'll have enough energy after practice to kick-start my bike."

Ransom bought Kano a drink to take back for his second set. It seemed time to go home. Already he was getting tense about tomorrow's practice. Night practice ran for a couple of hours at most, but Sunday was an endurance contest, four hours on asphalt in the sun. He should go home and sleep. As long as he stayed here, though, there was something in between him and practice. But the longer he stayed, the more practice began to infiltrate his attention, and the less sleep he would have to sustain him.

> Saturday I go out to play.
> Wake up Sunday morning, Lord,
> I get on my knees and I pray.

Five weeks ago Sunday Ito had kicked Ransom in the balls. He lay on the asphalt doubled over, choking and gasping for breath. He left the bike in the parking lot, and Yamada gave him a ride home, where he lay down on the tatami without unrolling the futon. Then he got up and puked in the sink. For two days he was down and still felt waves of nausea the third. When he returned to practice on Wednesday night, the sensei asked where he had been. Ransom had been in the dojo long enough to feel that he did not want to say he had been hurt. He said he had had to go to Tokyo on business. The sensei asked why he hadn't been told. He took for granted proprietorship of his disciple's schedules. Work did not take precedence, although as an excuse it had greater validity than pain or injury, in which the sensei seemed not to believe. Fortunately, the sensei didn't ask what business a part-time English conversation teacher would have in Tokyo.

Miles came over from his table. "They think you're Keith Richards."

"I know."

"I wouldn't stand for that."

"Why not?"

"That is one sorry-looking dude."

"Girls and boys of many ages would disagree."

"Do you know how ugly Keith Richards is? Keith Richards is so ugly, if he fell into a well you'd be pumping ugly for a month. Speaking of ugly, you haven't seen DeVito?"

"I doubt we will."

Miles squinted in the direction of the door. "Don't look now but here comes the vanguard of the revolution."

Yukiko sat down on the stool beside Ransom's. Her hair was cut very short, and she wore new, steel-rimmed glasses: the Trotsky look. She worked hard at being unattractive.

"Well, howdy, Yukiko," Miles said. "Was that you I saw on the news hijacking a 747? The stocking mask didn't do you justice."

"Maybe I should wear a cowboy hat. Are you still selling them in your little shop?" she said. Miles and Yukiko had a long-standing feud. Yukiko seemed to hold Miles personally responsible for the fate of the American Indians.

"I keep hoping you'll come in and buy a pair of spurs or something, but I haven't seen you around in a while," Miles said. "Where you been—summer camp in Beirut? Outward Bound in Irkutsk?"

"None of your business."

"Terrific to see you again," Miles said, moving off.

Yukiko turned to Ransom. "I was hoping I wouldn't see you here. Just because I was hoping you had started to use your time constructively. Or that you had gone home."

"Home. What's *home*? Home on the electric range? Where the buffalo roam? Where the heart is? Where you hang your hat? The buffalo are all in zoos, and nobody wears hats any more, which makes it difficult to locate this place— home."

"Please don't try to entertain me."

They had met shortly after Ransom arrived in Japan. She worked as a clerk in a bookstore and spent the rest of her time marching, organizing and handing out leaflets. Yukiko had studied at Berkeley for three years in the late sixties, where she was big in the student movement. Their first date was a protest march against the American military presence in Japan, organized by the Red Army Faction at Kyoto University. Yukiko was mysterious about her affiliation with this group, although Ransom suspected she was not as involved as she wished to be. She was unequivocal in her views, however, advocating socialist revolution. American imperialism and the programmed complacency of the masses were the main obstacles. Ransom was not unsympathetic to this view. His vague sense of disgust with his homeland had certain identifiable political components. In the march, he held a banner which he couldn't read. The other marchers were very polite to him. Many wanted to shake his hand. Yukiko told him later of the rumor that he was Tom Hayden.

For three months they conducted an uneasy liaison. Yukiko could never quite forgive Ransom for being American. Ransom could not quite buy into her program, although when he first arrived in Japan he was desperate to attach himself somewhere, and would have liked to believe in a system that would relieve him of his own confusion. He had once fought for C.O. status back when Vietnam was still an issue, although the draft had already ended and everyone pointed out to him that it was just a formality. He wanted to make a stand, but no one was interested.

Yukiko ordered a Coke and asked Ransom why it was that gaijin were inevitably attracted to all the quaint and reactionary aspects of Japanese culture. "Like the martial arts."

"I'm sure you have a theory."

"You know," she said, "I could never understand the route you took between my place and yours. It seemed roundabout. Then I figured out that you were avoiding the McDonald's on Kawaramachi-Imadegawa. It spoiled your idealized Japanese vista—pagodas and misty mountains."

Ransom didn't choose to argue the point. "What are you doing here, anyway? This isn't exactly your scene."

"I have an appointment."

"You mean a date?"

"It's none of your business what I mean."

She looked around significantly, then saw who she was looking for—Carl Digger, investigative journalist. He discreetly beckoned her over, and she merely nodded to Ransom as she was leaving.

Yukiko was a thorough bore, but then, so was Buffalo Rome. Ransom was angry at himself for not having gone home hours before, for having had an absurd affair, and now an absurd non-conversation with this would-be Madam Mao. Everybody in this place had a shtick, himself included. Suddenly his life felt like a shabby waste, as if a paper screen had been pulled back to reveal a vast landscape of pain and regret.

He ordered a scotch and drank it off. Without saying goodbye to anyone he headed out. The narc, at his post by the door, stopped him. "Do you know where I can buy some marijuana, man?"

"Sure."

"Groovy. Where?"

"Thailand."

Outside were some fifty bikes, Ransom's Honda 350 among them. He was putting on his helmet when he heard his name called. Marilyn was walking up the street on high heels, holding her long coat closed in front to conceal her skimpy cabaret togs.

"I was afraid I wouldn't find you."

"That's nothing to be afraid of."

"I tried to call you."

"I don't have a phone." Ransom fingered his keys.

"I know. Listen, we have to talk."

"You talk, I'll listen."

"Could we go someplace for a drink. Not here."

"I'm tired, Marilyn. I've got to get home." He threw his leg over the seat and unlocked his handlebars.

"It's about Miles."

"If you're feeling guilty about screwing Miles, I commend you, but I am not in the mood to commiserate."

"It's about his motorcycle. I think I know who did it."

"Join the club."

"It's not who you think. Can't we go somewhere?"

"I've got to go home." Ransom put his key in the ignition.

"It was yakuza," Marilyn said.

"Yakuza? Why would the yakuza demolish Miles's bike? That's a great idea, Marilyn."

A group of Japanese students emerged from Buffalo Rome. Two of them were supporting a third, who was moaning and comatose.

Ransom asked if he was okay.

Just drunk, they said. They rolled off down the street as a unit.

"It's my fiancé," Marilyn said. "He's yakuza."

"What fiancé?"

A few blocks over was an all-night donut shop. Ransom gave Marilyn the spare helmet and waited while she arranged herself on the seat behind him. She asked if she could put her arms around him. "Sure," he said, "but it's only three blocks." A beetle of some kind was riding the tachometer. Ransom tried to brush it away, but discovered that the beetle had somehow gotten inside the tach.

Dismounting, Marilyn ran one of her stockings.

At the door of Mr. Donut she said, "I'm not going to use the word *yakuza* and don't you either. Okay?"

Ransom agreed without much conviction. After they ordered coffee, she told her story. He knew she worked in a cabaret, and figured that gangsters weren't exactly uninterested in nightclubs, so nothing she said amazed him. He just wondered how serious this was for Miles.

She said she would spare him the whole trip, but she was in a refugee camp in Thailand, Samut Prakan, just south of Bangkok, when a group of Japanese businessmen came through, posing as journalists. She had a pretty good idea of what they were, but her options were few and this was no time to be choosy. She was among several women singled out for interviews. She had a good singing voice and a repertoire of American songs, and they seemed to like the way she looked. They asked her if she would be interested in working in Japan. They would arrange the necessary papers and visas.

They came for her at night, and the hurried, secretive departure led her to suspect that no visas or papers were involved. They made the last leg of the trip from Korea in the hold of a ship and disembarked at night. The girls, about fifteen in all, were hustled into the back of a truck and dropped off at various towns and cities along the way. She had seen two of the girls since then. One was working in a Turkish bath; the other looked wasted and wouldn't even acknowledge her. Marilyn was lucky—one of the head men liked her. She was placed in one of the best clubs in Kyoto, and her duties were aboveboard. The man put her up in a nice apartment and began to visit her with flowers. He was decent to her, but was violently jealous. A few months back he began mentioning marriage.

She lit a new cigarette and sipped at her coffee. "He had me followed. He found out about Miles."

"You think he wrecked Miles's bike."

"His men. He doesn't do anything himself. He's an oyabun."

"You're sleeping with a goddamned oyabun?"

She put her fingers to her lips. "Please, not so loud." Then she said, "It's better than sleeping with every man who has the price."

Ransom didn't know what to think. "Why are you telling me?"

"I don't want Miles to know. If he finds out he'll do something stupid. I thought maybe you could help me."

"How?"

"That's what I thought you could help me decide."

"There's always seppuku."

"What's that?"

"Ritual suicide. How do you talk to this guy? Your Japanese isn't too swift, is it?"

"I know you don't like me but I thought you'd want to help Miles."

"Is this fiancé of yours apt to hurt Miles?"

"I don't know."

"Miles almost deserves to get his head bashed but he's got a wife and a kid on the way. No doubt you're worried sick about them."

"Please, Ransom. I'm not even sleeping with Miles, in case you were wondering."

"Fine. There's your answer. Say Miles is just a friend."

"He won't believe it. He's convinced."

Ransom didn't really believe it himself. "Why don't you tell him he has the wrong guy?"

"Then he will want to know who is the right guy."

Ransom didn't want to think about this now. It seemed improbable and far away. He was still rattled by his lost evening at Buffalo Rome, and very soon he would be sweating his way through practice. But Marilyn was probably right to keep it from Miles, whose ax handle could land him in deep trouble. As little as he liked Marilyn, he was pleased that she had come to him first. If she was telling the truth, she was in a hard spot, and had no one else to help her.

"Well, tell the oyabun it's me. Tell him I'm the one you've been seeing. Don't come right out with it or he'll never believe you. Let him threaten and cajole for a while."

"But then he'll come after you."

"Better me than Miles. I'll think of something." Ransom didn't have a plan, but he had his reasons. His first thought was to protect Miles, who had more to lose than he did, but what grew on him was the challenge.

He put Marilyn in a cab and gave her the number of the coffee shop. They had agreed to meet at the Miyako Hotel at five the next day; he made her promise she wouldn't talk to Miles in the meantime.

6

SOUTH CHINA SEA, APRIL 1975

The Chinese sat at their own table. They ate different food, their faces buried in deep bowls, chopsticks waving in front of their heads like antennae. The children sat on their mothers' laps, tipping their heads back to receive morsels from the fat, boatlike spoons. The rich smells of their food filled the galley. At the third-class table Ransom ate overcooked food without taste or smell, the Hong Kong version of British cuisine. This morning it had been cold vulcanized eggs and limp toast, tonight a piece of untanned leather with gravy, flaccid gray beans, instant mashed potatoes, grilled tomato garnish. Ransom's fellow diners included an English schoolteacher on her way to a posting in Hong Kong, a quiet family of Indian Sikhs, and an American hippie whose girlfriend had not once left their cabin, being afflicted with dysentery, the progress of which her boyfriend faithfully reported.

Ransom had tried to buy fourth-class passage in Penang, but the man at the ticket window on the dock told him there was no fourth class. "What class are those people riding," Ransom asked, pointing to a Chinese family camped on a pile of bundles in the corner of the ticket office. "They're Chinese," the man, a Malay, had said. "I want the cheapest ticket you've got," Ransom said. "I don't mind sleeping on deck." The man said that fourth class was only Chinese. "You buy third class," he said.

Ransom had come overland from the subcontinent, travelling like a fugitive in third- and fourth-class train cars. He sometimes feared he was being pursued; when he rested his head against the hard wooden benches and closed his eyes, he envisioned Pathan drug runners from the Hindu Kush brandishing long, curved knives and modified M-16s with prayer beads wrapped around the stocks; corrupt Pakistani police familiar with instruments of torture loomed up behind them. Much worse were the apparitions of Ian and Annette. Because he did not know what had happened to Ian, who simply disappeared in Afghanistan, Ransom was unable to imagine anything but the worst: various states of mutilation and dismemberment. Annette he had seen— lying peacefully in the dank, putrid room they had occupied for three weeks, waiting for Ian to come back across the border. Stumbling in the moonlight, Ransom had carried her up the hillside above Landi Kotal. There was no question of going to the police. Annette was past help, which may have been where she wanted to be. Ransom was where he didn't want to be, on the border between

Afghanistan and Pakistan, a place without law. The authorities would have kept him in the country, subject to an investigation that would last as long as they thought they could squeeze out additional baksheesh. Ransom did what he had to do. But still.

He belonged on a ship like this: rusting, dirty, infested with rats. The rats seemed to be in command, confident of their rights. The steward, the cabin boys, the waiters were silent and distracted. The brass fittings had turned brown and green with neglect. Crew members were occasionally seen in groups of two or three, smoking in some corner. They fell silent and dispersed at the sight of a passenger. Ransom spent much of his time on deck, looking out over the curved sea. It would have been better, he thought, if the earth had been flat, if you could arrive at the point where the known stopped and the unknown began, where you could finally say—this is the end, or the beginning. He vaguely imagined Japan as such a place, a strange island kingdom at the edge of the world, a personal frontier, a place of austere discipline which would cleanse and change him.

The waiter had cleared plates and replaced them with dishes of green Jell-O when the intercom began to click and buzz. "Attention. Attention all passengers. This is the captain speaking. The republic of South Vietnam is just coming into view over our port bow."

The passengers drifted to the upper deck. Daylight was falling into the west over the stern. At first Ransom could see nothing but the crests of waves catching the last sun. Then someone called, "Look, there."

A thin sliver of land was wedged between sky and sea.

Within minutes the land was plainly visible, and above it, a random succession of dull yellow flashes.

"Lightning?" the schoolteacher said.

The hippie laughed.

The soft pink and gold illuminations were hypnotic. Ransom watched as the weird light grew brighter in the darkening sky. So that's it, Ransom thought. Later, when the boat docked at Hong Kong, he would learn that what he had seen was the final battle for Saigon.

The passengers watched the flickering show of lights in silence. Ransom stayed at the rail until the peninsula had crossed over their stern and the light was little more than a dim, pulsing glow.

7

From a deep sleep Ransom woke into a sovereign state of anxiety. For a moment he held back on the edge of waking, with the notion of slowing the inevitable. Sunday morning, once the start of the Lord's day.

Ransom slipped on a pair of boxers, washed, shaved and rolled up the bed. He pulled back the doors to the terrace and stepped outside, where two sets of karate gi were hanging from the clothesline. The view from the terrace was the backsides of the houses on the next street, rigged out like galleons with TV antennae and clotheslines. Above the tiled rooftops, the sky was overcast. If it rained, practice would be cancelled.

Beneath the terrace was Kaji's garden, an immaculate plot with stones and dwarf trees that gave the illusion of major landscape. Presiding over the ornamental puddle was a ceramic tanuki, an animal that the Japanese loved inordinately and that seemed to Ransom a bear-racoon hybrid. The buds of the cherry tree were swollen and showing pink, the tortured yellow branches of the trained pine tipped with a new green. As he looked down, a ferret darted from underneath the house with a piece of paper in its mouth and dashed across the pebbles to the water; it rose on its hind legs to examine the tanuki and test the air. Ransom whistled. The ferret looked up at him, then bolted underneath the fence, leaving the paper behind. Ransom tried to remember if a ferret was a good or bad omen. In Japan, everything was some kind of omen.

The first to arrive, Ransom changed into his gi and began to sweep the parking lot. They only trained inside during rainy season, when there was space reserved for them in the gym. The sensei had no use for padded mats and controlled temperature. Asphalt toughened the soles of the feet and gave you an incentive to stay on them. The winter had been cold and they had often practiced with snow on the ground. The biggest problem in winter was your toes; you couldn't feel them until you jammed one, and then it was like a dentist's drill hitting a nerve. The sensei had a shiatsu method of unjamming toes which involved yanking on them. In November Ransom had broken the middle toe on his left foot. He still taped the toe and favored right kicks. The doctor told him to lay off karate for two months. The sensei told him to tape it and forget about it.

He hoped he would have time to finish sweeping the lot before anyone arrived. He liked having the morning to himself. It would get violent and sweaty soon enough.

Ransom learned how to sweep when he started with the dojo. His first lessons were in bowing and sweeping. Ransom had been desperate to join. The sensei had not been eager to take on a foreign disciple. There were dojos that catered to gaijin but his wasn't one of them. He did not believe gaijin had the stuff. His reluctance convinced Ransom that he had found the right teacher.

Every night for a week Ransom watched them practice. He had not noticed the fighting so much as the grace of movement. The best of the students gave the impression of quadruped balance and intimacy with the ground. They conveyed an extraordinary sense of self-possession. For months Ransom had drifted across landscapes in a fevered daze, oblivious to almost everything but his own pain and guilt. The dojo with its strange incantations and white uniforms seemed to him a sacramental place, an intersection of body and spirit, where power and danger and will were ritualized in such a way that a man could learn to understand them. Ransom had lost his bearings spiritually, and he wanted to reclaim himself.

Finally Ransom approached the sensei with a speech he had worked up out of the dictionary. It was the only time Ransom would see him entirely at a loss. Later the sensei told Ransom that he would have gotten rid of him if he had known how. The sensei's English and Ransom's Japanese were equally poor; the sensei struggled to explain in Japanese that he was not equipped to handle a foreigner. His was a small dojo. The gaijin-san would feel more at home elsewhere. The sensei repeated this, speaking very slowly, and then retreated into the gym with his clothes under his arm. Ransom was back the next night, and the night after that. The third night, after practice, the sensei gave him a piece of paper with what turned out to be an address, written in both Japanese and painstaking roman characters. He pointed to his white suit, then to the piece of paper.

Ransom was waiting the next night in his crisp new gi, short in the arms and legs. When the sensei arrived he handed Ransom a broom. Ransom began to sweep the lot. The sensei stepped in several times to correct his technique. Ransom wasn't sure what to make of it. After the seated meditation, the sensei took him off into a corner of the lot. Through Suzuki, a college student who spoke more English than anyone else in the dojo, the sensei explained that bowing was the first skill to be mastered in karate. Suzuki demonstrated the proper bow. It looked simple enough—the all-purpose bob that Ransom had been seeing since he first arrived in the country. The sensei took Ransom over to the post wrapped in hemp. Ransom had seen the others punching it, but the sensei wanted him to practice bowing to it. He spent the next hour doing so, while the others leaped and kicked. The sensei came over several times to watch, shaking his head each time and demonstrating once more. Ransom watched and tried to determine what was different and crucial in the sensei's bow. He wondered if there was an exact angle of inclination, if the thing was codified that far; Ryder told him months later that department stores had machines designed to train their employees to bow correctly. Ransom concentrated on putting as much sincerity and humility into it as he could. After an hour his lower back was aching and his store of sincerity exhausted.

After a closing round of seated meditation, the sensei handed him the broom. Wondering why this was necessary after practice, Ransom swept the lot again from one end to the other.

The next night was the same. While the others followed their secret choreography, Ransom stood in the dunce corner bowing to his post. The sensei came around twice to measure his progress but offered no comment. Ransom's back ached so severely the next day that he could hardly get out of bed. He walked to the public bath hunched over like the old country women he saw sometimes at the bus stops, women who spent their lives bent doubled over in rice fields.

At the end of the third night he was convinced he was being systematically humiliated. The sensei hadn't wanted him in the dojo to begin with. When he came around to watch, Ransom was too stiff to bow fluidly, and the proper mix of humility and sincerity was out of the question.

Practice finished, he was changing into his street clothes when the sensei held out the broom. Ransom continued buttoning his shirt and didn't look up. When he got to the second-to-last button he saw there were three buttonholes left. The sensei saw, too. He held out the broom. Ransom rebuttoned and tucked in his shirt, then took the broom and snapped it in half over his knee. He laid the two halves down at the sensei's feet and was out in the street before he realized he had left his shoes behind.

The shoes were sitting beside the door of the gym when he arrived the next night, under a folded-paperbag tent. Ransom was fifteen minutes early. He had brought a new broom. The sensei arrived as he was beginning to sweep.

Ransom continued sweeping. The sensei walked over to the post and began punching. Ransom laid down the broom and approached him. The sensei changed hands and hit the post fifty times before turning to look at Ransom. Ransom drew himself up, clenched his fists at his side and bent deeply from the waist. He kept his head down.

Okay, the sensei said. *Good.*

Ransom had finished sweeping when Udo arrived. He walked like a sumo wrestler, with a semicircular swing of his legs, looking like he was carrying something between them. Udo had been a body builder before he joined the dojo and the hypertrophied pectorals and thighs that had won two Mr. Kyoto titles were no help with karate. He could bench-press two hundred kilos, but his punches were slow and ineffective.

Initially, Udo had refused to acknowledge Ransom's existence. The sensei forced him to do so by letting a match between them run on much too long. Udo went down three times. After the second knockdown there was blood all over the front of Udo's gi. Ransom had no heart to go on, but he knew better than to question the sensei's tactics. The next day Udo began to ask Ransom for pointers. Later, when Ransom had carburetor trouble with his bike, Udo brought him down to the service station where he worked, showed him all the features of the three-bay garage with hydraulic lifts, showed Ransom off to his friends and refused payment for the rebuild of the carburetor. Since then they had been out fishing a few times.

Ito arrived wearing his gi, as if he had no civilian life. He bowed to Ransom and to Udo and then began jogging around the lot. It still might rain, Ransom thought. Udo watched Ito circle the lot, then began running himself. He was scared to death of Ito.

The sensei was in a buoyant mood, smiling owlishly. Ransom bowed. The sensei nodded and asked if he thought it was going to rain. Ransom felt that it wasn't his meteorological intuition which was being checked, but his enthusiasm. Did Ransom want it to rain? seemed to be the question. Or maybe he was just paranoid.

When the sensei knelt down on the asphalt, the twelve of them fell into line according to rank—the sensei, Ito and then Ransom. Yamada was absent. Ransom had less seniority than others down the line but unlike most Japanese institutions the dojo was a meritocracy. The sensei didn't award belts—Ito's being the legendary exception—but the hierarchy was clear. Practicing seven days a week, at the dojo and on his own, Ransom had moved up through the ranks.

Kneeling seiza, butt resting on his heels, eyes closed, Ransom tried to drain himself of everything but will. To do this it helped to find an image. He pictured a box and held the image still while he filled it with the junk of his quotidian concerns: the broken English of student essays, Marilyn's problem, the bald rear tire on his Honda. Last of all he deposited his fear of injury. Then he tipped the box, slowly spilling its contents out into a void. When the box was empty he was clean. The box hovered in front of him, bare and luminous.

The sensei clapped his hands and it was time to begin. Jumping to his feet, Ransom felt ready for anything. Ito led the stretching and calisthenics, the others facing him in two lines. Ransom concentrated on duplicating his every move. With years of scrupulous imitation he might gain possession of the discipline.

The sun broke through an hour into practice but it didn't seem to cut the humidity. The front of Ransom's gi was soaked through. He was dragging by the third hour, then got a second wind which kept him going until the sensei called them in. They waited to hear if they would be sparring.

"Kata," the sensei said, to Ransom's immense relief. Kata were prescribed sequences linking offensive and defensive moves; performed individually, usually in slow motion, they choreographed one side of an imaginary battle. Although it was often difficult to summon the required calm at the end of such a long practice, Ransom liked the kata because no one got hurt.

The sensei demonstrated the swan kata. There were two aspects of representation. On the one hand, six imaginary opponents were dispatched. It was also a balletic sketch of a possible ornithological mating dance. Both had to be there at once, the fight and the grace of the swan. The sensei stood at attention in his white gi, filled his lungs and drifted through the sequence. The sweep of his arms was unmistakably winglike as he brushed aside attackers, not least in the slow, clapping motion of the hands which represented the popping of an opponent's eardrums. He finished on the same spot from which he had started.

The disciples formed two rows. The sensei signalled and they began. Halfway through, Ransom forgot the next move and lost his rhythm.

That was no swan, the sensei said to him at the end.

Ransom asked if he could try it again. The others watched him repeat the performance. After the third run the sensei said, *Not bad.* They worked on kata for almost an hour.

When the sensei kneeled, everyone rushed to his assigned place. Ransom took his time, feeling the operation of musculature up and down his calves as he walked over to kneel beside Ito. Now that practice was finally over, he wanted to continue. He would like to see what he could do with Ito today. But he was not unaware of being grateful at having been spared for another day.

Have you seen Yamada, the sensei asked him after everyone had showered.

I haven't seen him, Ransom said.

I thought you two were buddies, the sensei said. It sounded ominous.

I see him sometimes, Ransom said. *Not recently.*

The sensei said, *I think he's got a woman.*

Good for him, Ransom said.

Bad for his karate, the sensei countered. *You never would have made it this far if you had been thinking about women.*

I was thinking about them, Ransom said. *They weren't thinking about me.*

The sensei shook his head. *You made a choice,* he said.

At times Ransom considered the sensei omniscient, but he was wrong to think that Ransom had given up women for karate. He would have to understand the concept of penance.

8

After practice, Ransom had an hour and a half to kill before he had to meet Marilyn. He ate a bowl of noodles with the sensei and rode downtown to a public bath he frequented. Leaving his shoes with the others in the tiled entryway, he pulled back the door to the men's entrance, paid the attendant and asked for a bucket, towel and soap. In the changing room an aged man wearing the wraparound diaper favored by the prewar generation was dressing a young boy of three or four. The boy pointed at Ransom—"gaijin," he said—and the two of them openly watched him undress.

His clothes folded in a basket, he pulled back the glass door and stepped into the blue steam of the bath chamber. The sound of running water slowed and thickened as he closed the door behind him. Two men were submerged to their necks in the baths. Three others sat in front of the faucets along the far wall, one of them very dark-skinned. Closer up, Ransom could make out the dragon-and-flame motif of the tattoos which covered his back and arms. One of the attractions of the bath was that it was a yakuza hangout. The tattoos were worth the price of admission. Missing fingers were a bonus.

Ransom scooped his bucket in the warm tub and poured it over his head, then sat down on the tiles in front of one of the faucets. He rinsed himself down, lathered up his washcloth, and soaped himself, starting with the toes. Glancing sideways at the tattooed man, he observed the dragon getting doused. Yamada had come here with him recently and warned him not to stare, told him that yakuza were dangerous. Being stared at seven days a week, though, Ransom felt entitled to gawk himself.

Yamada's waning interest in the dojo disconcerted him. For two years Ransom had been putting nearly all of his energy and time into karate, hoping eventually to be as good as Yamada, who was three or four years older and had been at it for half of his life. Ransom believed that he would become a different person, better somehow, if he kept training. Without actually cataloguing imagined benefits, he felt that the discipline would tone all of his being. It was a way of knowing himself. He wished to be morally taut and resolute, and at the same time more at ease with his fellow creatures, to achieve a self-mastery that would reduce the complexity of transacting with others.

When he had finished rinsing, he went over to the first of four tubs arrayed in order of ascending temperature. In movies, the manly, samurai sort of man leapt immediately into the hottest tub, killing millions of sperm even as he proved his virility, but the sensible procedure was to work your way up. Ransom stepped into the first and submerged himself up to his neck. He lay back and closed his eyes. When the water began to feel cool he moved to the next tub, already occupied by two men who shared rough, peasant features and who openly scrutinized the invader. The tattooed man in the third tub stood up and lowered himself unceremoniously into the hottest. Ransom's two companions were conferring. The thickness of their Kansai dialect and the distortion of the echo obscured the conversation, but Ransom gathered they were talking about him.

Gaijin are bigger, one said, standing up, *but Japanese are harder.*

This, Ransom knew, was the common wisdom.

The laughter of women carried from the other side of the partition. The men eyed Ransom suspiciously: they knew he had come to steal their daughters and their sisters. These two were old enough to remember the Occupation. Ransom assumed an innocent expression—Nobody here but us eunuchs.

He lay back in the tub and considered the Marilyn business. Her cause was not exactly a noble one. She had been sleeping with two men—or at least thinking about it—one married and one a gangster, and she'd been caught. The only good thing she had done so far was to keep it from Miles, but her concern for his well-being was riddled with self-interest, a function of diverting shit from fan. Friendship was a motive for Ransom, but otherwise he was emotionally disengaged, which gave him an ethical vista. If

Marilyn were his lover, then there wouldn't be any moral dimension at all, only an erotic competition. The fact that he didn't particularly like her gave a clarity to the proceedings. He had no idea what he was going to do, but he felt that he had been waiting for something like this to present itself, a chance to act.

He moved to the third tub but passed on being parboiled in the fourth, finishing with a dunk in the cold water. The two men, now in the fourth tub, watched this procedure and perhaps observed that the gaijin anatomy exhibited a familiar response to cold water.

The drills did not feel real to DeVito. He knew this shit cold. He felt like he was sitting in the corner watching his body kick and block his partner. He wailed on the sucker, a brown-belt technician, driving him back on the attack, standing fast when he was defending, waiting for the drills to end and the sparring to begin. The drills were important, but combat was the point. Everything came together when you were fighting. Everything was real when you knew you could get your teeth smashed in, your balls delivered express to the back of your throat. Then you had to be all there and smash the other guy first.

Most dojos had a general hands-off-face policy, which obliged you to pull your hits just short of the head and neck. You only gained what you risked, was DeVito's view, and if you didn't put the whole works on the line, what was the point? That was one of the things he admired about the Japanese: they understood this. One of his buddies in the Marines had lent him a book about the samurai and he had learned about Bushido: the way of the warrior. They were prepared to die at any moment, and that, DeVito realized in a flash of enlightenment, was the way to really *live.*

After he was eighty-sixed out of the service DeVito came to Kyoto hoping to study kendo, the way of the sword, until he discovered that it was nowadays practiced with bamboo staves and protective gear. Karate seemed a more immediate and vital form of combat. After a protracted search he had found the kind of dojo he was looking for. The sensei was one of the toughest motherfuckers in Japan, or anywhere. Kuro-obi, seventh grade, national champion for three years, and the star of several karate flicks. The rumor at the dojo was that he had whipped hell out of Bruce Lee in an informal match.

The initiation almost killed him. Altogether it was about ten times harder than basic training at Camp Lejeune, although the memory of basic helped him get through it. For starters he had to run to the top of Mt. Hiei in December. It took six hours. Halfway up, running barefoot, he hit snow. A group from the dojo followed him in a car, jeering. The remaining trials were no picnic. In the dojo, he repeatedly had the shit kicked out of him. He understood what it was about. He would have endured worse. Now he was kuro-obi, second grade, having flattened and bloodied most of those who had presided over his initiation. The sensei, pleased with his progress, had named him second assistant.

Finally, the sensei banged the Chinese gong signalling the end of drills and the beginning of sparring. Everyone hustled to the sparring circle in the middle of the floor.

Any one who was perceived to dawdle would quickly regret it.

DeVito watched the early matches with a rising sense of excitement. He projected himself into each one, seeing missed opportunities, unprotected areas crying out for a hit, identifying with the clean arc of a kick hitting home. Finally the sensei called his name. He strode into the circle and slipped into his fighting stance as if into a warm bath, knowing as he looked into the eyes of the other that he had already won, feeling even before the match started the trajectory of his kick and the hard contact at the end of it.

Ransom crossed the river at the Sanjo-Ohashi Bridge and rode out through the Okazaki district, noted for temples and love hotels. The love hotels were tucked away on the residential streets, the word HOTEL in English indicating that the rates were hourly rather than nightly, that the beds might be circular or heart-shaped, the parking areas fenced and hedged so that patrons—illicit lovers, or husbands and wives whose domestic setup didn't afford privacy—could enter and exit discreetly. The Miyako Hotel was not one of these, aloof on a hillside on the western edge of the city, approached via a long, meticulously landscaped drive. Ransom chose it for their meeting because it was remote.

A flock of schoolgirls was milling around the front entrance, watched over by two cops. As Ransom passed through the group, he kept the visor of his helmet down so as not to excite the usual "gaijin" chorus. The Miyako was not the kind of place for a school outing. Nor was it exactly his kind of place. The maître d' in the lounge did not appear pleased with his jeans, but Ransom had the foresight to wear a blazer. He didn't see Marilyn. He asked, in English, for a table, and said a lady would be joining him.

"An American lady?"

"Not an American lady." Ransom didn't feel her ethnic or national origin was the management's concern.

"And would you like a drink, sir," the waiter asked after Ransom was seated.

"Yes. I would like a drink of water."

"Water?"

"On the rocks. With a twist of lemon."

Ransom found himself seated near an American couple, fiftyish, dressed for dinner.

"What was the name of the one with all the arms?" the man said.

"Kannon. Goddess of mercy. The arms were to help people into paradise."

"Right."

"Tomorrow I want to visit the Temple of the Golden Pavilion. And I hope the cherry blossoms are out soon. They were *supposed* to be out this weekend. Excuse me for a moment, Dave."

She stood up and walked away, an elegant woman, trim and tan inside an expensive-looking silk dress. When Ransom looked back at the table the man was watching him.

"Fuck the cherry blossoms," he said heartily. "And if we saw one temple, we saw a hundred of them."

"Only nineteen hundred to go," Ransom said.

"Stop! You're giving me nightmares. Don't tell the wife. She'll want to see them all." He took a swig of his drink, shook his head back and forth and sighed. "Been here for a while, have you?" he said.

"Just walked in," Ransom said.

"No, I mean—" He brightened suddenly and laughed. "Dave Constable's the name." He held out his hand, which Ransom shook. "That's quite a grip you've got there. Where you from? Back in the States, I mean."

"New York," Ransom said, preferring the city of his birth to that of his upbringing.

"What are you—over here on business?"

"More or less."

"So you know the ropes in this part of the world?"

"Not really."

He pulled his chair closer and leaned forward. "Say, what about these geisha?"

"What about them?"

"Where do you find them?"

"About a mile from here in an area called Gion. But that doesn't mean *you* can find them."

The man was spinning the hexagonal ashtray on the tablecloth, moving his index finger from slot to slot, dialling it like a phone. "What are they like?"

"Expensive."

"Do they . . . Are they . . . you know?"

"Not exactly," Ransom said. "You need an introduction just to get your foot in the door, and lots of money. What you would get for your money is conversation, mild flirtation, singing and dancing."

"No sex?"

"You'd have to spend months, and thousands; then, maybe."

"They sound like the girls I went to high school with."
Still dialling the ashtray, he looked wistful. "Are they beautiful?"

"Apparently to the Japanese. It's a question of packaging." Shortly after he had come to Japan, Ransom had gone once to a geisha house, the guest of a rich private student. He had been fascinated and appalled. The geisha had white porcelain faces and blackened teeth. They moved like marionettes, and their voices were high, almost mechanical, like the prerecorded messages on the subways and streetcars, artificial in the extreme. The wigs, the student told him later, weighed almost ten pounds.

"So much for Oriental nookie," Constable said with a wink. Catching sight of his wife, he put a finger to his lips. "Mum's the word."

He introduced his wife, Elizabeth, and said, "This young man here is an old Japan hand."

"Oh, wonderful. We can pick your brain for ideas. Would you recommend the Temple of the Golden Pavilion?"

"I'm afraid I've never been there."

"It's famous," she said.

"I've heard it's very nice."

"You know how it is, honey," Constable said agreeably. "People come to Rochester from all over the world to see the George Eastman House, but if you live practically next door, you don't even think about it."

"You probably know it as the International Photography Museum," the woman said to Ransom. She was waiting for a response so Ransom nodded. "Rochester is the home of Kodak."

"Don't forget Xerox," Constable said.

"Anyway, we'd be grateful for some pointers. We really want to immerse ourselves in Japanese culture."

"Your husband was just telling me that," Ransom said.

Across the table, Dave's face suffered changes, tending towards fearful and gray.

"Did he tell you about the tea ceremony we participated in?"

"He didn't mention it."

Mrs. Constable described the event in detail while her husband sat by silently, dialling the ashtray.

Ransom's first college roommate was from Rochester; it turned out that the Constables knew the family. They filled him in on the recent history of his classmate, who had just finished an internship at St. Vincent's in New York. The talk turned to the city: crime, restaurants, gentrification. The Constables went down from Rochester twice a year for a weekend, to do museums and theater. Summers they had a cottage in the Thousand Islands. While Mrs. Constable talked about an annual lilac festival, Ransom wondered how Ron Connors, former roommate and nerd, managed life or death decisions in the operating room. Ransom would just as soon operate on himself.

It was almost six o'clock, with no sign of Marilyn, when the Constables excused themselves to get ready for dinner.

"We're here for three more days," Liz said. "That's if we last it out at this hotel. There's some rock group staying on the floor above us and last night they practically tore the place down."

Ransom tried to imagine the country as they saw it: temples, gardens, exquisitely polite natives. They would welcome the inexplicable details—they had paid for some strangeness—although they probably wouldn't like the Kentucky Fried Chicken shacks. This was more or less how it had been for him when he arrived, except that he wasn't planning to get back on a plane at the end of the week. He was sick with Pakistani dysentery and guilt, having travelled three-quarters of the way around the world only to discover that everything he knew and believed was hideously inadequate to the task of living.

His ship from Hong Kong docked at Osaka. He took the train to Kyoto and found a room in a hostel. Three days later he met Miles in a coffee shop. Ransom had staggered into the place hoping to find a seat before he fainted, suddenly stricken with an attack of the cyclical fever he'd been fighting since India. He passed out just inside the door and when he came to he was looking up at a cowboy. Miles had taken Ransom home and Akiko had nursed him. Eventually they helped him find a teaching job and a place of his own. A Japanese doctor shot Ransom full of antibiotics and the fever stopped coming back. He enrolled in a language class, explored the streets of the city, and considered joining a Zen temple, until the day he wandered into a karate dojo.

Ransom began to wonder if something had happened to Marilyn. More likely, she had stood him up. He had given her more than an hour. The thing to do was make sure Miles was all right. He briefly imagined himself dispatching tattooed, heavily armed yakuza with his bare hands, and almost immediately realized that he was casting this scenario out of the kind of television fantasy that had made his father rich.

In the lobby a flash bulb went off in his face. A girl no older than twelve was pointing a camera at him and screeching. He pushed through the door and found himself looking at a hundred quizzical faces, all belonging to teenage girls. For a moment, nothing happened; he looked at them and they looked at him. Then someone screamed. Other voices joined in. The crowd pressed forward, hands outstretched.

Reflexively, he swept his arm in a mid-level block, clearing away several hands. The blazer slung over his shoulder was tugged down into the crowd. Then his shirt was torn at from all directions. He was pressed back against the glass door, which had swung closed behind him. The screaming pitched even higher when the shirt ripped and came clear of his chest. Hands were all over him, and he felt lips pressed to his arm. He watched his shirt dissipating in the mob, being torn into smaller and smaller pieces as it moved back. He was beginning to panic.

Fingers groped at his belt buckle, as Ransom spotted two policemen wading through the crowd, whistles in their mouths and clubs raised above their heads. Then he felt the door move behind him. A girl with pimples and pigtails seemed determined to write something on his chest with a ball point pen, and another flourished a pair of scissors. He felt his shoes go; then, lips on his feet.

He was being pulled back into the hotel. Two girls made it through the door with him, but they were pried loose and whisked away. A hotel employee stood in front of the door; and while the crowd still leaped and screamed, no one attempted to rush indoors.

A man in a blue suit was bowing repeatedly to Ransom. "I am so sorry for this misfortune. We did not know you would be using main entrance. Please accept my deep apology on behalf of hotel. Our security was at fault."

A knot of hotel guests gawked from the inner lobby at the half-naked gaijin. A woman in a hotel uniform appeared with a kimono which Ransom quickly put on. The man in the blue suit kept apologizing. Outside, the school girls began singing choruses of a song Ransom eventually recognized as "Satisfaction."

A limousine was placed at his disposal. Since his shoes were gone, he decided to pick up the bike later, and was escorted out the back entrance to a waiting car.

The driver had a broad face and drinker's complexion. He kept looking at Ransom in the rear view. "You Charrie Watts, *desu ne?*"

Ransom said that he was not a Rolling Stone.

"You know Mr. Kirk Douglas?"

"Not personally."

The driver reached inside his jacket and handed back a pocket photo album. The first picture showed him standing at the gate of Yasaka shrine with his arm around a man who appeared to be Kirk Douglas. The next one was similar, except that it was signed *Best wishes Lloyd Bridges.* Standing beside the car, Lloyd looked dried-out, not a spear gun in sight.

"I drive Jack Kneecross last year," he said.

"Say who?"

A crowd of schoolboys in uniforms had found their way

into the Nicklaus picture. The proud driver naturally had his arm around Jack, a baby-faced god and credit to his race.

Because he didn't want the neighbors asking questions, Ransom asked to be dropped a street away from his house. He had to stand next to the car while the driver found a pedestrian to take their picture.

He saw a shadow cross his as he approached the corner. He ducked, rolled on his shoulder and sprang back to his feet, but not quickly enough to dodge the second kick, which caught him on the chest and knocked him over.

Better, the sensei said. *But not very good.*

9

En route to Osaka, ancient headquarters of fish peddlers and sake traders, Ransom felt that perhaps the country had begun to go awry when it relaxed the four-tier caste system in which merchants and businessmen occupied the lowest rung, beneath farmers, warriors, and nobility. Kyoto was a museum; Osaka, once reduced to rubble by American bombing, was a collaboration of accountants and engineers. The commute between the two was forty minutes by train. Ransom went to Osaka, like everyone else, to make money.

Avoiding the rush, he caught a ten-thirty train, his fellow passengers women and children. He felt right at home with his book, a collection of historical tales for children written in childish hiragana, the phonetic system of writing. Though Ransom knew Americans and Europeans who were as devoted to the study of the language as he was to karate, he himself was content to dabble. He wanted to preserve the strangeness of his environment, keep himself just slightly off-balance.

For several days he had been working on one of the tales; his translation-in-progress was folded into the book:

The Lord Michizane lost favor in the court through the slander of his enemies and was banished. Not content with this, his enemies required the extermination of his family.

Spies from court searched the countryside and discovered Michizane's son and heir hidden in a small town. The son had been entrusted to Genzo, a former retainer of the Michizane family, now a provincial schoolmaster. An edict from the court arrived, commanding Genzo to present the head of the young heir to an envoy from the court.

Genzo was in despair. He could not disobey an order from the court. Nor could he kill his former lord's son, entrusted to his protection. A scheme occurred to him. He searched the classroom for a face that resembled the young prince. He would substitute another boy. But the others were rough peasant boys. None resembled the young lord.

Ransom's sleeve was tugged. When he looked up he was face to face with a boy standing in the aisle; he examined him for princely features. Meantime, the boy scrutinized Ransom before arriving at his verdict: "Gaijin."

Two seats back, his mother gestured frantically.

Who are you? the boy demanded.

I am a spy, Ransom said.

The boy nodded gravely. This seemed to be just what

he had suspected. The mother came forward, apologizing and blushing, and the kid bolted for the next car.

The envoy from the court arrived on the specified day. Genzo presented him with the head of a young boy. The boy's features were noble and aristocratic. The envoy took the head in his hands and examined it closely as if he were checking a persimmon for bruises. Genzo kept his hand on his sword. At last the envoy pronounced the head to be truly that of the young prince.

A final paragraph remained. Ransom wanted to know how it turned out. As the train emerged aboveground at Katsura, he took out his pocket dictionary and set to work; by the time the prerecorded female voice informed him that the train was coming up on Ibaraki, he had roughed it out.

Not far off, the mother of the dead youth waited. When she heard a sound at the gate she knew that it was not her son. She knew that she would never see her son again. The sliding door of the cottage was pulled back and a man entered. It was Genzo. He said, "Rejoice, my wife, for our son has been of service to his lord Michizane."

This was the stuff, Ransom thought, that turned brats like his little inquisitor into loyal salary men like those who had packed the train a few hours earlier. It might not be so bad to know where your loyalties lay, to have a distinct place in a chain of obligation and command. He wondered which was worse: having a master for whom you would cut off your child's head, or not having a master at all.

Outside the window a thin green fuzz showed on the rice paddies, lately flooded. Old women stooped, ankle-deep in mud, weeding and thinning the shoots.

At Umeda Station Ransom descended to the subway, a cheerful android voice welcoming him aboard and naming the stops. He arrived at the office a little after eleven-thirty, where the receptionist, Keiko, greeted him elaborately. Honda, his boss, president and director of the A-OK Advertising Agency and English Language Conversation School, was less effusive.

"Ransom-san," he called from his desk, as Ransom unloaded at his own. "Please to speak with me a moment." Desmond Caldwell, Ransom's British colleague, was hunched over in such a manner as to appear to be writing with one end of a pencil and picking his nose with the other.

Ransom wished Honda-sama good morning and performed a perfunctory bow before taking the seat in front of his desk.

"What happened to your face?" Honda said, indicating the scratches. "Karate?"

"Rock and roll," Ransom said.

Honda lit a Seven Star and asked how the weather was in Kyoto. For him this was a subject of genuine concern. Kyoto weather was notorious, the ring of mountains surrounding the city allegedly kept the good weather out and the bad weather in. Honda lived in Osaka, and couldn't understand why Ransom didn't. He claimed only gaijin and native Kyoto-jin could stand to live in the inclement ancient capital.

Ransom's report of partial clouds did not seem to satisfy him. "It's sunny here," he said, in case Ransom hadn't noticed, but he was clearly thinking of something else. He took a long drag on his cigarette and said, "I have had complaint from Mitsubishi."

"What kind of complaint?"

"They say you attack the Japanese family."

"How did I do that?"

Honda consulted a piece of paper. "They say you say there is 'double standard' in Japan."

Now he remembered. The phrase "double standard" had come up in the lesson. Perhaps because they were accustomed to multiple standards, they couldn't really get hold of the concept.

"I must to remind you that we teach English conversation. We do not teach ethics, American or otherwise."

"Language is shot through with values," Ransom said.

"Say again?"

"If I want to use Japanese correctly, I have to buy into the hierarchy. Talk to my boss one way and the receptionist another."

"I know nothing about that. I know that Mitsubishi account is very important to us. No more ethics. Ethics get you in trouble. Stick to business."

Ransom spent what was left of the morning rewriting a brochure for an air conditioner manufactured by their largest advertising account. Honda had written the original copy, which explained and extolled the air conditioner to Australian purchasers. Now the unit was being exported to the U.S. Across the top, Honda had written, "Does this need slight revision for American market?"

> The excellent thermal output machine of MODEL K-500
> TAKYO INTERNATIONAL as superb AIR CONDITIONING
> UNIT for your cooling pleasure, and permitting
> wonderful co-existence such as: 'high quality
> against low cost,' 'energy efficient with high
> performance approx 55 BTUs,' 'being efficient in
> mechanism plus operating under noises being
> extremely suppressed,' for cool relaxation feeling
> of fulfillment, "easy listening" in your beautiful
> home.

At the bottom he had written, "How about American theme headline: FOR YOUR LIFE, LIBERTY AND PURSUIT OF HAPPINESS." Ransom edited the copy as best he could, knowing that in the end Honda—who liked to say that Carlyle was his model in English prose—would take one or two of Ransom's changes, if any, and send it back to the client, who would never know the difference. Ransom had learned that he could not hold Honda to a rigorous standard of English grammar and usage. The boss grew testy if corrected too often. After all, Honda was the author of the Honda A-OK Business English Conversation textbook series. Ransom had to teach two classes a week ostensibly based on these texts, which were not as dreadful as they might have been, the actual author being an aspiring Great American Novelist who had been Honda's first employee. Honda, however, having interfered with the manuscripts just enough to insert several howlers in each chapter, had come to believe that he wrote the books himself, and consequently to consider himself an expert. Ransom had no great desire to disabuse him. He did the best he could under the circumstances, figuring that a misplaced modifier probably wasn't going to kill anyone. Ransom had developed a tolerance for bad English when he worked for his father as a script reader the year he graduated from college.

Desmond Caldwell looked up from his desk. " 'Ave you 'eard the Stones are in town?" Ransom nodded. Had he been in Japan too long, or did Desmond actually look like Keith Richards? Maybe it was just the snaggle teeth.

Ransom penned *Ave you eard about the Boston Strangler?* across the scratch pad, and Desmond hunched over his desk again in earnest labor.

At twelve-thirty he got a phone call from Rachel Coughlin, now a corporate something-or-other for a large American bank, and stationed in Tokyo.

"I'm in Osaka for two days. My lunch got cancelled. Have you eaten?"

"That depends," Ransom said.

"Don't worry—it's on the company," she said.

"I mean it depends on whether you're lunching as a friend or as my father's emissary abroad."

"Hey, come on. I was just trying to help. But I'm through being a go-between. Promise." She gave Ransom an address and said she would meet him there in twenty minutes. Honda wasn't around, so he left the edited air-conditioner copy on his desk and told Keiko he would be back by two-thirty.

The sidewalks were jammed with blue-suited businessmen, and Ransom was immediately caught up in the flow of the crowd. A brightly painted sound truck passed slowly, hawking a live sex show.

Rachel had befriended Ransom when he moved into her Bel Air neighborhood, and they had kept in touch after he went east to prep school. A year ago she had written to say she was working in Tokyo, and they had met for lunch several times since then. The last time he saw her, some six months ago, she was keen to know what Ransom's plans were, even insistent. She was going back to California for Christmas and she had a story about a special arrangement between the bank and an airline whereby she could bring a companion at no extra cost. It would be like the old days; he could spend Christmas at home and then join her at her family's cabin in Tahoe for skiing.

To Ransom it was clear that she'd been charged with this mission by his father. The free airfare story was made for TV. He had been getting letters from his father; impatient, fatherly letters: What was he doing with his life, what was he running from, when was he coming back to settle down, start a career? Ransom sympathized—the old man was fifty-something—but was nevertheless angry with him and Rachel alike for their manipulating. The improbably free Christmas trip was his father's idea; and, as Ransom suspected, his father planned to pay for the ticket on the sly. He had told Rachel that Ransom had clearly lost his faculties and sense to drugs in India, that he would not listen to reason.

In Yodoyobashi he passed a coffee shop with the name, written in English over the door, *Persistent Pursuit of Dainty*.

Waiting for a light, he found himself beside a businessman carrying a GROOVY CAT shopping bag, a relative of the FUNKY BABE:

> GROOVY CAT: Let's call a groovy guy a "Groovy Cat."
> Guys tough, check out the scene, love to
> dancing with Funky Babes. Let's all strive
> to be Groovy Cats.

Surrounded by so much twisted English—in advertising, embedded in Japanese sentences, in conversation with non-native speakers like Honda and Kano—Ransom sometimes felt a kind of aphasia setting in: a student or client would present him with a crippled English sentence and he would be at a loss to fix it.

He turned into a covered alley lined with noodle and yakitori stands. A boy in a white uniform dodged through the crowd on his bicycle, three trays of noodles balanced in his left palm. He seemed headed for disaster but kept threading the openings, one-handed, between pedestrians and finally turned the corner. Farther up, in front of the tobacco stand, a man talking on the red pay telephone bowed repeatedly to his invisible confidant.

Among the plastic models in the glass case beside the door of the restaurant was a mournful, inflated *fugu*, poison blowfish, an occasionally fatal delicacy which by law could only be prepared by licensed chefs.

Ransom was shown to a table, and Rachel came in a few minutes later, breathless, trailing strands of her involvement with the world of commerce. She kissed Ransom and then dropped into her chair, her jacket flaring then sub-siding around her like a parachute, attracting the attention of all of the blue-suited diners, the only woman in the restaurant and blond to boot.

"Exchange rates are going wild," she said.

Ransom smiled, "I can hardly keep up."

"It's exciting, now that all the currencies are floating, but life was probably a hell of a lot easier when they were fixed. Anyway, you're looking very good."

"You too," Ransom said.

"What are you up to tonight?"

"I teach a class. Then karate practice."

"I have tickets for the Stones."

"You and ten thousand Japanese teeny boppers. I met some of them the other day."

"Join me."

"No can do."

"Skip your practice."

He shook his head.

"What's so vital about one karate practice?"

"This could be the night I break somebody's nose. You wouldn't want me to miss out on that."

"When are you going to get serious?"

"About what?"

She sighed, raised her hands as if to strangle him. "You know. I mean, about everything. About your life."

"Going to see the Stones is serious?"

"You know what I mean."

"I thought you'd retired as my father's agent."

"Forget your father. You're my age, Chris. You're bright

as hell but pretty soon people are going to say, Well, Mr. Ransom, what's this three-year gap in your résumé? Kung-fu and the Kyoto experience won't open many doors."

"Karate," Ransom said.

"What's the difference? There's a lot going on here besides head-bashing. Listen, the business ideas of the next decade are going to come out of Japan. Why do you think I'm here? I requested this posting. The Japanese are starting to set the pace. Resource depletion, population density, miniaturization—an American who comes here with his eyes open is going to be in a position to learn. The new logos is right here. It's beyond socialism and capitalism. We are talking the Tao of Capital. Jesus, Chris, the choice isn't working in television or living like an impoverished monk in Japan. There are other options."

"All the world lies before me, eh?"

She leaned back in her chair and sighed. "I don't know why you're doing this romantic exile routine. What are you running from? Your father?"

"I'm not running, Rachel."

"Why can't you forgive him?"

"Forgive him for what?"

"That's *my* question. What is it?"

"I hate television."

"Very sophisticated, aren't we. You blame him for your mother, don't you."

"I blame him for thinking that he's the director and other people are just players—Mom, me, all those promising young actresses. Other people aren't real to him."

"No one was more devastated by your mother's death—forgive me, but I mean this—than he was."

"The cleaning lady was more devastated."

"He's not that bad, Chris."

"That Christmas scheme was typical. He'd rather dream up a bad plot than just ask me to come home."

"It was for a good cause."

"That's what Nixon said after he got caught."

"He loves you."

"Did I ever tell you how he got me into Princeton? I told him I wouldn't even apply unless he promised not to get his friends and fellow alums to pull strings. My junior year I find out, accidentally, from a friend in the records office—he thinks it's a big joke, right?—that my old man donated a very considerable sum to the university the year I applied."

"Don't be ridiculous. You got in because you were smart. Your father probably needed a tax write-off."

"Right."

"So he was trying to help. Sue him."

"Well, I don't want his help, thanks. What pisses him off is that he can't help me when I'm over here. Limits to his power and all that."

"He's not young anymore, Chris. And you're his only son."

"How do you feel about the blowfish sashimi," Ransom said, seeing the waiter hovering.

She sighed, looked down at the menu briefly and said, "Okay. Live dangerously."

After they had ordered he said, "Do you like your job?"

"Sure. Why?"

"What do you like about it? I'm curious. You really seem

enthusiastic. Are you in it for the money or is there something else?"

"It's challenging." Rachel said without hesitating.

"How?" Ransom said. "The way a crossword puzzle is challenging? Maybe I just don't get it. When I got out of school, I couldn't think of anything I really wanted to do. There were options, but there weren't any reasons."

"What are your goals?" Rachel challenged.

Ransom thought about it. "I don't know. I think maybe I want to become a blank slate. Forgive and forget."

The blowfish arrived, thin, salmon-colored wafers on a black lacquer tray. "I don't know," Ransom said, "whether it is more polite to offer it to you first or to test it myself."

Rachel snagged a piece with her chopsticks and deposited it on her tongue. Ransom followed suit. The chewy flesh slightly numbed his lips.

Rachel explained rising interest and inflation rates to him. While she was in the Ladies' Ransom paid the check, but she was so upset about it that he let her pay half.

"Can I walk you somewhere?" he said, when they were outside.

"I've got a meeting." She put her arms around his neck and kissed him. "Why don't you ever come to Tokyo?"

"I don't like Tokyo much."

"We'll stay indoors."

"You could come to Kyoto. See the sights."

"Do you have a phone yet?"

"I'll call you."

Out on the street, he flagged a cab for her. As it moved off into the traffic Ransom felt a twinge of sadness and wondered if they might have been more than friends under different circumstances.

At five o'clock, after fruitless negotiations with Honda over the air-conditioner copy, Ransom was in a conference room on the fourteenth floor of the Mitsubishi Shoji office, looking out over the city. A receptionist brought him a hand towel and a cup of tea. The students entered in twos and threes, and he greeted them by name. Roughly Ransom's age, they were all male, young sub-managers who might someday find themselves in New York or London on Mitsubishi business.

When everyone was seated, Ransom opened his book and called out a page number. The students looked alarmed: jumping right into the lesson was a departure from the norm. Generally he opened class with an informal discussion. A standard question was: what did you do this weekend? The bachelors drank and played mah-jongg with their buddies. The married men drank and played with their children. Wives didn't rate a mention. Every once in a while, someone would visit a sick relative in Tokyo.

Ransom was not pleased with them for complaining about his comments last week, so they could have it straight from the book this time. He slowly repeated the page number and they reluctantly opened their books, the cover of which featured a wavy-haired executive behind a Bauhaus desk and a blond secretary taking dictation, blouse buttoned up to the neck but showing a bit of knee. This was Level Two of the A-OK system. Adorning the cover of Level One was a prim, less attractive secretary taking dictation from a less commanding executive. Several students had asked him about the cover of Level Three, no doubt hoping to hear that the blonde had shed her clothing and crawled across the desk on her hands and knees.

Ransom read: "Lesson Seven: Talking Business the American Way. Dialogue One: 'Wanted, A Real Go-Getter.'" He anticipated the hands that shot up around the table. Mr. Hayashi asked, "What is go-getter?"

Ransom's father often employed the phrase as a term of great approbation, but his son knew he would have trouble explaining why to people who had been raised on self-effacement and group thinking. "Okay. A go-getter is someone who . . . is very aggressive. Who knows what he wants. And goes . . . and gets it." He thought this last a nice touch.

The faces around the table showed puzzlement tinged with alarm. Hayashi, class bird dog, raised his hand. "Is this a bad person?"

Ransom pondered the inherent value judgments. This note of aggressiveness and self-assertion was disturbing to his students. "I think," he said, "that in America, such a person would be considered a very good businessman."

More puzzlement. Proceed.

"Okay. Hayashi, you start. You are Mr. Robinson. As we all know, Mr. Robinson is the Personnel Director of Vidco. Right?"

Hayashi beamed, fingers spread, palms down on either side of his book, ready to assume executive responsibility.

"Mr. Sato." Sato jumped at the unmistakable syllables of his name, then slumped lower in his chair. Lazy and reluctant, Sato would make an intriguing go-getter. Ransom wondered briefly if it was Sato who had ratted on him, then realized that Sato would not have understood the conversation in question.

"Mr. Sato, you are Jim Banks. You are applying for a job. Remember, you are a real go-getter. Self-assured. Aggressive. All right, go get 'em."

Hayashi cleared his throat, pressed his palms down hard on the table.

Hayashi/Robinson: "Come right in, Jim. Have a sheet."

Ransom: "That's *seat*."

Hayashi/Robinson: "Have a sit."

Sato/Banks: "Thank you."

Hayashi/Robinson: "Frankly, Jim, I'm quite impressed with your . . ."

Ransom: "Résumé."

Hayashi/Robinson: "Your résumé. You seem to have a track record of proven sales performance. I see you decided fairly early on that sales was your bag."

Sato/Banks: "That's true, Mr. Robinson."

Hayashi/Robinson: "Call me Flank."

Ransom: "Frank."

Sato/Banks: "Well, Flank, I believe I mentioned working my way through college with my own . . . perfumé . . ."

Ransom: "Perfume."

Sato looked up, his face expressing surprise and injury; he had correctly applied the pronunciation of "résumé" to a word that looked almost identical, only to be told he was wrong. He shook his head sadly and looked back at the book.

Sato/Banks: "Perfume distributorship. On graduating I sold the business for a handsome profit."

Hayashi/Robinson: "Very enterprising. You seem to be a real *go-getter,* Jim. And I see you haven't been idle since then."

Pause.

Ransom: "Sato, you're on."

Sato/Banks: "*Doko?* Okay, okay. Well, I joined the Unifax sales force three years ago and I'm now regional sales manager for an eight-state legion."

Hayashi/Robinson: "Unifax seems to have done really well by you."

Sato/Banks: "They have, but frankly, I'm looking for a new challenge. I think my talons could best be utilized in a national sales position with an aggressive, growth-oriented firm."

Hayashi/Robinson: "Well, Jim. The Vidco sales team could certainly use a prayer like you."

Utter bafflement. The clock over the door said 6:26. Another hour to go.

10

Night practice had an air of ceremony. Under the spotlight the parking lot took on the aspect of a stage or an altar. Men in white robes. The sprawl of the day was reduced to a circle of light.

Ransom led calisthenics, taking care not to rush the stretching; there were enough ways to get hurt without pulling a muscle or popping a joint. They worked up the body—toes, Achilles tendons, ankles, knees, thighs. Facing him, the others moved as if they were shadows of a single figure, perfectly in sync. The sensei sat on the steps of the gym, smoking a cigarette. Ransom proceeded to drills: middle kicks, high kicks, right and left, fifty each. He watched the Monk and Yamada in the front row, tuning himself to their rhythm until it seemed to him that the kicks were not rising out of any volition of his own but as a manifestation of a collective effort.

The sensei told them to pair off for drills, directing the Monk, Yamada and Ransom to work with the junior ranks. A motorcycle pulled into the lot as the sensei was demonstrating a three-kick combination. Ransom paired up with Udo, the bodybuilder. As they moved off to their spot, Ransom saw DeVito remove his helmet and lean back against the seat of his bike.

He tried to ignore him, but found himself working Udo much harder than he might have. He was impatient with Udo's offense; the flash of impulses in Udo's eyes telegraphed his attacks, and the actual contact was an anticlimax. In such a mundane context Ransom was unable to show his abilities, and when he took the attack he pounded Udo back across the lot, knocking him over before he realized what he was doing.

After fifteen minutes they changed drills and partners. Although Ransom didn't look at DeVito, he knew he was there. Working with Tadashi, another undistinguished opponent, he wished that the sensei would give them something more interesting to do. Usually the sensei participated in the drills, but tonight he was slouching around the sidelines. He came over once and told Ransom to stop favoring his left leg. Several times he shouted admonitions at Yamada.

After an hour of slogging through drills Ransom hoped for sparring, an occasion for performance. At the same time, his habitual anxiety about sparring was aggravated by DeVito's gaze. By the time the sensei called them in from drills he was thoroughly disgusted with himself. If he couldn't keep DeVito from clouding his mind, then he hadn't learned anything.

Two points, no restrictions, the sensei said. He called Yamada out first. Beginning with a schoolboy who had joined the dojo only a few weeks ago, Yamada fought five easy matches in order of rank, although his last opponent almost caught him with a middle kick and the sensei told him twice that he was looking sloppy. Then the Monk came in, quickly dispatched Sato, Ichii, and Minamoto, all of whom were competent, but looked scared and clumsy against Ito. Next was Suzuki, a thin high school student with a DA haircut and a good front kick. As soon as the sensei started the match, he threw himself at the Monk with a flurry of limbs and then crumpled, lying jackknifed on the asphalt, a clicking sound in his throat.

The sensei hoisted him to his feet, held him by the ribs, and explained that his stance was too high. The Monk stood with his hands folded in front of his crotch, eyes half-closed. Once Suzuki recovered his wind, the sensei told him to try again. This time he attacked with his hands. The Monk stepped back and inserted a delicate front-thrust between Suzuki's moving arms, pulling it just short of the forehead. The sensei called the point. Suzuki tilted his head and squinted at Ito's fist, as if the outcome might look better from different angle. He bowed and retired with a fatalistic shake of the head.

Now was Ransom's turn. He stepped out to take Suzuki's place, fixing his eyes on the Monk's, holding the gaze through the bow. The Monk settled back, way down in cat stance, all of his weight back on the rear leg, folded nearly double, while the lead foot barely touched the pavement.

He made an L with his forearms in front of his chest, the left vertical, the right horizontal. It seemed to Ransom that Ito's eyes were like pools in which no fish were showing; he would have to throw out some bait. He kicked. The Monk swept the kick away with his forearm. Ransom threw another kick, two jabs, and got knocked sideways by a kick in the ribs.

His breath was short and there was a dull pain in his ribs. The sensei told him to straighten up and fight. The ache in his ribs was either going to slow him down or serve as his weapon. He straightened up, then lowered himself into a crouch facing the Monk. When he inhaled, he drew the ache into a fine, hot wire extending from his side up into his right arm. He aimed it at the Monk. He saw the wire pointing toward the Monk's chest. When the Monk came at him he drove it home, feeling the impact of his knuckles against the Monk's sternum travel back to its point of origin in his ribs. The pain dissipated and then it was gone, as if it had travelled from his own body into the Monk's.

The sensei called the point, the first time Ransom had ever scored on the Monk. He was trying to remember how he had done it, as they squared off, when the Monk kicked him in the chest for the match.

When he remembered to look for DeVito, he was gone.

After practice, as Ransom was folding up his gi, he felt a hand on his shoulder.

Very nice, said the Monk. *I congratulate you.*

I was lucky, Ransom said.

The Monk shook his head. *All of your training was in that punch.* Then he said something about focus.

Ransom smiled foolishly. Ito, the Monk, smiled back. They stood this way, face to face, for a moment; Ransom vaguely anticipating a benediction, a word or gesture that would seal the transfer he felt had taken place. The Monk bowed, turned and walked off, his white gi slung over his shoulder, rolled and tied in the ragged black belt, plastic sandals flopping.

Ransom drifted with the others across the street to the noodle shop where the toothless sobaya-san could not welcome them enough. Yamada was already sitting at the front table with a beer. When he saw Ransom he put down his glass and began to clap.

Nice move, he said.

Lucky move, the sensei called out from the counter.

Yamada pulled out a chair for Ransom, poured a glass of beer and told him to drink it off. Ransom complied. Yamada ordered two more of the big half-liter bottles. Ransom thought about DeVito. Sizing him up. What he saw tonight would probably make him terribly confident. Ransom told himself that he didn't care what DeVito thought, but his presence seemed to promise trouble.

Yamada came back with beer. *Time for sex crimes,* he announced, and changed channels on the television. The room went quiet. The host and hostess of the show welcomed the home and studio audiences, then traded double entendres which the noodle shop audience thought hilarious. Most of them were over Ransom's head.

What do we have tonight, the host asked. He was wearing a pink tuxedo, a blue boutonnière and several pounds of hair spray.

One gang rape, the woman responded brightly, *one double suicide, and a love-triangle murder. We'll be right back.*

An ad for instant noodles came on, followed by back to back detergents. Yamada told Ransom to drink up. The sensei, who had ducked out to the bathroom, returned and asked what the lineup was. Ransom wondered what the Monk was doing. He imagined Ito in a bare, monastic cell, two tatami mats and a small table at which he performed occasional calligraphy, sitting cross-legged, mentally reviewing the evening's practice, every motion, every contraction of muscular tissue, every neuron explosion. Yamada enthusiastically described last week's ax murder, voted best episode of the week by the studio audience, which was asked, at the end of the show, to select their favorite of the three dramatic re-enactments of true life sex crimes, taken from the files of police precincts all over Japan.

The noodle shop audience was not especially impressed with the first episode, a standard love-triangle deal. A young salary man conceives a passionate attachment for a bar hostess; his parents arrange a marriage for him with an unappealing stranger. He marries, which event scarcely interrupts the serious business of his life, including his affair. However, one day a Korean businessman proposes to the hostess, who accepts. She informs her lover of this one night when they are lying in bed, post-coitus, in a love hotel. They remain in the hotel for days. The scene switches to the front desk of the hotel, to which the salary man, increasingly haggard, keeps returning to pay for another few hours on the room. The staff jokes about the honeymoon couple, takes bets on how long they can keep it up. Until, finally, after a week, they begin to notice the smell.

No one is impressed; this was standard material. Yamada said that they always saved the best for last. Ransom said he hated to miss out on the good stuff, but he had to be going.

11

His karate sensei gave him a letter of recommendation to a kendo dojo. DeVito couldn't read all of it, but the sensei said it commended him for his true spirit of Budo, the Martial Way. He brought the letter to the budokan and watched a practice session. Looking like enraged baseball umpires, some thirty men in padded blue smocks and helmets whacked each other with bamboo staves. All in all, this seemed a little tame. When the session ended DeVito appoached the sensei, bowed deeply and presented the letter. The sensei had a face like a drill sergeant, lips like knife blades. He glanced at the letter, balled it up and tossed it over his shoulder.

Why do you want to pursue kendo? he said.

DeVito had been prepared for this. He bowed again and said that the way of the sword was the highest expression of the spirit of Budo. He made his grammar deliberately awkward, hoping this would add to the impression of humility.

There's some garbage on the floor over there, the sensei said, indicating DeVito's recommendation. *Pick it up.*

DeVito bowed and scuttled over to the letter, picking it up, wondering why he kept submitting himself to the same kind of tyrannical authority—his old man, Marine officers, senseis. But in the Corps he had begun to understand that you had to eat some short-term humble pie to get to be one of the guys who dished it out. Living in Japan, he had learned that you could say *Fuck you* on the inside and *Yes, sir* on the outside. Maybe this was knowledge that came to the silver-spoon set mixed in with their Gerber baby mush, but DeVito learned his lesson the hard way, and he was going to make up for lost time. It was easier to do it in a foreign country, especially Japan, because you could play ignorant whenever you needed to, and people tended to cut you plenty of slack.

He did his faithful-dog number, retrieving the ball of paper for the sensei. He knew that this guy was the best, and he was willing to do what it took to enroll as a student.

Garbage can, the sensei said, indicating the location with a nod of his head.

Some of the students stood by watching the spectacle, helmets under their arms. Laugh now, DeVito thought, returning from his garbage run.

How often can you practice?

Every day.

It was the right answer.

The sensei called out to a young boy who had just finished sweeping the wooden floor and was putting the broom away in a closet. *Broom,* he said, and the boy raced over.

The sensei told DeVito to sweep the floor.

DeVito thought, Surprise me, why don't you? Taking the broom from the boy, he bowed and thanked the sensei before undertaking his humble sweeping routine, polishing the floor with a vengeance. When you were ambitious, you did what you had to do. Ambition had brought him this far, half a world away from his dirtball hometown in Oklahoma. He wondered where he'd gotten it; not from his old man, who thought he'd made the big time when he opened his own barber shop, and whose idea of travel was twenty-seven holes in a golf cart. *Get yourself a trade,* was his great advice. That and *Be your own boss,* as if the old man didn't kiss ass on every banker and lawyer and oilman that walked into the shop.

DeVito swept every inch of the floor while the sensei looked on, and when he was done he scurried back and bowed. The sensei scrutinized the floor before turning to DeVito. *Come back in two months.*

This guy was hard-ass deluxe. How would you like an instant nose job, he wondered. He said, *Yes, sensei. Thank you very much.*

12

The kid reached up and tugged at the brim of the Stetson, edging it lower in short increments toward a precise but elusive position over his brow. When he had it right, he dropped his hands to his sides and then lifted them away from his body until they were a foot from either hip. Then he was ready.

You could see it in his eyes: the sun was high, the shadows short on the dusty street. Below the false-fronted second stories, doors and windows were bolted and shuttered. It was just the two of them now, the kid and the tall stranger in the dark clothes staring him down from thirty paces. A dry wind stirred eddies of grit around their legs. A lonesome tumbleweed rolled past. In the hills at the edge of town, rattlers and scorpions bellied over warm rocks in search of prey. The kid wouldn't be the first to draw. He would wait all day if he had to.

For Miles Ryder, watching from his stool behind the glass counter at Hormone Derange, the drama being played out in front of his full-length mirror was not entirely without suspense. Maybe this time the kid, a Japanese schoolboy, would buy the Stetson. This was his third shootout in four days. So far the kid has been lucky. But the odds got shorter every day.

Ryder turned to Ransom, who was leaning with his elbows on the counter thumbing through a Japanese cycle magazine. He said, "These Jap bikes all look like sewing machines to me."

Ransom said, "The seven fifties are quicker than a big Harley, and they've got a faster top end."

"Statistics don't impress me."

"They're a hell of a lot more reliable, too."

"They've taken the balls out of biking. It's like sex. Give me a little stink and smoke and noise between point A and point B. Give me a woman who howls and shouts. Give me that deep bass of a Harley."

"Suit yourself," Ransom said.

"Speaking of getting from point A to point B, I always wonder why it is we say 'I'm coming' and they say 'I'm going'? How come orgasm is an arrival for English speakers and a departure for Japanese? The first time I got laid here, this girl starts shrieking *iku! iku!* I knew from my *Japanese Made Easy* book that this meant 'I'm going,' and I couldn't figure out where she was going, and why. That's one problem with these mixed Japanese-gaijin marriages, not knowing whether you're coming or going."

"How is Akiko?" Ransom said, wondering if Miles was still seeing or, for that matter, screwing Marilyn.

"All right. She's past the morning pukes. It's hard to know how she's feeling—she never complains."

Miles Ryder tilted back on his stool. Above him, on the wall, was a mounted boar's head, its flared tusks suggesting a sneer; beside the boar a poster showing a cowboy sitting on a split-rail fence, a woman draped like saddlebags over his shoulders. *Are You Ready for Boots?* read the caption.

"Problem is, it'll take months to find a new Harley and the insurance won't come close to covering it."

"I saw DeVito the other day," Ransom said. "He dropped in at my dojo."

"And you let him walk away?"

"Why are you so sure it was him?"

"It's your basic fox-and-chicken situation. You don't need testimony from the cows to figure out the blood and feathers. What do you suppose he was doing at your dojo?"

Ransom shrugged, "He doesn't have any reason to bother me."

"He has plenty of reasons. You just don't think they're good ones."

Ransom turned the page. A woman in a bikini was tied provocatively across the frame of a Ducati, wrists bound to the handlebars, ankles to the spokes of the back wheels.

"I'm going to get him," Ryder said.

"Let it go," Ransom said, handing him the magazine.

Hat in hand, the quick-draw kid approached the counter. He asked, for the fifth or sixth time, how much it was.

Then he turned it over and peered inside the crown, as if looking for an oracle. Finally he said he would take it. Ryder told him it was a good choice, put it in a box and explained the care and feeding of the hat. He said he hated to sell a hat this good to someone who wasn't going to take care of it. The kid said he would. Ryder told him to come back for boots, when he was ready.

13

The yen was rising, auto exports were up, the Giants had beaten the Carp in extra innings after a home run by Sadaharu Oh, who was only eleven short of Hank Aaron's 755. The Japanese debated the significance of the imminent new world record, given the difference in field size, playing season, pitching styles between the two countries. Ransom thought Babe Ruth would always be King.

Otani, the coffee shop owner, poured Ransom another glass of water, complaining bitterly about an umpire's call earlier in the week. When the phone rang, Otani removed his apron and went around the bar to pick it up. He said *hai* five or six times, bowing repeatedly as he did so, and finally held out the phone for Ransom.

"I'm sorry I couldn't meet you at the hotel," Marilyn said. "I had some trouble."

"What kind of trouble?"

"I'll tell you later. Can you meet me tonight?"

"After practice," he said, and arranged to meet at the Drive-in downtown at ten.

Stuck in an alley off Kawaramachi Street, the Drive-in was actually a walk-in. The cars were inside—fiberglass mock-ups of '57 Chevies and other classic models, parked in rows on a precipitous, stepped floor. Ransom's father had once owned a '57 Chevy Bel Air; Ransom still had a picture of himself, a crewcut seven-year-old, and his mother, her blond hair tamed under a scarf, both smiling from the passenger seat of that car. This was in Bel Air, shortly after they'd moved west; the fact that their car and their new town had the same name seemed to ChrisRansom a remarkable coincidence which could only be fraught with great meaning. He remembered his father washing the car every weekend with the garden hose and a pail of soapy water. Sometimes Chris would be allowed to wash the fierce chrome eagle on the hood. The last time he had seen a real '57 Chevy had been two years ago, on the Pakistani side of the Khyber Pass.

Ransom was late. Marilyn was waiting in the lobby, wearing sunglasses. He asked if they were going to see the movie and she nodded.

They walked down about halfway. Overhead, the ceiling was painted to resemble a nighttime sky, with lightbulb stars and a fluorescent half moon. Marilyn pointed to an aqua '56 T-bird. Ransom held the driver's door open for her while she crawled across to the passenger seat. A stylish young couple took the module beside theirs: cuffed black jeans, leather jacket, and pompadour for him; ponytail, pleated skirt and bobby socks for her. Ransom got behind the wheel and closed the door, thereby activating the lighted dash. The side and back windows were tinted for privacy.

Meanwhile, Ransom thought, armadas of Datsuns and Toyotas were cutting the Pacific, bound for American highways.

The credits rolled down the screen to the accompaniment of a brooding symphonic overture. Then Marlon Brando was yelling up at a tenement window, "Hey, Joey!"

"I'm sorry about Sunday," Marilyn said. "When I got back to my apartment Saturday night he was waiting for me."

"Who?"

"My fiancé. I've never seen him so angry. He called me all kinds of names and said he was going to take care of the cowboy. So I said what you told me. I told him it wasn't really Miles. I pretended to hold out but finally said it was you and told him what you looked like. And when he left on Sunday morning he put a man at my door. That's why I couldn't make it to the hotel."

Listening to her, Ransom noticed something about the way she was holding her head. He reached over and lifted her sunglasses. Even in the dim light he could see the bruises around her eye.

"He hit you."

She looked down at her hands.

"This has gone way too far. You've got to move out. Obviously you can't stay with me, but there's a hostel near my place."

She shook her head. "I can't leave."

"Why the hell not? If you're going to tell me you love this guy then I wash my hands of the whole thing. And you're crazy."

"It's not that. It's my job."

"Then get another job. We'll find you one somehow."

"I can't—I don't have a visa. I don't even have a passport. I'm in the country illegally, Ransom."

"You must have a gaijin card."

"It's a fake. He had it made for me. If I leave him he will tell his friends in Immigration. I can't get a job, an apartment or a plane ticket without the card. They'll throw me out of the country."

Ransom was stumped. It was easier to think about dealing with yakuza if one held the card of possible legal recourse. He tugged at the steering wheel, which spun freely in its socket.

"You're really between a rock and a hard place."

"Pardon?"

"And now your gangster is looking for me." He was suddenly angry as he realized the hopelessness of her dilemma.

"You told me to tell him it was you instead of Miles."

"I know. But you didn't tell me how bad things were. It would take the CIA to get you out of this."

She put her glasses back on and turned to the screen. "I'm sorry," she said, more angry than sorry, Ransom felt. He watched the movie, which seemed written, directed and acted to provide ironic commentary on his conversation with Marilyn: honest people, including the reluctant Brando, standing up to the mob. Why *On the Waterfront* tonight, he wondered. It was a weird coincidence, unless it wasn't a coincidence at all. She had chosen the meeting place, which afforded privacy, not easy to find in Japan— but he wondered if the feature had been an additional incentive. But it seemed unlikely that she had even *heard* of the movie; this atmosphere of conspiracy, amplified by the plot, was making him paranoid. These days it was difficult, he thought, to live as if you weren't in a movie.

He turned to her, and hesitated for a moment. "Does he really *love* you, or what?"

"He wants me," she said.

"Maybe he'll get sick of you after a while."

"Maybe. But he wants to marry me now."

"What do you mean *now*?"

"Soon. As soon as possible."

"At least that would solve your legal problems, wouldn't it?"

"In a way. It would make me his property. Japanese law."

Ransom was looking for openings, weak spots. "How about money?" Ransom had some, his father's checks. Maybe he could buy the guy off.

"That's what he expects to get from me."

"What do you mean?"

"After we're married, he gets all the money I earn."

"Are you going to earn that much?"

She had been studying the dashboard. Now she turned toward him, her eyes hidden behind the glasses. "Do you think I'm attractive?"

He thought this rather shameless, until he put it together

with the part about earning money. "You think he's going to pimp you." Ransom felt a thread of panic rising along his neck.

"They all do, all his friends, the yakuza."

"I thought you said he was jealous."

"He is. He's jealous of my pleasure. But business is different."

"You seem to take all this for granted."

"Please don't judge," she said. "It's not as if I have a choice." She turned back to the screen. "I shouldn't have involved you."

"It's about time I got involved in something."

"Wait," she said, "watch this. I love this scene. When Brando says he could have been a contender."

"You've seen this before?"

"Shhh. Of course."

"Where?"

"Who knows?" All her attention was focused on the screen.

"They show these old flicks in Vietnam?"

She looked over at him blankly, as if she had forgotten who he was. "What did you say?"

"You saw this in Vietnam?"

"Sure. Saigon." She turned back to the screen. "The Bijou."

When the movie ended and the lights came up, they waited in the car. "Tell your fiancé that my father is a very important man in the government."

"He is?"

"No, but he won't know that. Tell him my old man's a congressman. That should take a while to check out."

"What does he do, your father?" Marilyn asked, as they got out of the Thunderbird and began walking up the aisle.

"He underestimates the intelligence of the American public and they pay him handsomely for it."

"What does that mean?"

"He works in television."

"Is he rich?"

"Apparently not rich enough to be happy."

"You are angry with him."

"Maybe so."

"Why?"

Ransom stopped. "Have you ever watched American television? What am I saying? Everyone in the world watches American television." He started up the steps again. "It's more than that. I hate his cynicism. He turned his back on things he used to believe in, and now he likes to bad-mouth those things and pretend they don't exist. Everybody has a price, as he's so fond of saying."

He stopped, wondering why he was suddenly confiding in this woman. They mounted toward the exit. The last few couples, in various stages of dishevelment, were emerging from their stationary hot rods.

"We better split up here," Marilyn said, at the top of he steps. "He has a lot of friends around here who would recognize me."

"Just like in the movies," Ransom said. "Give me your phone number."

She shook her head. "He answers. I'll call you."

"I'm going away for a few days with Miles. Are you going to be all right?"

She frowned, her face narrowing with disapproval. "Going away? Where are you going?"

"Japan Alps. Just for a few days. Do you want me to call it off?"

"Would you?"

"If you want me to. If you're worried."

She took a deep, whistling breath, as if trying to summon courage. To Ransom it sometimes seemed that she was imitating emotions instead of feeling them. She had a very dramatic sense of gesture.

"Really," he said. "I'll stay here. Why don't I do that?"

Marilyn shook her head. She said she would be fine. She might even be better off with Ransom and Ryder out of town.

He lingered after she left. A kid in a white linen suit, his hair tinted red, flashed him the peace sign.

Ransom left the theater, approaching all corners wide, checking the street behind and in front. He felt conspicuous, a tall man in a short country.

14

They took the bullet train to Nagoya, then the express to Matsumoto. It was dark by the time they reached Matsumoto, so they missed the scenery on the cab ride to their inn; but Ransom could feel the mountains out there, their brooding gravity, as the car slalomed the valley road.

"Are we the fox or the hare?" Ryder said, after being thrown against Ransom for the third time. "This guy drives like you ski."

"As if his life depended on it," Ransom said, smiling. "I admire that in a man."

"I admire a cabbie who thinks about *my* fucking life."

Akiko had packed lunches for them—rice balls, smoked fish and fruit, neatly compartmented in wooden boxes—but Ransom was hungry again and hoped they wouldn't arrive too late for supper.

The proprietor and his wife greeted them elaborately at the door. They were honored to have the gaijin-san return to their negligible inn. The couple appeared to be in their fifties, both gray and permanently stooped with arthritis or labor, broad faces creased and folded. They seemed to remember that Ryder was the fluent one, or the funny one, directing their welcome to him, and he obliged by saying something in dialect which pleased them immensely.

Dinner had been kept warm. After carrying their bags up to the bedrooms, they came down to find two places set at the long, knee-high table in the main room. In a far corner, the grandfather sat in front of the television. Ryder and Ransom appeared to be the only guests, this being off-season. A kerosene heater glowed in the middle of the room, dispelling the chill of the house. As the hostesss began to serve up the dishes of rice and the mountain vegetables that Ransom had never seen elsewhere in the country, their host filled the shallow sake cups from small flagons heated in a pan of steaming water on top of the stove, urging them to drink, which Ransom did, feeling that one could be too fastidious and not wanting to be rude. By the time the woman brought out the post-prandial buckwheat noodles, a speciality of the region, they had killed the better part of a two-liter bottle.

Inhaling a mouthful of noodles, Ryder said, "Does this taste better than any food you've ever eaten in your entire life, or am I just a cheap date?" He rephrased and translated this remark for the woman, who blushed and deprecated her cooking.

It's the mountain air, she said.

"I wonder if sex is this good up here," Ryder said. He

asked the old woman if it was also the mountain air that made the people so friendly and hospitable. Their host beamed and filled their cups again, while the old woman went to the kitchen to see what she had to offer by way of evening the score on compliments. In his corner, the silent grandfather changed channels.

"The mountain air does good things for this sake," Ransom said. Thinking to steal some of Ryder's thunder he told the host that it was the best sake he'd ever had.

Ryder told the man that while Ransom wouldn't know good sake from vinegar, in this case he was right.

The host explained that it was a Kamikochi brand, made just a few kilometers down the road. He was not a man who had travelled widely but in his estimation the local product was pretty fair. Of course, he might be prejudiced. So saying, he opened another bottle and filled the battery of miniature flagons, then immersed them in the hot water.

Ryder lay back with his elbows on the tatami and belched—the polite thing to do.

Ransom spread his legs out in front of him. He could feel his skin glowing from the combustion of food and drink within him and on his back the cold night air beyond the circle of heat from the stove.

"The mountain air," said Ransom.

"I could sleep right here," Ryder said.

"I could sleep forever."

"My needs are simple. Food, drink and sex. How did I ever get such a complicated life?"

The woman asked if they were ready for their bath. Ryder answered that a hot bath would be the crowning touch on one of the finest evenings he had ever spent. To

Ransom he said, "The altitude must be getting to me. Our hostess is starting to look good."

The man led them to a big, steaming cedar tub in a chilly room at the back of the house. They undressed and washed with hot water in the chilly room, then eased into the scalding tub. Submerged to his neck, facing Ryder, Ransom said, "Wet and dry. Hot and cold. I like these perfect dichotomies."

"Sometimes you're hot and sometimes you're not."

"Sometimes you're drunk."

"It's the mountain air."

"The mountaineers."

"Mountains don't have ears. They're just there. That's why we like them. That's why we climb them."

"Because they're there."

"Exactly, Mr. Ransom."

"Why do we ski on them?"

"Because they have chairlifts."

Ransom propped his head back against the rim of the tub and closed his eyes.

"All we need now are some mountain girls," Ryder said.

Ransom looked up. "You've got a wife, for Christsake, Miles. Why do you have to be such a pig?"

Ryder eyed him warily through the steam. "What is it with you, man? What makes you such a righteous guy?"

Ransom suddenly felt sober. "I don't know. I guess I should mind my own damn business."

"I don't even know how you can stand to be around me." Miles's voice was booming and echoing within the walls. "I'm such a bad guy." Miles stirred the surface of the water with his hand, watching the eddies and ripples.

"I came to Japan to get away, and one morning I wake up all fenced in again."

"Nobody made you get married."

"Thanks for the compassion, padre. You're absolutely the weirdest guy I know, Ransom, and here you are telling *me* how to live *my* life. Who made you the fucking Pope?"

"You have to take responsiblity for your actions."

Miles looked at him sympathetically, as if Ransom were the actual subject of the conversation.

"I'm sounding like an asshole," Ransom said. "I guess I'm drunk. Let's drop it." Miles continued to look at him. Ransom said, "My old man ran around on my mom, and I guess that's not something you forget."

"Mine did, too. I used to tell myself I'd never be like that." Miles shook his head. "I wonder what happened?"

Ransom liked spring skiing best, the combination of cold nights and warm days. The spring snow was the distilled essence of all the snow that had fallen through the winter, hard and granular, but soft enough to slice under an edge. The cold nights preserved it and the sun softened it up. They had almost waited too long. Only the highest runs were still skiable. But they didn't have to share them with the entire population of Tokyo.

They got a late start, waking under huge goose-down quilts with their breath hanging in the room, Ransom acutely hungover. Once they got moving the hangover seemed almost benign, making him receptive to discrete sensations: the temperature and smell of the air, the amazing bulk of the mountain peaks against the cloudless sky. Their fellow passengers on the bus trip to the slopes were two student mountaineers in tweed knickers and waffle stompers and a changing cast of old women with indigo scarves on their heads and bundles on their backs.

After renting skis, they rode to the top of the first chairlift and were still below the snowline. On the second lift the run beneath them was punctuated with patches of dirt and rock, but otherwise promising. At the top they stood in their skis and looked out at the mountain peaks: the sky was clear in all directions, except for the indolent puffs of smoke and steam above the barren cone of the semi-active Mt. Yake.

"How much do you want to wager on this first run," Miles asked. Miles was not a great skier, but he was fearless. Somewhere he had picked up the idea that getting to the bottom as quickly as possible was the sole object of the sport.

"Let's make it interesting, as long as you think you're going to cut a handsome figure on crutches."

"That's the whole point of a wager. To make it interesting."

"I'm talking big."

"How big?"

"Let's say you won't so much as speak to any female save your wife for—well, let's start with a month. I mean not even a friendly chat."

"Good Christ." Ryder dug his pole into the snow and worked the basket back and forth. "Not even Marilyn?"

"Especially not even Marilyn."

"What do I get?"

"Make me a counter-offer."

Miles tugged at his crotch and looked out over the valley. "A binge in Tokyo, paid for by you. We stay at the Otani, and you match me drink for drink. No restrictions, plenty of girls."

"Deal."

Ryder hesitated. "Wait a minute, I've got a better one. If I win, you tell me the story of those two markers you put in the little graveyard down in the valley last year."

It was Ransom's turn to pause. Miles's eyes were on him like surgical tweezers. "Why do you want to know that?"

"I don't know. Maybe because you don't want to tell me. Maybe because I'm your friend. Maybe because it would be good for you to lose this bet."

Ransom assessed the ribbon of snow beyond his ski tips.

"You wanted to make it interesting," Miles said.

"All right," Ransom said. "Two months on your end, though."

"A monk for life. Are you ready?"

Miles corralled a nearby skier to count off the start, and jumped between *three* and *go*—a Texas head start. The open bowl near the top of the lift narrowed into a trail between rock outcroppings a hundred yards below, and Ransom couldn't get past Ryder's flailing poles. The patches of rock and dirt and the other skiers on the trail prevented either one of them from schussing straight down. You had to stay on your edges. Miles narrowly missed a rock and wobbled dangerously as he tried to regain balance. Ransom cut inside, and beat him to a narrow chute between tree stumps; behind him he heard Ryder's edges clatter over rock. Ransom narrowly threaded two skiers doing snow-plows, and dropped into a racing tuck as the trail opened up again. Ryder was screaming "Banzai!" right behind him, as the trail narrowed again; with his weight advantage he could easily catch up.

Miles was a ski length ahead when he turned to taunt Ransom, caught an edge, and went down in a windmill of limbs and skis.

At the bottom of the slope, shaking the snow out of his hair, Ryder said, "Two goddamn months?"

"You got it."

"Well, the joke's on you. I haven't seen Marilyn in two weeks."

Ransom decided to leave it at that.

They were returning on the afternoon of the third day. That morning, Ransom told Miles that he was going to Hotaka alone, but Ryder insisted on coming. The innkeeper drove them in his van. The serpentine valley eventually spilled into a broad cirque, where, on a rise, the Alpine Lodge was situated above a huge parking lot. Behind the lodge, the long ridge of Hotaka extended across the sky like a rusted saw blade.

Ransom bought two bottles of sake in the lodge. Ryder bought one for himself. "You want me to wait here," he asked.

"You can come if you want."

They went out through the parking lot, past families snapping pictures of the peaks, and followed a footpath into the woods. Ryder asked if he remembered the way, and Ransom nodded his head. After ten minutes they came to the clearing. It looked just the same: some forty stones huddled together in a small meadow, each one engraved with a name, memorial gifts of sake and flowers placed beside many. An informal shrine commemorating climbers who had died in the mountains, it was started and maintained by their families and friends. The bodies were elsewhere; some had never been found. At the edge of the clearing were two newer stones. One said *Ian,* the other *Annette.* A local artisan had done the engraving.

Ransom placed a bottle of sake beside each stone. He ran his eyes across the letters, trying to separate each chiselled character from the others in the vague hope that the familiar names would yield some new meaning, finally looking up at the face of the mountain, and at the pale sky. "Okay," he said to Ryder, who was standing back in the trees, and started back up the path.

That afternoon they took the train back to Kyoto.

15

"And where is your beautiful wife this fine day?" the Pathan said, when Ransom found him at his stall in the bazaar. The woman in question was not Ransom's wife, and by his lights it was not much of a day: no wind, the sun a degree higher in the sky and hotter than it had been the day before, and still no sign of Ian. The Pathan's question had an ironic spin, as if the man understood all of this and found it slightly amusing. But then he always sounded that way to Ransom. He replied that Annette was back at the fort where she was relatively safe from lecherous Pathans. He meant this as a joke, but the anxiety of waiting two weeks in a place where he didn't want to be put a sharper edge on the words than he'd intended.

The Pathan's thin smile faded.

Something bumped Ransom's thigh. He looked down

and found a sheep nosing at his jeans. The sheep turned and waddled off down the bazaar, poking into the stalls as if shopping.

Ransom had insulted the Pathan, a stupid thing to do. Pathan tribesmen with Enfield rifles strapped over their shoulders and bandoliers of ammunition around their baggy shirts strutted past the stall. The man Ransom was talking to had a revolver holstered on his hip.

"You have heard from your friend?" he said after a minute.

Ransom shook his head, relieved that his indiscretion had been passed over.

"He was not Australian?"

"American."

"Ah." The Pathan nodded. "There is an Australian passport for sale."

It took Ransom a minute to sort this out, and to construe the warning. He thought he knew where the passport had come from. A few days earlier, in the bazaar, he had met an Australian who had mined opals in the Outback for two years. He had dry, brick-red skin against which his green eyes and the gaudy opal pendant on his chest glistened. A man who had lived alone in a trailer in the desert, seventy miles from the nearest settlement, he showed the tentative volubility of the rescued castaway who is not quite certain if language still works. Over kebabs in the bazaar he told Ransom, who hadn't asked, about his plan. He was in Landi Kotal to score hash oil. He was going to swallow it, in condoms, when he flew out of Karachi, and shit out a small fortune when he got back to Sydney. That was it. When he had finished talking, he beamed as if he were the first person to have penetrated the mystery of supply and demand. Ransom felt obliged to tell him that it was an old trick, and people had died that way; any residual alcohol that hadn't been boiled off in the processing of the oil would eat through the condoms, and once that happened it was permanent deep-space. But the Australian smiled and rubbed the opal to his chest. "My lucky amulet," he said. Ransom left the Australian licking chili sauce from his cracked lips and that was the last he saw of him. Yesterday he'd seen the opal pendant for sale at a stall not five yards from where he stood. He felt awful then, thinking of what might have happened, thinking he might have been more sympathetic, or at least more persistent.

It was an object lesson, Ransom thought. The Pathan was reminding him of what could happen.

"Excuse me," he said to the Pathan. "My humor was crude."

The Pathan nodded. "Your wife. She is still sick?"

Ransom nodded. A convention of their transactions was that Annette was sick and that the junk was a temporary analgesic. This was, in fact, the way Annette viewed her habit.

"There is anything else I can do for you," the Pathan asked, after they'd made the usual exchange.

"How about a fifth of scotch?"

"I am sorry. You know I am a devout man."

Ransom nodded. He thought it was a funny kind of devotion that traded in smack and balked at booze, but he didn't say anything.

"I hope your wife will be well soon," the Pathan said. "A good woman is a pearl of great price."

They'd met the Pathan two weeks earlier, the day after they arrived in Landi Kotal. Ian was planning to leave for Kabul later that afternoon. The three of them spent the morning in the bazaar. This was Annette's first time in Landi Kotal and she wanted to look at everything. The close-packed stalls displayed bolts of Scottish tweed, Swiss watches, Indian ivories, sundries with the initials of French and Italian designers, Levi's, Japanese cameras and radios, Buddhas in bronze and clay, vintage British cavalry swords and U.S. Army–issue Colt 45s. They found a handtowel embroidered with the legend *Grand Hotel, Mackinac Island, Michigan* laid out beside a stack of Tibetan prayer rugs, and in the next stall a Peugeot ten-speed bicycle. Smuggling was the main industry of the region. Some of the contraband was what it appeared to be, but the smart buyer began with the assumption that the Western goods were Asian counterfeits, the handcrafts and antiques mass-produced. You never took the first price quoted.

At one of the stalls, Ian and Ransom examined some pale, crumbly hash. Ian shook his head. Water-pressed, he said, the dregs of the last season's pressing. He was confirmed in his decision to cross the border and get the pick of the crop in the mountain villages outside of Kabul.

A small boy with a large knife sheathed in his belt stepped into their path waving his arms. "I got stone, man," he announced. "I got stone. Very hot stuff. Brand new. Crazy tunes." He reached into a pocket and drew out a cassette which he pressed into Ransom's hand. The blocky, Roman letters on the inner lining read, "Excite on Main St. by Rolling Stone." The boy wiggled his shoulders and hips vigorously. He took Annette's arm and coaxed them over to his rock-and-roll emporium, a stall with boxes of bootleg cassettes and several Japanese cassette players. A Fender Stratocaster was mounted in a gun rack at the back of the stall.

Annette wanted to buy a cassette player. Ian told her that if it wasn't confiscated at the border when they went back to India they'd end up paying more duty than it was worth. Ransom reminded her that their money was tight. Annette slammed down a tape she'd been looking at. "Always you and Ian gang up on me," she said, stalking off into the bazaar. Ian went after her while Ransom bargained for the cassette player. Annette had been clean for three weeks and Ransom wanted to keep her happy.

Finding Ian and Annette was easy because they'd gathered a crowd. Annette's red chamois shirt was on the ground and she was trying to tug her T-shirt up over her head. Ian was trying to restrain her. Men and boys in turbans were closing around them.

Earlier in the morning they had counseled Annette on keeping herself covered no matter how warm it was. Annette didn't like being told what to do. And she didn't like clothes. In Goa they'd spent the days nude on the beach. But Goa was not Moslem.

Ransom pushed through the onlookers. Ian had her arms pinned. Annette had a mouthful of her own sleeve and was trying to rip the fabric with her teeth. When Ransom grabbed her shoulder she kicked him in the shin.

"Bastards! Beat up on me!"

They each took an arm and pushed her through the crowd. Annette was laughing now.

"Fook these dirty people," Annette said. "They have never seen teets before?" Ransom was hoping that no one could make out the English behind Annette's French accent. The eyes of the crowd were already hostile.

The crowd followed them. Annette tried to wrench herself away from Ransom. He dropped the new cassette player, which had been pinned under his arm. The turbans hissed and muttered behind them. Ransom looked back and saw a man pick up a stone from the side of the road. Some of the men carried rifles. A young man darted forward from the crowd and grabbed at the neck of Annette's shirt. Ransom turned and kicked him in the knee, provoking angry shouts from the mob.

"Don't look back," Ian said.

Annette was no longer resisting. Her face was pale.

In front of them a man emerged from one of the stalls. Ransom raised his fist.

"Please follow me," the man said. "This way." He took them through a narrow passage between two stalls. "Here," he said, holding back the flap of the tent.

"They will not come here," the man said, closing the flaps. He lit an oil lamp and beckoned them to sit.

The first thing Ransom noticed about the man was that his eyes were blue. The sharply hooked nose seemed to be placed a little too high on his face. He wore a pale-blue turban and had a long, wispy beard, which he stroked with his left hand. Ransom saw that the ring finger on his right hand was missing, nubbed below the first joint.

"An accident," the man said, catching Ransom's eyes on his finger. He introduced himself. Ransom missed the name. He said he was of the Afridi tribe of Pathans and that it was the code of his people to offer shelter and protection to strangers.

Ransom was stroking Annette's hand, watching her.

"She is your woman," the man asked Ransom.

Ransom didn't say anything.

Annette said, "I am nobody's woman. Nobody cares about me." She was pale and her hands trembled.

"She is very beautiful," the Pathan said.

Ransom put his arm around Annette and began to knead the muscles in her neck. He stopped suddenly when he saw the way the Pathan was looking at Annette. It was a look he had seen in the faces of the crowd in the bazaar.

Ian said, "I think we should be pushing on."

They thanked the man. He assured them that he was always at their service. He was a merchant, a broker of commodities, and if they should require anything, anything at all, during their stay in Landi Kotal . . .

To Ransom he offered the advice that you did not display a jewel in the bazaar unless you intended to sell it. Then he looked again at Annette.

Ransom and Annette saw Ian off a few hours later. The taxi stand at the edge of the bazaar had a fleet of pre-'60 Chevies. When a sufficient number of passengers had presented themselves, the cabs rattled off over the Khyber Pass. A taxi was nearly ready to leave when they arrived. The driver had seven fares in the cab itself and intended to put four more in the trunk. Four of the passengers were Caucasian. A woman with matted blond hair and dirt in the creases of her face was leaning out the back window of the cab moaning. The man beside her was holding her hair back behind her neck. While Ian dickered with the driver, she vomited. "That's the way," the man said, "that's the way." Inside the cab someone with a heavy southern accent was telling a story about a guy from Ohio who had his balls cut off at the border when the guards found a ball of hash taped underneath his scrotum. A Pathan with an automatic rifle on his shoulder was securing a canvas bag to the pile of luggage on the roof.

"Well, that's it," Ian said, after he'd paid the driver. "I've got a seat on the observation deck," he said, indicating the trunk. He turned to Annette and opened his arms. "How about a kiss for the soldier going off to the wars?"

Annette allowed herself to be embraced, then kissed him on the cheek.

Ian hugged Ransom and said, "You take care of her. That's your job."

Ransom nodded and tried to smile. He was suddenly very nervous. He felt there was something they were forgetting. They'd been planning this for weeks, but now that the time had come he didn't like the idea of splitting up. The blond girl leaning out of the cab heaved again, and Ranson felt his own stomach shrink in on itself. "You'll be back in a few days?"

"A few days, maybe a week. Just as soon as I can."

Ian had done this before. He liked to buy direct from the tribes in Afghanistan because it was cheaper and the hash was better than anything that came into Landi Kotal. He had a third of the money in his boot heel. Ransom, who had never done anything like this in his life, was holding the rest. Ian would catch a bus from the border to Kabul, hire a guide into the hills, arrange the buy and make a down payment. He would come back through customs clean, and they would wait for the Afghanis, who did not believe in borders, to bring the stuff over the mountains. That was the plan.

The taxi driver told Ian they were ready to go. Ian climbed into the trunk of the cab and settled himself among three old men in pink turbans. A cloud of smoke engulfed the rear of the car as the driver gunned the engine. When he popped the clutch the car lurched violently and died.

More than an hour later, the driver still hadn't managed to get the car running. Ransom and Annette had waited with Ian as the sun dropped through the cloudless sky toward the jagged ridge of mountains to the west. Ransom could feel the dry rasp of high-altitude sunlight on his face even as he was slapping his arms and chest for warmth. Annette said she was freezing to death. Ian said they shouldn't bother to wait.

"I've been thinking," Ransom said. "Why don't you stick around another day, get a fresh start tomorrow." To him the signs did not seem auspicious—the near-riot in the bazaar, the sick blond girl, the taxi breaking down. He was not eager to see Ian go.

"I'd hate to lose a day," said Ian, whose augury did not recognize ill omens. He acted as if he believed that he had been born under a fortunate sign, and that his luck would hold.

Ian went to talk to the driver, who had just climbed in behind the wheel of the cab. The engine turned over and sputtered back to life. Ian jumped into the trunk of the taxi. He waved as the car pulled forward. Ransom put one arm around Annette and waved with the other as the taxi disappeared into the dust.

Annette and Ransom were staying in a fortified house on the hillside just off the main road. Surrounded by high walls for protection against bandits, it looked like a two-storey pillbox. Ian had arranged for them to stay there; the family, he said, was on a pilgrimage to Mecca. The heavy wooden door on the ground floor opened into a dark space rank with the smell of animals, the quarters of the family sheep. A stairway led to the second level, where the small, vertical windows, suitable for returning rifle fire, admitted little light. There was no escaping the residual odor of the animals. *"Le château des pourceaux,"* Annette said, holding her nose, when they first surveyed the place.

Things had gone sour after the incident in the bazaar. Annette had seen all she cared to see of Landi Kotal and wanted to move on. She began to talk about Katmandu, where she and Ransom had first met. Ransom didn't want to be reminded of Katmandu. They had spent a month together there, Ransom having just arrived in Asia, looking for freedom in the homeland of fatalism, looking for he didn't know what—but something more vital than the pallid choice of career. He had never met anyone like Annette, unless it was Ian, so profligate with her energy, staying up all night talking, racing from city to city, friend to friend—the kind of person who seemed too expansive to gather all of her affection into a package and present it to one other human being. Ransom instinctively admired this abundance; and the more he admired it, the more important it became for him to have it all to himself. He had never wanted anyone so much, and his wanting made him awkward and jealous. Annette had gone off one night with an Italian, and Ransom hadn't seen her again until she showed up one day in Goa, three months later, hundreds of miles from where she had ditched him.

Fed up with Landi Kotal, with more reason than she usually had for wanting to move on to a new place, Annette spoke wistfully now of their month in Katmandu, of the pastel-colored temples and the tall, crooked houses with hex eyes painted on the lintels.

"And the monkeys," Ransom said absently. "Don't forget the monkeys." The two of them were lying on a single pallet inside the fortress house. Ian had been gone three days.

"I hate the monkeys," she said. "Nasty, ugly things. I hate them."

"Sorry," Ransom said. There was no telling when some little thing would set her off. He didn't remember any special antipathy toward monkeys. He turned onto his side and looked at her. Her face was rigid. He stroked her shoulder; she pushed his hand away.

"It smells like pig in here."

"Sheep. It's sheep."

"Pig. Pig pig pig. Big-time, big-deal businessmen. They make a big deal and they stay in a pig house. Pig time. Pig deal. Pig guys."

"Annette."

"Pig!"

Ransom leaned over and kissed her neck. "Once we

finish this we'll have lots of money. Then we can go anywhere."

"We go now."

"We have to wait for Ian."

"Ian. Always Ian. Ian Ian Ian Ian—"

Ransom clapped a hand over her mouth and she bit him.

She resumed the chant, her voice rising until she lashed
out at Ransom with her arms and legs. When Ransom tried
to cram the blanket into her mouth, she kneed him.

He got a handful of her hair and rolled her off the pallet.
He thumped her head, hard, against the wooden floor. She
stopped struggling and began to cry.

After a while she said, "Do you love me?"

Ransom said that he did.

"Do you love me more than Ian?"

"Do I sleep with Ian?"

"Maybe," she said.

He wondered if she really believed this, then decided
that it was shorthand for her jealousy of Ransom's friendship with Ian. They had known each other in college, not
close friends, Ian being two classes ahead of him, but Ransom had admired Ian's reckless vitality, feeling himself to
be far more cautious than he wished to be. While most of
his classmates prepared for gainful employ, Ian seemed to
be training for adventure. Ian took his junior year off to
travel Asia, and though Ransom never told him so, it was
his example and the articles he sent back to the college
paper that inspired Ransom to do the same thing. They
had run into each other, a year after Ransom graduated,
at a pie shop on Pig Alley in Katmandu, and after Annette

ditched Ransom they had started to hang out together, eventually travelling south through India to Goa, where they rented a beach hut for the winter. Annette had reappeared—everybody showed up for Christmas in Goa. In Annette's version of Katmandu, Ransom had cruelly abandoned her, and when she moved in with them she made him promise he would never run out on her again. For a few weeks everything was fine. Ian liked Annette and Annette liked Ian, to the point that Ransom felt almost like the third party, their dispositions curiously complementary: Ian believing in the power of his own will to shape the world to his needs, and in the inherent value of his own desires; Annette profoundly fatalistic, what Ransom later saw as a junkie mentality, acting as if nothing she did mattered, and therefore she might as well do anything she pleased. They shared a belief in the primacy of their inclinations. At first, Ransom considered them kindred spirits, but then Annette had turned petulant and jealous of Ian, quizzing Ransom with hypothetical situations in which he had to choose between the two of them.

Now Ian was somewhere on the other side of the Hindu Kush trying to score some dope, and Ransom said to Annette, "Ian's not my type."

"What is your type," she demanded.

"French, female, blond and manic."

"What's manic? *C'est manie?*"

"Sexy. It means very sexy."

The next day Annette stayed in bed complaining of cramps. Ransom went to Peshawar to check on bus schedules. When he got back Annette was high. He could see it in the way she greeted him, giddy and languorous, and

in the slight drop in register in her voice. She'd had a habit
for two months in Goa, and he knew the signs.

"Where did you get the stuff?"

"Come hold me," she said.

"Where did you get it?" Even as he asked, he didn't
know why he bothered. The point was, she had it. But he
couldn't think of anything else to say.

"Only a little bit," she said. "To make the sickness go
away." This was her way, calling the disease the cure.

She nodded off before sundown. He stayed with her
through the next morning. By noon she was sweating and
trembling. He held out until three, when he could no longer
stand to watch her. She told him she'd bought the stuff
from the Pathan who'd helped them that day. Ransom went
to find him, and returned an hour later with her fix. There
would be time to straighten her out when this business was
all over.

Ransom went outside the moment she started to tie off.
He bought it, but he would not watch her put the needle
in her arm. He looked out over the barren gray peaks. The
afternoon sun cast crisp, angular shadows. There was no
vegetation in sight. To the west, the road threaded its way
between the jaws of the pass. Three eastbound vehicles
crawled like beetles toward the bright mosaic of the town.
Possibly Ian was in one of them. Ransom wanted to think
so. But he felt that a landscape like this didn't have anything
very encouraging to say about the fate of individuals.

16

"Your Cheating Heart" was on the jukebox and Miles Ryder sang along, sitting on the bar displaying his new boots, when Ransom came in.

"This weather is getting me down," Miles said.

"It's bound to get worse."

"I don't think I can take another rainy season." Miles raised his leg, hooked his ankle over his knee, and brushed repeatedly at his boot heel, although it was clean. "The baby isn't born yet and the house already feels crowded. Akiko never complains, but just looking at her makes me uncomfortable." He let go of his foot; the boot banged loudly against the bar. "You coming from practice?"

"Yessir."

"I could understand if you were going to use it. On DeVito-san, say." He jumped down from the bar to answer the phone. Ransom ordered a cup of tea. When Miles came back, Ransom asked him if he was faithfully adhering to the terms of their skiing wager.

"Didn't you see the sign over the door: *Ladies not welcome*? I catch one whiff of gardenia cologne and I run in the other direction. Why are you looking at me like that? What ever happened to trust."

"Good question. You haven't seen Marilyn?"

Miles shook his head. "I don't know, maybe it's my breath." He took off his hat and stroked the feather in the band, then looked toward the door. "Here comes our favorite satori hound," he said.

"Greetings," Brad Russell said, as he took the seat beside Ransom. "The old hangout hasn't changed much." He looked around with the air of a man returning to the hometown after ascendant years in the city, although Ransom was certain it was a matter of weeks at most since he had last seen Russell here.

"Been away," Ransom asked.

"I've been on a *seishin*."

"Isn't that one of those sex tours," Miles said, "where the Jap businessmen do all the whorehouses from Seoul to Taipei?"

"It's a Zen retreat, you idiot," Russell sputtered. "We went to a small temple in the mountains outside Arashi-yama for ten days. Woke up every morning at four and went outside to sit zazen for twelve hours. Twelve hours! The roshi walked around with a stick and if your posture was bad he clubbed you until you straightened out. My knees and my back are killing me."

"What did you do at night?" Miles said.

"We slept on the floor in our clothes. It was freezing."

"Sounds like big fun," Miles said. "Serious craziness."

"I really feel like I made a breakthrough out there," Russell said. "How about you?" he said to Ransom. "Still a follower of the martial way?"

"Ransom follows the Way of the Tourist."

"Funny."

"I'm serious. It's his own school. You've never heard him lecture on the subject?"

Russell was trying to determine whether he was being taken for a ride.

"Tell him, Ransom sensei. Speak to him of the Tao of the Tourist."

"You tell him."

"The disciple will attempt to convey the teachings of the master. The Way of the Tourist consists in not letting yourself sink into the swamp of familiarity. It's not a vacation but an arduous way of life, requiring constant vigilance. Objects and people will try to attach themselves to you and become intimate. Rooms in which you take shelter and rest will ask you to call them *home*. Habits will try to impose themselves. And when that happens, you stop seeing and thinking altogether. Am I in error, Ransom-sensei?"

Ransom nodded his approval.

"The Tao of the Tourist cannot have a headquarters, but Japan is a suitable country in which to practice it, for those of us who weren't born here, because we will always be gaijin to the Japanese and because just when you think you've got the place figured out something happens and you're on strange terrain again. *Home on the strange* is the motto of the Way. The Way of the Tourist can't have a headquarters, but Kyoto is a good provisional encampment because it's a genuine tourist town. All these old temples and shrines, busloads of part-time tourists being herded through every day. These last, of course, cannot be considered true followers of the Way."

"You're a real jerk, Ryder," Russell said.

"Hey! Do they teach you that kind of language at your Zen school?"

"You're going to lose most of your customers this way," Ransom said, after Russell had stalked off.

"He's already lost, and he doesn't drink. You're the only nondrinker I can stand."

They watched the band setting up onstage.

"Maybe I should go home early tonight," Miles said. "See how the wife and fetus are doing." He showed no inclination to pursue this plan.

Ransom stayed to hear the band's first set, Kano pulling high lonesome notes out of his big hollow-body Gibson, singing against all odds with feeling, scrupulously reproducing lyrics that were casual and occasionally incomprehensible in the original, reaching a peak of frenzy in a version of Robert Johnson's "Hellhound on My Trail."

> I got to keep moving, got to keep moving
> Blues falling down like hail, falling down like hail
> I can't keep no money, Hellhound on my trail.

The set over, Ransom was thinking of leaving when Yamada came in, jovial with drink. He joined Ransom and ordered Suntory.

I hoped you would be here, Yamada said.

You look happy, Ransom said.

Not really. Yamada drank off half the whiskey. *How old are you?*

Twenty-six.

Are you going to get married soon?

I don't think so.

My parents want me to get married. I'm twenty-eight and in Japan that's time to get married.

You have a girlfriend, don't you?

My parents want me to marry someone else. They've already decided.

Who?

A daughter of my father's boss. I've never met her.

Why don't they like your girlfriend?

Maybe because they didn't pick her for me. I asked the sensei for advice. He said I should marry the girl my parents want me to marry. He's very traditional. He doesn't believe in love.

He thinks your girlfriend is the reason you've been missing karate.

He's right. Yamada sipped at his drink, his face slack and tired. The band played "Last Fair Deal Gone Down." *She works at my office. She's very nice. They don't think she comes from a good family.*

Ransom was wary of giving advice. It wasn't his family, his country. He could leave any time, but Yamada had to live here, and he was in a better position than Ransom to know the price of deviation from the rigorous demands of convention.

Is it customary in America to choose your own wife?

That, Ransom said, *was the usual practice.*

It's different here, Yamada said. *You don't choose anything for yourself.*

Groping for vocabulary, Ransom suggested that following inclinations didn't necessarily make one happier in the long run. He mentioned the divorce rate in the States, and tried to say that having no rules at all could be terribly confusing.

Have you ever been in love, Yamada asked.

Ransom said he had, and then heard his name called out over the microphone. DeVito was standing onstage, holding the mike with one hand and pointing to Ransom with the other.

"I hereby publicly challenge Ransom-san to a duel, a karate match for the purpose of answering aspersions on my character. I challenge him in front of all these witnesses, so that everyone will know that he is a coward and a liar if he does not answer my challenge."

Miles came around the bar with the ax handle; DeVito grabbed the microphone stand. When Miles took a swing at him he blocked it and swung back with the stand, the blow glancing off Ryder's shoulder.

Before Ransom could move, the narc posted at the door jumped between the two of them, identifying himself as a police officer.

"Do you have an answer for me, Ransom?" DeVito shouted, as the cop returned the mike stand to the anxious-looking Kano.

"Pesticide," Ransom called back.

"You'll fight me. You wait and see."

The cop marched DeVito off the stage. "You'll fight me," he yelled again, as they disappeared out the door.

17

Guys like Ransom had been jerking DeVito around ever since he could remember. They had a way of dressing and talking, these guys. The lieutenant who had busted him out of the Marines was the same breed of cat. Although it was Ryder who bushwhacked him, he blamed it on Ransom, with his altar-boy face and his superior attitude. He thought he was so cool that he only used his last name. DeVito sussed him out the first time they met at Buffalo Rome, the night he was celebrating getting his black belt. Ransom sat there not drinking, in his baggy khaki pants with the cuffs, and he says with his thick girlish lips that his sensei doesn't believe in awarding belts. Like he thought there was something sleazy about the whole thing.

Busting up Ryder's bike had settled the scorecard with the cowboy nicely; stomping a mudhole in his ass would have been too easy. But Ransom he wanted to take apart with his hands, the way he had taken the Harley apart, except that he'd needed a pipe wrench to help with the Harley. In his mind DeVito rehearsed the various ways he could hurt Ransom. After watching him practice, DeVito knew exactly where he was coming from. If Ransom had been a pansy there would be a quick limit to the kind of abuse he could take, and that was no more fun than shooting an old dog. But he was competent enough to drag out his own beating a good long time.

Someday he'd find that lieutenant and fix his wagon. Davis, Stuart, L., Atlanta, Georgia. He couldn't stay in the service forever. He had those same lips as Ransom. Like that Okinawan girl who brought him up on charges. Acting all of a sudden like she was a virgin.

DeVito paid a modest rent to the monks, who did not own enough art treasures or historically significant buildings to attract as many tourists as they would have liked, and who didn't seem to mind the women coming and going, or the music from his system. The stereo had everything; he kept it up-to-date researching new developments and travelling to Tokyo to the electronics shows, selling off his castaways to the incoming gaijin. He had soundproofed one of his two rooms with fiberboard, asbestos panels and industrial carpet. By now he was running two hundred watts per channel. Even with the soundproofing he couldn't begin to use it all. The tunes room was also the weight room; he had reinforced the frame under the tatami and laid down a gym mat. He would seal himself in there, slap weight on the bar, the Dead on the system, and crank the volume while he pumped some serious iron. He had everything the Dead ever recorded, which was a good thing because you weren't apt to get any at Buffalo Rome, all that blues, whining about going home—who the hell wanted to go home?

One afternoon an apprentice monk came over and asked to hear "Sympathy for the Devil." A kid from the country, his heart wasn't really in Buddhism, but he said that his family were patrons of a big temple in the north and he was expected to become the roshi. He was big for a Japanese, really porky, and it turned out he had done some sumo wrestling. Over the next few weeks DeVito worked out with him when the kid was supposed to be sweeping the grounds and pumped him for everything he knew. DeVito's ambition was to master all of the martial arts and then develop a new system incorporating the best aspects of each. He could open his own chain of dojos worldwide. If he needed capital, there was always the yakuza; they knew how to make a buck, and they could relate to the samurai traditions. A new kid at his dojo had explained to him that the finger-chopping business went back to the samurai; back then when a warrior lost a finger he lost some finesse with the sword. Lose enough fingers and presto—dead meat. Even in the days of yore, especially then, there was no free lunch. This, he thought, was something guys like Ransom would never understand.

The fat-kid monk one day told DeVito about the temple's sword collection. Trying not to show his excitement, DeVito asked dumb questions. The swords had accumulated over the years, the legacy of samurai patrons of the temple. It had once been illegal for anyone but samurai to wear swords; it was now illegal for anyone to possess them without a license. DeVito had applied for a license, but hadn't heard anything. The red tape, especially for a gaijin, was impenetrable. He had seen the old blades, blades that could slice a three-inch oak like butter or a man from shoulder to waist, that sang when they parted the air, forged by hand out of layers of native steel, heated, stretched and folded over again and again until they held the finest edge known to man. He had seen them in licensed shops and in museums and he owned more than a dozen volumes in English and Japanese devoted exclusively to katana. He owned a prewar officer's sword, something he'd picked up in a card game at the base on Okinawa and later smuggled to the mainland in a guitar case, but it was basically a piece of shit.

The kid eventually let drop where the katana were stored, adding that no one had taken them out of their chests in years. The building, a relic of a previous century, was padlocked, but one night, when he knew the roshi was away drinking, DeVito scouted it out and found a crawlspace underneath the structure, which stood on posts two feet above ground. He slipped through the opening, and it was a simple matter to push up on the tatami mats which constituted the floor and climb inside. The chests were not even locked. It was an unbelievable cache—about ten katana, wrapped in silk, in each of the chests. He took only one, the best, a treasure which he determined by the tag attached to the scabbard was forged in 1525. He left the rest where they were and took care to make sure that the chests looked undisturbed. He went out the way he came in and stashed the katana beneath the floor of his weight room.

Sometimes, at night, he took the sword out. The blade, when it was finely polished, showed a wavy layered pattern almost like wood grain along the line of the temper. In one of his books he had read the instructions of a fifteenth-century swordmaker to his apprentice: "Heat the steel at final forging until it turns the color of the moon about to set out on its journey across the heavens on a June or July evening." The scabbard was finished in rich black lacquer without any ornamentation, in keeping with the austere spirit of the period of warfare in which it had been born; the guard, however, made of iron, was elaborately engraved with a chrysanthemum design inlaid in gold, clearly a later mounting. The hilt was traditional sharkskin bound with silk cord.

Engraved on the steel tang, DeVito found characters that related the history of the sword. He made a crayon rubbing of the inscription and showed it to a leading Kyoto egghead who hung out at Buffalo Rome, claiming that it came from a sword in a private American collection. This guy, who would believe anything, dutifully translated the inscription: the maker's name, the date it was made, the province and the name of the owner of the sword. The second inscription, added seventy years later when the sword was shortened, especially interested DeVito, recording the results of a cutting test performed by the craftsman who had customized the sword: *mitsu-do setsudan: three bodies with one stroke.* The custom of the time was to test the sword on bodies; usually corpses, sometimes condemned criminals. *Three bodies with one stroke.* Somehow DeVito felt certain that living men, lined up side by side, had constituted this test. He imagined the arc of the sword, the sound of cleaving flesh and bone.

Every morning DeVito ran ten kilometers, did one hundred push-ups and one hundred sit-ups. That was his warm-up for working out in earnest. The first thing he saw when he opened his eyes in the morning was the sign tacked to the wall at the foot of the futon:

> When one thinks he has gone too far,
> he will not have erred.
>
> —*Hagakure*

18

Sunday morning came around again. Ransom woke with a dread reminiscent of his childhood, when he could look forward to sitting on the hard pew between his parents, who seemed particularly unhappy with each other on Sunday mornings; later, alone with his mother after his father had stopped pretending to be a Catholic. He had learned to hate Sundays. Now, years after he had set foot in a church, it was the day he could expect to get his ass kicked by the Monk.

He rolled back the sliding doors and walked onto the terrace. There was a fresh smell in the air, and when he looked down he saw the pink blossoms on his landlord's cherry tree. The odor of cherry blossoms was, for Ransom, inextricably associated with that of vomit. For the past two years, under the sponsorship of his English students, Ran-

som had participated in the annual custom of cherry-
blossom viewing, a ritual which consisted of bivouacking
en masse at one of the designated parks or temples, pro-
visioned with enough food and drink for a week; then,
under the canopy of cherry trees, singing songs, drinking,
vomiting and pissing as the petals fluttered down and span-
gled all. The tree in Kaji's garden, which had blossomed
only hours ago, was already losing petals, and Ransom was
touched by the melancholy that informed the old haiku
about the transience of this life, and then by the awareness
that he was still susceptible to the tender emotions. This
was not bad in itself, but neither was it good.

The sky hovered low over the city. On a terrace across
from his own, a young wife was hanging laundry. Ransom
had found her uncannily accurate as a forecaster; he gave
up any hope of rain and cancellation of practice. She started
with the smallest of children's socks, working up to her
husband's; then the larger items precisely in order of size.
Ransom wondered what the imperative was behind this
acute organization. Would her world collapse if the socks
were pinned at random? Or was there a secret stain in her
laundress's heart, a calamity that compelled her to make a
ritual out of the humblest task, fighting chaos with order?

Inside, he washed at the sink and boiled water for shaving and tea. After shaving, he rolled up the futon and swept
the room. Out in the street he heard the plaintive wail of
the tofu man's horn. With almost two hours to practice
there was time to eat; if he didn't eat he would be in rough
shape by the middle of practice. Taking a bowl from the
cabinet, he ran downstairs and halfway down the street
before he caught up to the big tricycle. The tofu man

dismounted decorously and bowed several times. Ransom asked for a block of the soft.

Back in the kitchen, he grated some dried bonito over the tofu and wet it down with soy sauce. Knowing he would burn this off in an hour without carbohydrates, he found a bowl of rice in the refrigerator. Breakfast of champions. He ate all of the tofu and half of the rice, having learned to find the middle ground between eating too little and fainting, and eating too much and puking.

An hour and twenty minutes left. Ransom sat cross-legged at the table and tweezed grains of rice from the side of the bowl with his chopsticks. The master swordsmen and karate-ka of old were said to be able to pluck flies out of the air with theirs.

The bowls washed, he rummaged in the desk drawer for the bound typescript of his father's play. Ransom had tried to read it several times in the past year, getting no farther than the first act, wanting it to be a masterpiece and finding it uninspired. It was not respect for his father that made him want to like it. For years he had judged the old man harshly, using this play as the standard of excellence from which he seemed to have fallen; the possibility that it was no good complicated the question of his father's career integrity.

Restless, he put the manuscript back in the drawer and set his calligraphy box, a cup of water, three brushes and a calligraphy pad on the table. Opening the black lacquer box, he picked an ink stick and wet down the iron ink tray, then rubbed the stick along the tray until he had a dark gray wash. He dipped his brush and made a horizontal stroke. Horizontals first. The procedure was strict and rhythmic, dictated by economy of motion. He did *kara* of *karate*. He filled the first sheet with seven or eight of them, following the same sequence of strokes, filling his brush from the tray, then tore it off and started a new sheet. After two sheets the repetition became tedious and his attention drifted while his hand continued to perform; the almost identical nature of each sequence gained interest with each tiny individuation and gained suspense with the unfulfilled possibility of a major change or variation, until Ransom couldn't have said what the word meant; it was no longer a word to him at all, if it ever had been. Because his Japanese was so limited, the characters were objects more than words, pictures corresponding to nothing at all.

When it was time to go, he got his gi from the terrace, where it was airing out, folded the pants with the shirt, rolled them together and tied them with the belt.

He was three blocks away from the dojo when his bike began to kick and misfire, finally choking off just short of the driveway. Ransom walked it the rest of the way. Out back the Monk was belaboring the punching post. Udo was sweeping the lot, and waddled over for a look. He climbed on and tried to kick-start it, then got down on his knees and started poking into the machinery. Others arrived and assembled around the bike, proposing diagnoses. Then Suzuki, who went to college with Yamada's younger brother, came in on his moped with the news that Yamada was going to be married. It was a "love marriage," Suzuki said, using an English phrase for a foreign concept. This announcement excited no small amount of surprise and comment. Ransom was pleased, although worried about the price Yamada would pay for his independence.

The sensei marched over and told everyone to change, no dawdling. Suzuki asked if he knew of Yamada's engagement; he said he did, in a tone that indicated no felicitation. Yamada had probably visited the sensei to ask his blessing and to explain his decision, a conversation Ransom would have liked to have overheard. The sensei appeared to be in a foul mood. Ransom took it as a bad sign that he was wearing his black gi.

The Monk directed the stretching and calisthenics. He spread his feet apart and lowered his butt until it touched the asphalt. Ransom could not follow all the way; he had pushed as far as he could, feeling the tendons and muscles inside his leg stretching toward what seemed a tearing point, when he felt a foot on his back, forcing him lower; the sensei was standing over him, saying, *I could drive a truck between your legs.* Losing balance, pain mounting on either side of his groin, Ransom pushed out on his right heel and registered a sudden burning in his left thigh.

Lower, the sensei said.

I can't, Ransom thought, I can't possibly, but he did not say it.

He felt hands on his hips and then a flash of fire arcing up his left leg and across his groin and he concentrated on stifling the cry that had risen up into his throat and threatened to come out of his eyes and his nose and the follicles of his scalp. When the sensei released him, he drew a long, slow breath and wondered if anything was permanently ripped. He straighted up slowly. The high kicks, which followed shortly, were painful, but the pain faded. Ransom fixed his eyes on the Monk and tried to synchronize himself. The Monk seemed to be made of a perfectly elastic but diamantine material; the liquid rhythm of his limbs was hard to reconcile with the sensation of actual contact, when he was suddenly as hard and solid as teak. This was a grinding, no-frills practice in which the sensei took an active role. Half an hour after they paired off for kicking and blocking, the sensei began harassing Ransom. He watched as Ransom attacked Suzuki, then told Suzuki to step aside.

I want you to kick me right there, the sensei said, pointing to his belly.

They faced off. Ransom kicked, a hard left and then a harder right, keeping his eyes on the small black pupils of the sensei, driving his kicks into the target which would have been the sensei's belly if he had not stepped back and blocked the hole with his forearm. The sensei drew Ransom forward as he retreated around the lot, timing his retreat so that Ransom's kicks seemed almost powerless as they connected. When Ransom came at him faster, lengthening his stride and picking up the tempo of the kicks, determined to hit him hard, the sensei slowed his pace and forced Ransom to slow. Ransom kicked as hard as he could, telling himself that he would at least make him yield ground, beginning to hate the sensei's eyes and seeing in them, he thought, a recognition of the desperation which was beginning to show in his own. He wanted to break the sensei's arms.

The sensei stopped retreating altogether and fended off Ransom's kicks from a standing position. It became difficult to keep his back leg bent and maintain fighting crouch; from a standing position, his kicks became even less effective. His calves ached. The sensei kept telling him to stay down. The tops of Ransom's feet and his shins were swollen and numb from the pounding. He didn't think he could keep it up much longer, but the less he put into it, he knew, the longer the sensei would work him. He felt dizzy and he could hear a faint buzzing in his ears. The back of his neck was hot and itchy and he focused on that, to the exclusion of the pain in his feet and the pain in his calves, commanding himself to summon his energy and deliver it all at once, in one direction, like a center-fire rifle cartridge. As it was, he was wasting himself slowly. At the same time, he wondered why he was doing this: karate, boys in white suits kicking each other as if something were at stake. He could walk away, right now, no need to go on, tell the sensei to piss up a rope or whatever they pissed up in Japanese, kiss his gaijin ass.

Suddenly enraged at his own body for betraying him so easily, Ransom began to court the pain plaguing him and to almost gloat as his feet pulped up and his calves burned. Then the sensei looked aside, hearing or seeing something that Ransom was too exhausted to register, or perhaps out of boredom; or maybe, it occurred to Ransom later, handing him a chance. Ransom broke his rhythm, holding back for a second, then kicked harder than he had yet kicked, finding a small chink in the sensei's defense and driving through the block until he felt the yielding canvas of the target.

It was a good, solid hit, and though the sensei was not visibly impressed he shifted on his feet in order to retain his balance. This was something. Ransom had been present once when the sensei had stood in the middle of the parking lot, arms folded on his chest, and invited each member of the dojo—except the absent Monk—to try and push him over. The sensei resisted only to the extent of not moving; no one, including Ransom, was able to budge him. Ransom had not known what to make of this, he still didn't, but this time he had succeeded in moving the immovable sensei.

Okay, the sensei said, after Ransom had delivered a few more kicks, and walked off.

When Yamada arrived, less than an hour of practice remained. He apologized, bowed to the company and quickly changed. No one mentioned his engagement. He joined Ransom for the final drills.

Congratulations, Ransom said.

Yamada blushed and nodded.

Ransom planted his feet, inhaled deeply and then emptied himself of air. Yamada punched him in the gut, ten times with his right arm and with his left, Ransom taking and expelling another breath in between. Then they switched.

The sensei called, and they gathered in a circle around him. Ransom was tired and sore, his gi drenched with sweat. In his clean white gi the Monk looked rested and fresh. Ransom didn't want to face him. Not today. Not now. Maybe some other time.

Sparring, the sensei said. *Two points, no restrictions.*

He looked around the group until his eyes fell on Ransom. Ransom looked back, trying to appear undaunted, disinterested, ready for anything. Still looking at Ransom, he called Yamada's name. Yamada shouted *Hai!* and stepped forward.

The sensei sent the junior members of the dojo to face Yamada first. The smallest boy flailed away valiantly. Yamada tapped him twice for the match and worked through the next five without incident. At this point Ransom expected the sensei to call the Monk, since the sparring was often split between the two black belts. But the sensei worked up the roster sending them in against Yamada. No one had scored on him—a foregone conclusion with his earlier opponents—but by the time he had dispatched Suzuki, ranked just beneath Ransom, Yamada was beginning to tire, his round face red and filmed with sweat.

It was Ransom's turn. They bowed. Ransom could see that Yamada's stance was loose. He was taking it easy, standing a little high to relieve the pressure on his knees. He threw Ransom three kicks and the third found an opening, catching him in the solar plexus and knocking him backward, although Ransom reacted quickly and didn't lose much wind.

Point, the sensei said.

They faced off and Ransom attacked, kicking low, high and low before getting punched in the chest. The sensei didn't call the point. Instead, he waited until Ransom looked over and then dangled his arms like an ape.

Wide open, the sensei said. *Attacking doesn't mean you can forget about your defense.*

Ransom nodded, ready to limp away with his chagrin, when the sensei said, *Best out of seven.*

Pardon, Ransom said, pretending he hadn't heard, and the sensei repeated his command almost mockingly.

Yamada bowed to Ransom once again. The sensei must have been disciplining them both, Yamada for being late and perhaps for getting married and Ransom for what—presuming to be a black belt?

Ransom took the next two points, both on straight front kicks, after protracted exchanges. Yamada's cheek was bleeding where the nail of Ransom's big toe had grazed it. They were both slowing down, just out of immediate kick range from each other, and the sensei called them on it. Ransom was breathing hard; Yamada appeared to have his breath under control. He came at Ransom with a combination of thrusts, but suddenly fell back; as Ransom set himself to attack he saw an insect, a bee, had flown into Yamada's eye. Yamada was shaking his head, frantically, and Ransom stopped himself mid-kick.

Attack, the sensei shouted, but Ransom hesitated. Yamada had dislodged the bee and resumed his stance, his left eye closed and weeping. He kicked Ransom in the stomach.

Doubled over, trying to regain his breath, Ransom felt indignant, betrayed. He heard the voice of the sensei, lecturing him, a fool, an idiot. Without bothering to listen, he knew what was being said. Never break off an attack. Practice as if your life were at stake, live as if you were practicing. Expect the unexpected, whether in the form of a knife or a winged insect.

As he gasped for breath, Ransom tried to master a desire for revenge with the proposition that Yamada had performed admirably, by the book, and that he had screwed up. The nicest thing you could do for your opponent in the dojo, the sensei liked to say, was to hit him as hard as you could.

He tried to hurt Yamada, perhaps for his own good, but

he was badly winded and after a few exchanges Yamada hit him square on the chest, though without much damage. They bowed. Yamada did not look as bad as Ransom felt, but he looked tired, and now he had to fight the Monk.

Yamada held his own for a short time, but the Monk was relentless. The Monk's strategy was aimed at Yamada's endurance. Usually he waited for his opponent to attack, but today he took the offensive. Yamada went down.

Ransom had never seen him go down. The back door of the gym opened and, before it closed again, the buzz of voices from within made the subsequent silence awful. Yamada jumped to his feet and resumed fighting stance. He was being punished, Ransom thought, for falling in love.

Finally it was over. Yamada bowed at the end and knelt beside the Monk. Afterwards it was very quiet, someone asking for soap, a frightened-looking new boy sweeping the lot, Udo's voice lowered as he asked Ransom when the trouble with his bike started. Over by the showers, Yamada was pulling on his pants. Suzuki asked him if he was okay, then congratulated him on his marriage, but the others, as if by agreement, kept their distance. The Monk was jogging around the lot to wind down.

When Ransom came out of the shower Udo held up a carburetor for his inspection.

Look at that, he said. Udo pulled on the intake so that Ransom could get a glimpse of the inside, but Ransom couldn't see much.

What is it? Ransom said.

I think it's sugar, Udo said.

Sugar?

Udo nodded.

Ransom asked, *How would that get there?*

Udo asked if he had any enemies. He wasn't certain it was sugar, though. He told Ransom he'd have the bike picked up and taken to the garage, and call when he found out. Ransom gave him the number of the coffee shop.

Walking downtown, Ransom reviewed the suspects. The gesture seemed a little pissant for the yakuza. DeVito was promising, and there was always the possibility of random juvenile delinquency.

Among the shoes at the men's entrance to the public bath were a pair of Italianate lizard loafers. Ransom left his sneakers beside them. He paid the old woman for the bath and accessories and took a basket for his clothes.

Inside the bath chamber, two heavily tattooed men were squatting on the tiles along the row of faucets. Ransom sat down a few faucets away. Today the yakuza did not seem as quaint as in the past.

He heard the word *gaijin* several times. He ignored them as long as he could. Then a piece of soap hit him in the head. When he looked over, they were delighted, as if they had just discovered that he was animate. The smaller of the two, whom Ransom observed to be missing two fingers, began making faces at him.

"I reft my heart in San Franshisco, *desu ne?*"

Ransom turned away and lathered up his wash cloth.

"I am a boy. My name is. How do you do? I am fine shank you."

They were still at the faucets when he went to the tubs. Without making a very conspicuous detour he would need to walk directly behind them to get to the water. They both turned and stared as he walked past. He felt that holding the washbucket and cloth in front of his crotch would be a concession of some kind, so he didn't. The smaller one said something nasty that he couldn't make out. He lowered himself into the first tub.

They began directing all of their comments at him. He couldn't hear all of them, but one refrain was how bad gaijin smelled.

He moved to the second tub. The two men stood up and sauntered over. They looked down at Ransom.

My friend wants to get in that tub, the little man said. His chest was taken up with a tattoo of a geisha in a long flowing kimono. On the larger man's chest a dragon roared, brilliant in red and green, and there was a scar on his right cheek. Both had wide, fleshy faces and crewcuts. The taller one was in decent shape; probably a budo-ka of some kind, kendo or karate. Ransom was tired of their shit and he would have liked to see if he could knock them around, but it wasn't worth it. He climbed out of the tub and stepped into the third, lying back and closing his eyes. The two men splashed water over the rim from the next tub and discussed the erotic utility of gaijin women.

When Ransom abruptly stood up they fell silent. He turned to look at them, and for a moment saw fear in both. Then he wasn't sure what he was going to do. He did not want to retreat in cowardly fashion, nor did he want to put up with any more of their talk. He got out of the tub and stepped over to the fourth and hottest. Steam drifted and curled over the surface. He stepped in as casually as he would onto a subway car.

The shock seized his lungs and the next sensation that

separated out from a solution of pain was the waves, made by his entry, abrading his flesh like sandpaper. He kept a stoic demeanor, resisted the urge to move; motion increased the heat. Once the water was still it became almost tolerable. He wasn't sure if he had done this for himself or for them, but he stayed in until it was no longer painful, ignoring them, their words swamped in the watery echoes, and then he stood up, walked over to the cold tub and submerged himself completely until he felt cool on the outside.

Ransom picked up his gear and walked out, not looking back, though he could hear their taunts. Inspired, he towelled off and dressed quickly. There were two baskets of clothing on the floor beside the lockers, and one Funky Babe shopping bag. He emptied both baskets into the shopping bag.

The old lady thanked him as he slipped out the door. He picked up the shoes in the entryway and added them to the bag. Out on the sidewalk, he felt lightheaded. The noise of traffic seemed to reach him from a great distance. He walked to the corner and deposited the shopping bag in a trash can, pausing for a moment to admire the velour lapels of a maroon sport jacket, then walked out to Kawaramachi Street to the bus stop.

19

"What's the weather in Kyoto," Honda asked.

"Muggy," Ransom said.

"Muggy? What is this?"

"*Mushi atsui.*"

"You should move to Osaka. Be closer to office."

Ransom grunted noncommittally.

"I do not mean to criticize, but Mitsubishi class wishes to know why you do not go out drinking with them? As you surely know, relaxation drinking is an important part of business scene in Japan."

"I have karate practice every night. Besides which, I don't drink."

"You could join them sometimes."

"The last time I did my head ached for three days.

Everybody had to sing a song and I got 'I Did It My Way.' "

"Flank Sinatra." Honda smiled. Then he became serious. "Please. Make a date to join them for drinking."

"I'll check my calendar," Ransom said. A Japanese standoff, this. For the moment they would leave it vague.

Honda had to go out and pitch the A-OK Business English System to a new company. The sulky and unkempt Desmond Caldwell was accompanying him as a live exhibit. Caldwell was wearing a tie and jacket for the occasion.

Ransom sat down at his desk and opened a letter from his father, which he had transferred directly from the mail slot to his breast pocket on his way out of the house. On the train, he had not been eager to open it. He did so now to delay reading the ad copy Honda had left for his comments, which was probably even worse than a fatherly epistle.

The letter was mercifully brief, drifting in tone between high-patriarchal and boys'-night-out: "Although I haven't been in touch of late, my thoughts are often with you . . . breakfast at Polo Lounge . . . Lara Lavalle, the silicone queen, who uses her finger to read her lines off the monitor . . . Hoping this finds you well, Chris. Your loving father." No lectures about wasting one's life, turning up one's nose at all the golden opportunities. Ransom junior was relieved, and chastened at the thought of the bad-mouth he had put on his dad for both Rachel and Marilyn.

Again he felt the onslaught of panic and regret—he could nearly smell it—and turned in self-defense to the ad copy, a pitch for a new chain of saunas. The art showed a bikini-clad Japanese girl against the Manhattan skyline:

I LOVE SAUNA

Let's Sauna

Let's Sauna for my happy

Let's Sauna for your happy

Let's Sauna joyful life

Let's Sauna for our happy

Oh beautiful day, healthy day, nice a day.

Let's Sauna all happy.

Honda's note indicated that the copy would also serve as the lyrics to a song which would saturate national radio to mark the grand opening of the sauna chain. Ransom didn't know where to begin. Despairing of the language, he decided to evade the issue by consulting with Miti-san, the art director, who because he had scored low on his preschool tests was rejected by the best kindergartens, and subsequently did not get into the best schools, including Tokyo University, thus was unable to get a job at Dentsu, the top Japanese ad agency, and therefore ended up in charge of design and layout for A-OK textbooks and ads.

Miti was holed-up in his cubicle, separated from the rest of the office by a sheet of glass. When Ransom knocked, he was sitting in front of his drafting table reading a magazine. Looking alarmed, Miti-san slipped into his shoes and straightened his tie. They exchanged pleasantries—Ransom asking about the wife and kid, Miti about karate—and then Ransom asked what was the thinking behind the bikini and the New York skyline.

Miti shrugged and looked down at the artwork again, as if he hadn't seen it in a long time.

Don't they have saunas in New York, he asked, fearfully.

Sure they do, Ransom said. He was just curious if New York was particularly associated with sauna bathing in the minds of the Japanese.

New York is like sex, Miti said, relaxing a little. *You can sell almost anything if you attach it to New York.*

Ransom finally convinced Miti that he hadn't come in a spirit of criticism so much as a spirit of curiosity. Miti became almost loquacious.

The principles of Japanese advertising, he said, were really quite simple. Gaijin were glamorous. If you were selling a luxury product—liquor, perfume—you used a gaijin, preferably a blond model, a New York, London or Paris backdrop, and an English slogan. If you were selling a household product, you used a domestic-looking Japanese model. The interesting cases were those in between. Miti had decided that the sauna, being a service, ought to have some racial identification as well as gaijin glamour.

Miti asked Ransom what he thought of Sadaharu Oh, the home-run heir apparent.

Ransom said he was a fine ballplayer.

Miti said, *Hank Aaron is a Negro, isn't he?*

Ransom said he was, unsure of the significance Miti attached to this fact. He went back out to his desk and struggled with the sauna copy, the construction of which was brought back to him that evening as he worked through Lesson Nine of Level Two with his Mitsubishi class, Ransom reading and the class repeating, books closed.

I make a deal.

"I make a deal."
You make a deal.
"You make a deal."
He makes a deal.
"He makes a deal."
She makes a deal.
"She makes a deal."
Mr. Smith makes a deal . . .

20

On Tuesday night the sensei asked Ransom to stay after practice. The cool night air was a relief from the mugginess of the day, which Ransom had spent in Osaka, untangling English words from Japanese constructions, correcting pronunciation in a smoke-filled room in the Mitsubishi building.

Practice had gone well. In sparring, Ransom had given the Monk a hard time for his two points. The Monk, now smoothing and folding his gi on the steps of the gym, was among the last to leave. Finally he cinched the compact bundle with his obi, the kuro obi, bowed to the sensei and Ransom, who remained in their gi, and walked off, looking as if he were closing down a movie.

Ransom watched the sensei walk out to the center of the lot, marvelling at his grace and ease. In one of their first after-practice sessions, the sensei worked on Ransom's gravity. First he imitated Ransom's walk, bouncing up and down, swinging his arms, swivelling his head. *That's how Americans walk,* the sensei said, and months later, seeing a group of American tourists sauntering up Shijo Street, Ransom saw what he meant: moving as if they were trying to launch themselves into space, confident that the air would part to let them pass, without a worry about the ground beneath their feet. Over a period of months they worked on lowering Ransom's center of balance, bringing it down from his chest. During practice the sensei would clamp a hand over Ransom's head to fix it level as he moved. Sitting on chairs, he said, contributed to the terrible top-heaviness of Americans. Ransom complained that he was never going to get any shorter—that was what it came down to—but his walk had changed.

Now Ransom stood facing the sensei, hands crossed, waiting for instructions.

The sensei poked at the asphalt with the ball of his foot. Then he said, *I don't believe in fancy moves. Triple backward upside-down kicks* . . . He twisted his body preposterously to illustrate. *Movie stuff, that jumping around.* He jumped. *Understand?*

Ransom said he understood.

Also, he said, *it took me two years to get you down closer to the ground. But, when one masters the basics, there are other techniques . . . useful . . . understand?*

Ransom nodded.

He said, *I've been thinking about a new technique for you. For your build, some techniques don't make sense. But I think this one will suit you. Ready?*

They assumed fighting stance.

The sensei jumped up and let loose a kick at Ransom's chest. Ransom blocked it easily, then saw the other coming at him, sweeping just past his nose, brushing hair over his forehead, the sensei in mid-air in front of him, coming down lightly, all at once.

You spring from the back leg, the sensei explained. *The first kick is a fake, but you use it for upward momentum. The first kick is chest level, but it's the second that has the power, head level.*

The sensei reached inside his pants and adjusted himself.

It's dangerous, though, the sensei said. *Dangerous for the attacker. If you don't spring hard enough, if you're blocked hard on the first, you can land on your back. Also dangerous for the opponent. If you connect with the head kick . . .* He paused.

In practice, we lower the level of the second kick till we can control it. Understand?

Ransom assented eagerly.

It was a matter of combining moves he was already familiar with and extending them. After half an hour the sensei seemed satisfied with his progress.

Let's get a drink, he said as they were changing.

To say that you didn't drink, Ransom figured, was especially foolish when your sensei was the one asking.

Okay, Ransom said. *Where?*

Gion, the sensei said.

Ransom said, *I've got an extra helmet,* indicating the shoddy old 250 Scrambler Udo had given him to use until he could clear the sugar out of Ransom's bike.

We can take a cab, the sensei proposed.

Why waste the money, Ransom asked.

I'm not getting on the back of that thing, he said.

Ransom asked him if he'd rather drive.

He shook his head. *I'm not crazy,* he said. *Those things are dangerous.*

They left the bike there and took a cab. Traffic thickened as they approached Gion, and at Sanjo Street, on the northern edge of the district, the sensei paid the cabbie and hopped out. The gaudier establishments, cabarets with neon signs and loud music, circled the district. Further in, the streets narrowed into one-way alleys and tributary passageways. Drunken businessmen in blue suits stumbled from doorways singing and holding each other up. The signs became more discreet, the architecture more domestic as they walked in, passing tea houses and member's clubs.

The sensei had a bottle at a little nomiya, a tunnel of a place with eight seats along the bar, two of which happened to be empty. The hostess made a fuss over the sensei and the patrons greeted him deferentially; Ransom was subjected to the pet-gaijin treatment. The sensei proclaimed Ransom a real samurai. A bottle of J&B, decorated with the sensei's name and the stylized profile of a clenched fist, was placed in front of them, along with a set-up of ice and soda.

They talked baseball. The sensei demonstrated tricks with matches and coins. But once their sashimi arrived and Ransom started in, the sensei grabbed Ransom's chopsticks with one hand and the back of his head with the other. He showed how easy it would be—given the position of the chopsticks, pointing directly back into the mouth—to skewer Ransom's skull, then demonstrated the safe technique, keeping the chopsticks off to the side of the face so that at worst your cheek was pierced.

The whiskey tasted harsh at first, but the second one was better. The sensei insisted. Two seats down a man was passed out with his head on the bar. As if on tracks, the hostess and her daughter glided back and forth from one end of the bar to the other. The stereo played hokey love songs. Suddenly, the sensei wanted to sing. He asked the hostess to play the instrumental backup tape to "Onna Hitori." The other patrons applauded. He pushed back his seat and stood up, as the music began. He closed his eyes and sang:

> Kyoto ohara sanzen-in
> Koini tsukareta onna ga hitori
> Yuki ni shioze no sugaki no obi ga
> Ike no mizumo ni yureteita

He had a fine voice. It was a song about lost love, a woman alone, snow falling on a temple, on the woman. When the sensei finished they all applauded enthusiastically.

Did you understand it, the sensei asked.

Not all the words, Ransom said. *But I liked it.*

Good. The words aren't so important. It's the feeling—he patted his belly—*that counts.*

Ransom remembered something: Love to feel everything rather than think. The sensei was a Funky Babe.

When the bottle was dry the sensei said it was time for a bath. The hostess walked them to the door, telling them to be careful and to come again soon. They walked east, toward the river.

The whiskey had given Ransom a headache. The sensei was in fine form, smiling and humming. He asked Ransom if he had ever been to a Turko Buro. Ransom said that he hadn't. *It's time you did,* the sensei said.

Ransom tried to think of an excuse.

What do you say in English, the sensei wanted to know.

"Turkish bath," Ransom said.

Do you have them in America, the sensei asked.

Not really, Ransom said.

Either you have them or you don't.

He could plead hydrophobia, Ransom thought.

The sensei stopped in front of a doorway and knocked. A buzzer sounded and the sensei pushed the door open. The empty reception area might just as easily have been a dentist's waiting room: Naugahyde couch and chairs, coffee table, magazine rack. The sensei told Ransom to sit down.

A wooden panel, set into the far wall, slid back revealing a small window and a face. The man shook his head. They were closed, he said through a speaker. The sensei stepped up to the window and held a conference with the man. Ransom sat down on the couch. He could not bring himself to tell the sensei, who would not understand, and would probably be offended, that he didn't want to do this. He tasted something metallic in the back of his mouth.

The sensei joined Ransom on the couch. He said, *I had to convince them you were a good gaijin. Normally they wouldn't take one. They don't want any trouble.*

Thank you, Ransom said.

I paid for the bath, but for the hon-ban you have to pay the girl once you're inside. It's three thousand yen.

He picked up a magazine and kicked off his sandals.

Then he suddenly turned back to Ransom. He asked, *Do you know about the bubble dance?*

Ransom nodded. *I've heard about it.*

It costs extra, the sensei said, *but it's worth it.*

A door beside the window panel opened. A man with a samurai haircut stuck his head out and looked them over; his face was like a side of beef. He stepped into the room, displaying an improbable tuxedo. The folds of his neck hung over the starched white collar.

"Konbanwa," the sensei said.

The man grunted unintelligibly. He stared for a moment and left, closing the door behind him.

The sensei had just swapped magazines when a girl in a pink bathrobe appeared in the hall at the other end of the room. *Welcome,* she said. She looked like a well-fed schoolgirl, with a face that was all horizontals.

The sensei turned to Ransom and told him it was his choice: He could go with this one or take his chances on the next one. Feeling queasy, Ransom stood up and followed the girl, not wanting to prolong this further. She led him by the hand down a brightly lit hallway, turning corners until Ransom thought he must be back where they started. The hall was carpeted and everything except for the buzz in his head seemed muffled. She stopped in front of a door she unlocked with a key, then knelt down and removed his shoes.

He followed her into a tatami room furnished with a bed and a standing wardrobe, which opened onto a tiled bath chamber with turquoise tub and ceramic Cupid fountain.

Undoing the buttons of his shirt, she asked his name.

Hers was Haruko. She hung his shirt in the wardrobe and helped him out of his pants and shorts. Ransom was glad, at least, that she wasn't a talker. She removed her robe, revealing a plump body, and a pair of black lace panties.

She led him into the tiled room and seated him on a plastic bath stool. Cupid was pissing into a golden oyster shell. The tub was empty. She turned on the water, holding a bucket under the spigots, then soaked him down and told him to relax. Ransom looked her over for signs of abuse, bruises, needle tracks, tattoos—anything to confirm his sense of the involuntary nature of her line of work, the kind of work Marilyn might be forced into. But she looked healthy enough.

She shampooed him first, then soaped up a washcloth and worked her way down. He looked very strong, she said, and again told him to relax, he was as tight as something that wasn't part of Ransom's vocabulary. She massaged his shoulders and back.

When her hands went below his waist, she was as thorough as she had been elsewhere. She looked up briefly at him and asked Ransom if he would say that he was an average gaijin.

There was no such thing, Ransom said, as an average gaijin.

She said she meant, was he average physically?

Ransom knew what she meant, and shrugged.

Suddenly coy, she asked if he wanted the bubble dance.

Ransom shook his head.

She ran her soapy hand down the inside of his thigh. *I do it very well,* she said.

I'm sure you do, Ransom said.

Are you sure? she said, running her hand back up between his legs.

Ransom said he was sure.

She finished with his feet, washing and massaging each of his toes. Finally she rinsed him off and gestured toward the bath. He eased himself in, Haruko adding a burst of cold water. The water was fine but the whole procedure was happening to someone else and Ransom wanted only to be outside, headed home. She started kneading his shoulders again. He was sorry that she had to wash and fuck strange men for a living, but his sympathy wasn't going to do a thing for her. She told him again how tight he was.

When the bath was finished Haruko asked if he would like the hon-ban, gesturing toward the bed.

No, thank you, he said.

Most of the younger men get the hon-ban, she said.

I'm sure they enjoy it. Ransom felt ridiculous, standing nude in the middle of the changing room, trying to be polite.

You're the first gaijin customer I've had, she said. She looked him up and down as if committing the details to memory, then she went to get his shirt. He tried to tip her, feeling that he had been a financial disappointment, but she wouldn't accept it.

He waited for the sensei in the reception area and after a few minutes heard his voice. A woman on his arm, he strode through the doorway, nearly radiant. He and the woman bantered for a few minutes, and Ransom received his fair share of comment.

Once they were out on the street, the sensei asked what he thought of the bubble dance.

Terrific, Ransom said.

They turned a corner into a narrow, covered passageway and caught sight of a geisha, ghostly in her white makeup, framed in a doorway. She froze, looking at them, and Ransom was reminded of a deer caught in headlights. Then she turned, hurried across the street with tiny pigeon steps and disappeared in another doorway. Ransom and his teacher stood in the passageway, both looking at the door.

21

For two years Ransom had been watched wherever he went, and he had gradually stopped noticing that conversation paused when he entered a restaurant, that all heads turned when he boarded a train. But now, if he was glanced at by a man in a suit, his first thought was that he was under surveillance. Where before he had felt only curiosity, he now detected hostility. These people didn't want him in their country, and some of them might feel more than a vague resentment. According to Marilyn, Kyoto was owned and operated by the yakuza; the police were in on the take, every bath operator and street vendor paid protection, and every third-rate entertainer on television was in their pocket, not to mention government officials.

More and more, Ransom found himself watching his back. The sensei, he remembered, told him that the old karate masters never approached a corner directly, but always moved out and around. Taking immediate inventory of people in public places, Ransom suddenly noticed that the proprietor of his local newsstand was tattooed. In the Osaka subway one morning, he glanced at the overhead strap beside his and saw a hand one finger shy; that same night, riding home, a man in a brown suit and hat had stared at him from Osaka to Takatsuki, sitting directly across from him, his gaze never wavering when Ransom looked up from his paper.

Ransom addressed him: *Is something the matter?*

The man raised his eyebrows and said nothing.

Find something else to do with your eyes, Ransom said.

The man acted surprised, even sheepish, and when he trudged off at the next stop Ransom feared he had overreacted.

Maybe, he thought, it was the weather: the air thicker and wetter by the day, the barometer plunging.

Marilyn called him at the coffee shop the next morning, Saturday. He didn't want to meet anywhere in the city, and if they were followed, the country wasn't safe either. Deciding that crowds provided good protection, Ransom gave her the number of a bus and told her to take it to the end of the line to Arashiyama. They would meet at six in the park beside the river, where people gathered to watch the pelican-fishing, but not likely anyone they knew.

At five-thirty Ransom set out, riding east along the Arashiyama road. The Scrambler lagged and surged, and Ransom wondered how Udo was making out with the 350. The city thinned and gradually disappeared, soon giving way to temples and rice fields, knee-high in green in the late afternoon sun. Turning into the parking lot, he smelled fried food from the stalls along the riverbank. The unpaved lot was unattended, but the Nissans and Toyotas were parked in perfect rows.

The riverbank was carpeted with tatami mats on which families camped with picnic gear. Roman candles and rockets hissed and sputtered over the water. Ransom picked his way through the crowd, looking for Marilyn. Hawkers in the food stalls invited him to buy grilled squid, barbecued corn, chicken parts on sticks, hot dogs fashioned from mysterious animal and fish products and binders. As the Kyoto bus rattled to a stop in the parking lot, the first boat rounded the bend upriver.

Ransom waved to Marilyn, who walked cautiously, in high heels, toward the river.

"Where are we," she demanded.

"Relax, it's a festival. One of my students told me about it. We're just a couple of tourists watching the pelicans."

"What kind of festival?"

"Beats me, maybe an equinox or something."

"It smells terrible."

Ransom untied the rolled tatami mat from the back of the Scrambler and coaxed Marilyn to a spot upriver where they could spread out. He bought a handful of Roman candles from an old man and fired one out over the water.

"You really know how to show a girl a good time," Marilyn said.

"I guess you had all kinds of festivals in Vietnam."

"Sure, lots of fireworks during Tet—grenades coming through restaurant windows, car-bombs in the street." Although she was wrapped in a fox jacket and the temperature was easily seventy, Marilyn sat stiffly on the mat, hugging her body with her arms.

"I just wanted to meet someplace out of the way."

"I'm kind of edgy," she said, fishing a cigarette from her purse. "I've been thinking. It was nice of you to try to help, but I don't think we better see each other anymore. I had a hell of a time getting away today and my oyabun, he might do something crazy."

Ransom looked out at the boats coming down the river. "Someone put sugar in my gas tank."

"Gas tank? What are you talking about?"

"My motorcycle's. The sugar pretty much screws up the bike."

She stared out at the water. "That means he's found you. Please, I don't want you to get hurt."

"Maybe it wasn't him."

"You have other enemies?"

"Somehow sugar in my gas tank doesn't quite strike me as a yakuza move."

"Well, one day he threatens to kill me and the next day he brings me flowers and cries in my lap." She drew on her cigarette. "He says we're going to get married soon."

"What do you say?"

"You seem to forget that I don't have any choices. Anyway, why don't you get out while you still can."

The sun had fallen behind the mountains, and Ransom watched the silhouettes of the boats against the river. Marilyn looked at him. "Whose lap do you cry on?"

"I keep a ten-gallon bucket handy."

She lay back on her elbows in the grass. "Do you have any girlfriends?"

"Not really."

"Are you, do you like men? I mean, gay?"

"No, not hardly."

She sat up and took his hand in both of hers. "I like you, Ransom."

"Thank you," he said.

"I don't even know your first name."

"Chris Ransom. I don't like the Chris much."

"You don't like me at all, do you?"

"I like you just fine. And I can help you more if we leave it at that."

"What is it with you?" she said. "If you live long enough with a hurt, then you'll start liking it."

"My disappointments," Ransom said, "are none of your business."

Downriver, the boats had gathered in a small flotilla. Marilyn squinted. "What are *those?*"

"Pelicans," Ransom said. "Come on, let's go down."

They walked to the main landing, and above the noise of the crowd they heard the weird voices of the birds. Perched shoulder-to-shoulder along the gunwales of the boats, the pelicans looked like clowns in a chorus line, all noses and feet. Guiding Marilyn in front of him, Ransom pressed ahead until they stood among many others around the lead boat. The man astride the boat held the ends of the leashes fastened to the pelican's legs. He addressed the birds in a crisp, military tone, cuffing them and jerking the leashes when they became unruly. *Get in line. Knock it off.*

He then lit a torch and fired up the wood-filled iron basket hanging over the bow, the captains in the other boats following suit. A cheer rose from the crowd. Rockets arched over the water. The pelicans bobbed and shook their heads in anticipation.

"What's going on?" Marilyn said.

"You'll see."

The fires drifted out over the water. Ransom couldn't make out if the birds jumped into the water on command or if they were pushed, but the leashes trailed them, stretching out on the water then sinking as the pelicans dove under. The man up front hauled them back, one by one, and held them upside down until they had disgorged their catch into the boat. Iron rings around their necks prevented them from swallowing.

"That's disgusting," Marilyn said, when Ransom explained.

He heard his name called, and turned. DiVito was standing in the trees along the bank above them.

"What does he want?" Marilyn said.

"To fight."

"Here?"

"Promise me you'll get back to the bus."

"You're not going to fight him, are you?"

"No. But I'm not leaving until you get clear. Go down along the bank and then up to the parking lot. Keep close to people."

"Let's both go."

"He'd follow us."

"Are you coming up here," DeVito called, "or do you want me to chase you?" He started down the bank, and

Ransom told Marilyn to get going. The throng around them provided temporary insulation, but her progress seemed incredibly slow. DeVito was shoving his way through the crowd, which was swelling as the boats headed back toward shore. Ransom slipped out of his shoes. Beside him, a young father hoisted his son up on his shoulders. Moving toward the water, Ransom turned to see DeVito's samurai haircut advancing above the darker heads, getting closer. Two boats were sculling in to show their catch as Ransom stepped into the river, then spun around.

"What exactly do you want?" he said. DeVito was almost within spitting distance.

"You know what I want. So why run? A fair fight, hotshot."

The boatmen had started to tie up at the dock, calling at the crowd to make room, while the pelicans gurgled and clapped their beaks. Two boats were waiting just a few yards out from Ransom, who dove into the water between them. When he came up, with the two boats between him and the shore, the clamoring at the dock had increased in pitch, and he heard splashing behind him. He swam out into the river, turning gradually downstream, slowed by his jeans. When he looked back, the flaming basket at the prow of the boat farthest from shore was swinging wildly, and the boatman was flailing at the water with an oar. Ransom thought he saw someone in the water, amid the splashes of the oar. He glanced downriver, and the foundations of the Arashiyama Bridge were arching up above him.

Below the bridge he clambered up onto the road, breathing hard, watching for movement behind him. Once in the parking lot he crouched between cars and surveyed the area, wondering if DeVito would recognize the bike that Udo had lent him, wondering for that matter how DeVito had found him.

Two young men, drunk and happy, were looking for their car, and Ransom asked what all the noise was about. A crazy gaijin, they said, jumped into the river and got tangled up with the pelicans. Possibly two gaijin, but in any case it was the funniest thing they had ever seen. The pelicans flapping in every direction, the gaijin cursing and tearing at the leashes, and the enraged boatman trying to brain him with an oar. Only now did they really see Ransom—a wet, barefooted gaijin—and immediately both stopped laughing. He wished them good night, located his bike and rode off.

22

The heat built up, collecting at first in certain areas—behind the refrigerator, in the bright patches of sunlight over the tatami—and then spreading throughout the bowl within the mountains that ringed the city. The beer gardens on the rooftops of the big hotels reopened, and the air itself fell into lassitude; the kites flying over the river gradually disappeared, and with the burden of growing humidity, the sky seemed to lower itself on Kyoto like a canvas tent sagging with the weight of rainwater. The point of saturation would be reached by the middle of June, and the sky would open up in earnest to begin the *tsuyu,* the rainy season.

To avoid the hottest part of the day, the sensei changed Sunday practice from noon to ten. No one in the dojo sweated so profusely as Ransom, who nevertheless was

satisfied by his progress. He scored two more points on
the Monk and managed to keep himself from getting injured. At the same time, he felt he was moving, or being
moved, toward some crisis point of his own. Marilyn's yakuza
had given her an ultimatum: she would marry him in June
or he would turn her over to immigration, of which the
only possible result was deportation.

At the U.S. consulate in Osaka, Ransom asked what
could be done. The young man he talked to, who was about
Ransom's age, was cheerfully discouraging and seemed to
relish his thoroughly realistic interpretation of this bleak
situation. Political asylum was highly unlikely. Almost two
hundred thousand Vietnamese had entered the States in
the last two years, way above the quota set by Congress.
Tens of thousands more were seeking entry from camps
in Malaysia, Hong Kong and Thailand. He managed to
convey the impression that even though affairs of state
required his immediate attention, he was willing to devote
his valuable time to this small matter. About the only way
Marilyn could get into the States, he said, would be for an
American citizen to marry her.

Ransom had suspected more than once that this was what
she was angling for all along. He thought it conceivable
that there was no yakuza boyfriend, that she had invented
him for her purposes and that she was just another Asian
girl who wanted out.

She had mentioned the name of the club where she
supposedly sang and Ransom decided to check her out.
The club, on the edge of Gion, was a flashy establishment
whose doorman and awning were somebody's idea of the
Las Vegas style. Inside, the walls appeared to be covered

with polished aluminum. A hostess in a sequined minidress escorted him to his table, where within minutes he was joined by another hostess who nearly sat in his lap as she fed him slices of octopus and ran through her repertoire of English. He endured these ministrations for over an hour, aware that all this was costing him a fortune, and tried to ignore the exuberant performances of a female impersonator and a male duo. As he was leaving, Marilyn appeared on the stage, and from the door he listened to her sing "The Sound of Music." He listened just long enough to decide that, as far as he could judge, she had a good voice.

Walking into Buffalo Rome the next night, he sensed immediately that something was wrong. The frequency and quality of the noise was different, the voices frantic. Aikido Eric walked up and grabbed Ransom's elbow.

"Miles is in the hospital," he said. "Beat up."

"What?"

"He's in a coma."

Everyone but Ransom was certain that DeVito was responsible, and he kept his doubts to himself. No one, it seemed, knew for sure which hospital he was in.

Phoning Ryder's house, Ransom got no answer, so he rode over but no one came to the door. Finally an old woman came out of the house next door, and reluctantly gave Ransom the name of the hospital. Where gaijin were involved, she seemed to feel, there was no telling what would happen.

At the front desk a nurse explained they were giving details only to immediate family. Ransom explained that he was a brother, and was given directions to the room. The hospital was small and dingy, and Miles's room was at the end of an especially dark hallway. Miles lay on his back in one of three beds, taped up, his head above the eyebrows concealed by bandages. Akiko sat in a chair beside him. The elderly man in the next bed, rigged up with intravenous bottles, noted Ransom's arrival with obvious interest, while a middle-aged man snored loudly in the bed by the window.

"He's asleep," Akiko said.

"What happened?"

"I don't know, Chris. He went out this afternoon and the hospital called this evening. When I got here he was sleeping." He had a broken arm, cracked ribs and a concussion, she added, but the doctors claimed he'd be fine in a few weeks.

"How about you?" Ransom said. "Anything I can do?"

"Nothing thanks, really."

"You're due soon, aren't you?"

She looked at her feet—"Perhaps one week"—then looked up. "Is Miles in trouble?" she asked.

"I don't think so," Ransom said. "He didn't say anything?"

She shook her head, and her expression touched Ransom deeply: resignation that had passed beyond sadness.

"Hello, hello," the old man offered. "I am a boy. Sank you very much."

Ransom said hello, then turned to Akiko.

"I'm going to take care of this, Akiko. Nothing like this will happen again."

She nodded—without conviction, it seemed to him. Though he knew she didn't mean to, Akiko made him feel implicated in this violence, responsible in his genes, in his nationality. Gaijin, she must think, are all so strange and violent.

From the hospital Ransom went to a sushi bar not far from Marilyn's club. He ordered a nigiri tray, which he wanted delivered. Ransom was a frequent customer and the sushi master was glad to see him. A red-faced businessman at the counter was looking Ransom over as if he expected him to change form any minute.

He speaks Japanese, the master said.

Really? The businessman sounded doubtful.

Ransom sat at the bar over a cup of tea and while the master prepared the tray he wrote a note to Marilyn. Ransom explained that the sushi was for a woman friend, and asked if he could send a message along with the tray.

You have to watch out for those nightclub girls, the master said. *They'll empty your pockets before they unzip your fly.*

Ransom told the delivery boy it was important that he hand the tray directly to Marilyn, and that nobody was around when he gave her the note.

Almost an hour had passed before she came in, wearing a long coat over one of the sequined outfits. The businessman was favorably impressed. Nudging Ransom, he said, "Pretty, okay?"

"What's so urgent," Marilyn asked, after ordering a beer.

For a moment she seemed not to understand what he said. She hadn't expected them to bother Ryder, she said, but then added, "His underlings, the kobun, most of them are so stupid they wouldn't even know they had the wrong gaijin."

"But they had the right one."

"No, I told him it was you."

"Maybe they're getting at me through my best friend, is that it?"

"That's not impossible," she said.

"Hello," the businessman said, leaning across Ransom to address Marilyn. "My name is Yamaguchi Sato. Okay?" He reeked of sake.

The sushi master came around from behind the counter, pulled the businessman into an upright position and convinced him to move to a stool farther down the bar. "Goodbye," the man said, waving.

Ransom turned back to Marilyn. "You don't seem too terribly concerned about Miles. You haven't even asked how he is."

"I'm sorry," she said. "It's just—"

"Don't be sorry. I thought you liked him, that's all."

"You're impossible to please, aren't you? When I was going out with Miles, you didn't like it at all. Now that I've stopped seeing him, you don't like that either."

"He's my friend."

"You blame me, don't you?" There were tears in her eyes. She took a cigarette and a Kleenex from her purse. "I didn't ask for any of this."

"Has your oyabun said anything recently?"

"That he'd kill you if I saw you again."

"That's ridiculous."

"He's a jealous man."

"He'd have to be more than jealous. Can you imagine all the shit a murdered gaijin would bring down? He still wants to marry you?"

"June tenth."

Ransom looked at the scenic Kyoto calendar behind the counter: May 29.

"What are you going to do?"

"I hoped you'd have an idea." She lit the cigarette. "I'm sorry I got you involved."

"Don't be," Ransom said. "You do want to leave, don't you?"

"Of course I do."

He leaned close and lowered his voice. "Listen, I have a passport, a woman's passport. And I have a friend who can probably doctor it for you. Which leaves money. Do you have enough for plane fare to the States?"

She looked bewildered. "A passport?"

"It's French, but at least you can get in as a tourist. Now is there some money you can get at?"

"Are you coming with me?"

"No."

"I'm not going alone."

"I'll put you in touch with my dad. He'd help if I asked him. He could get you a job, singing or something."

"Come with me, it's too dangerous to stay. You don't know my fiancé."

"He's not going to do anything."

She held her face in her hands, and Ransom couldn't tell if she was crying or thinking. Then she began to sob, her shoulders heaving more and more violently until she was gasping for breath. Ransom laid his hand on her shoulder. She drew away.

The businessman looked deeply troubled, as if he were about to start crying himself. Tentatively, he said, "Let's all be funky babes, okay?"

Finally, Marilyn looked up, wiping her cheeks with the Kleenex; all at once she was composed. "Where did you get a passport?"

"What difference does it make?"

"I'm just curious."

"I don't think we should be hanging around in public in your boyfriend's neighborhood," Ransom said. "Call me tomorrow at the coffee shop. Get a passport photo and I'll see if I can get the thing fixed."

23

Ransom went daily to the Pathan, buying Annette's fix and checking for news from the border. Afternoons, while she slept, he returned to the bazaar and lingered over tea in one of the shops. Evenings, he read to her from a coverless paperback copy of *One Hundred Years of Solitude* that he had bought from a broke Canadian in Delhi for a few rupees. Annette didn't like to read but she liked to be read to. Ransom wasn't sure how much she was following; it was a strange book even if you weren't wrecked on smack.

On the thirteenth day, he saw the Australian's pendant for sale in the bazaar. It seemed like an omen. He went immediately back to the fort, and waited until Annette was on the declining slope of her afternoon fix to tell her that he wanted her to leave. If there was going to be trouble, he wanted Annette to be free and clear. Worrying about her was sapping him. He felt that he would have to do something soon, and her presence limited his options.

"Listen," he said. "This is important. Do you still have friends in Katmandu?"

She shrugged and smiled. "I have friends in Katmandu, I have friends in Goa, I have friends in Paris, friends *partout. Trop d'amis.*" Annette laughed. *"Amis de trop."*

He took her by the shoulders. "Annette, listen to me."

"You know where I have no friends? *Le Japon.* No friends in Japan. It is why I want to go there. Because I know no one and no one knows me. When I was a little girl my mother said, *They live in paper houses in Japan.* And I wanted to go see. Paper houses. I tried to imagine it. Can we go there?"

He gripped her shoulders tightly. "Annette, this is serious. Things could get bad here. We have enough for a plane ticket. You go to Katmandu and stay with your friends. I'll meet you there as soon as I can."

She frowned. "Not alone."

"I have to wait for Ian."

"You want to give me the dump again."

Ransom shook his head. "I just don't want anything to happen to you. I'll come get you as soon as Ian shows up."

"I rest here with you."

Ransom knew she wasn't going to change her mind. He also knew that his idea wasn't practical. She was in no shape to travel alone. Yet it seemed more dangerous for her to stay. He'd been having nightmares about the incident in the bazaar.

That evening he brought the subject up again, but Annette put her hands over her ears and began to sing whenever he tried to speak.

The Pathan was more discursive than usual on the morning of the seventeenth day. He inquired after Annette and took note of the weather, getting hotter.

"Doesn't it ever rain around here," Ransom asked.

"Not often."

"I wish it would, just for a change."

The Pathan wanted to discuss the business climate. The government was stepping up border patrols. Rival tribes were fighting over the smuggling routes. Ransom guessed he was being softened up for a price hike.

"It is especially dangerous for amateurs," the Pathan said. He shook his head slowly and frowned.

Ransom registered a new note in the conversation. He felt his heart in his chest, as if it had just started pumping a moment before.

"You've got news for me?"

The Pathan raised his eyebrows in a way that indicated amazement, either at Ransom's acuity or at his lack of tact in coming so abruptly to the point. He scrupulously smoothed the baggy folds of his sleeves.

"There is a rumor."

Ransom waited.

"The men your friend contacted across the border are not honest men. They require a payment for his safe return."

"Why haven't I been approached," Ransom demanded.

The answer came to him without any hint from the Pathan, who looked out impassively over the bazaar, as if he had lost interest in the conversation.

"How much?" Ransom said. He guessed that whoever had Ian would know exactly how much he was planning to pay on delivery and would ask for a little more. For a moment Ransom was almost relieved, knowing finally what the situation was, and what was required, but at the same time he didn't feel that he knew anything for certain.

"If you wish, I can look into the matter," the Pathan said.

Ransom doubted that an inquiry was necessary, but he had to observe the Pathan's ritual. That he appear to trust the Pathan was crucial, now that he didn't know if he could.

He went back to the fort, finding Annette awake.

"Une maison de papier," she said. "We will have to be so careful not to smoke in bed."

Ransom didn't know what she was talking about.

"I will write on the walls, I think. *L'histoire de ma vie.* At night our home will be like a lantern—we will be shadow people moving across the light." He had always loved her imagination, the way she had of investing the hard edges of the world with an aura of fantasy, but at the moment she just seemed like a junkie. He didn't tell her about his conversation with the Pathan.

That afternoon Ransom was told that the kidnappers would settle for nothing less than two thousand dollars. Ransom had a little more than eighteen hundred in his money belt, and wondered if the Pathan had any way of knowing this.

"I don't have that much."

"Then your friend is dead."

"Tell them I have fifteen hundred." This was the amount Ian would have promised on delivery of the hash.

"I do not believe they will change their minds."

"What if I wired for money?"

The Pathan said, "Where do you think you are?" He was looking at Ransom intently now, having shed the bored manner of a man performing an unwanted and unprofitable office.

"I need proof." He could think of no way to get the two hundred, but felt he had to keep the process moving forward.

"I was asked to show you this," the Pathan said. He reached into a leather pouch on his holster belt and removed a gold signet ring.

"That doesn't prove anything. Why didn't he send a note?"

The Pathan shrugged. "These are not literary men."

"But how do I know he's alive?" Until that moment it hadn't really occurred to him that Ian might be dead. Even if he came up with the money he had no guarantee except the Pathan's word.

"I believe he is alive," the Pathan said.

"I have to think this through."

"Do you have the money?"

Ransom shook his head. "Not all of it."

"Perhaps," the Pathan said, "I could assist you with the balance."

And then Ransom realized that he had been waiting to say this.

"In exchange for what?" Ransom said.

Annette was sleeping on the pallet with her mouth open.
Ransom knelt down beside her and pushed her hair away
from her eyes. He timed her breathing: twelve a minute,
low even for an addict. He watched an insect work its way
up the earthen wall beside the pallet, its shadow large and
oblong in the lamplight, and wondered if there was a right
thing to do.

"Ransom?"

"I'm here."

"*Quelle heure est-il?*"

"Afternoon."

"I think it is time."

"There's something I have to talk to you about."

"Not now."

"Yes. Now."

She turned to look at him. Her face was slack. He tried
to remember her as she had been in Katmandu. The out-
lines of beauty were still there. But in Katmandu her eyes
had a fire that seemed to illuminate whatever they touched.
When she pointed to her favorite of eight identical arms
on a temple statue, it became obviously the one that might
begin to move at any minute. She herself was always moving, and would explain what she was doing even as she was
doing it, as if she wanted to ensure the reality of her actions.
She hardly seemed to sleep, and when she woke she immediately shook Ransom awake to relate her dreams in
astounding detail. She wanted to do and see everything,
but now she looked like she'd seen enough.

"You're killing yourself," he said.

"So American for you to say it," she said. "Christopher

Ransom, yankee cowboy, *non?* You think we choose to do
things. You think you control your fate."

"You don't have to be a junkie."

"It makes me happy. I *choose* to be happy, you say. I
say, it chooses me. The only thing is I accept the conse-
quences."

"Even if it means dying?"

She shrugged.

"Do you really think we're not responsible for our actions? You wouldn't blame me if I began to beat you? If
I killed you?"

Annette shook her head. She seemed to have lost interest in the conversation.

"You are crying," she said, when she looked up. She
reached up and wiped his cheek.

Ransom said, "Annette."

"Don't be sad," she said. "Maybe you take a little fix
with me."

Ransom shook his head.

"Give me one. I want you to do it."

"Ian's in trouble," he said.

She sighed dreamily. "Don't worry. You will think of
something, *non?*"

"I need your help"

"You do what's best."

"Listen to me."

"Please. Not now. Give me a fix." She reached down
and stroked his knee. "Then we make love, maybe." They
hadn't since she started shooting up again. The drug had
swallowed all of her desire, and he found he didn't want
her as she was now.

She walked her fingers up toward his crotch. He pushed her hand away. "I'm trying to talk to you."

"Please."

Ransom had no illusions about his complicity in Annette's habit, but he felt that some last shred of principle was upheld by his refusal to stick the needle into her arm. Now it seemed a cheap distinction. Annette was beyond thinking. He had allowed her to do this to herself. For this he had to accept responsibility, and for the rest of it.

"All right," he said.

Annette sat up on the pallet. She had rolled up the sleeve of her shirt. The arm was thin and pale, speckled near the joint with needle marks. Ransom took the bandana from around his neck and tied her off. He swabbed her arm with alcohol, then wiped the needle.

"A little more," she said, when Ransom started to heat the spoon over the flame of the oil lamp. "Okay?"

A little more, then. Ransom wanted her to be out of it for the next few hours, didn't want her to know what he had to do. He wished her a long, cool rush that would lift her beyond the clammy mud walls, beyond the gray hills outside to a white, featureless place. He wished he could join her there. He shook more powder from the packet into the spoon. When the powder had melted, he put the spoon down on the pallet. He drew the liquid into the syringe, then held it up to look for bubbles.

He missed the vein on the first try. His hands were shaking. When he tried to pull it out a peak of white flesh rose around the needle. He clutched her elbow tighter. The second time the needle slipped easily into the vein. He raised his thumb and depressed the plunger.

Where he drew the needle out, a tiny red bubble blossomed and burst. Annette's face unclenched and she sank down onto the pallet with a sigh.

Ransom staggered down the stairs. Outside, he got down on his hands and knees and vomited.

He found the Pathan in the bazaar.

"You have decided," the Pathan asked.

Ransom nodded. There was nothing he could say.

"You have somewhere . . . to go?"

"I won't bother you," Ransom said.

The Pathan nodded solemnly. He reached under his shirt and held out a dirty white envelope.

"Two hundred dollars," the Pathan said, "as a token of good faith. When I return you will have the rest of the money for me, as agreed."

Ransom let him stand there, holding the envelope. The Pathan waited; he would not insist. Finally Ransom took the envelope and shoved it into his pocket.

"Two hours," the Pathan said. He turned and walked off through the bazaar. Ransom imagined rifle sights on the receding blue turban.

24

Sweat stinging his eyes, Ransom ran along the river, sunlight glancing from the ripples where a tree stump broke the surface. Everything shimmered, the sandy expanse of the flood plain blanching out like a snowfield and losing all features and solidity even as he felt the hard dirt under his feet; the trees along the levee receding, the Imadegawa Bridge appearing too frail and insubstantial to bear traffic. The white noise of his brain merged with the high whine of cicadas.

Halfway between the two bridges he dropped and did fifty push-ups on his fists. In the middle of the sit-ups he began to lose his bearings. Eyes closed, he had the sensation that he was suspended upside down and then began to feel that he was sideways. Seventy. The ground was coming up from all directions to slap at his back. Eighty-five. He was spinning, not unpleasantly. He thought he could probably make it to a hundred, but at ninety-eight he could not possibly do one more. He dropped flat on his back and lay there, catching his breath, feeling the sunlight on his face. Pulled at the back of his head with his linked hands, raised himself, touched. Ninety-nine. At one hundred he opened his eyes, then closed them again, stunned by the light. What if he were to stay there, never get up? Lie there and wait for the night, and then for the winter to come and cover him with snow. Layers and layers of cool snow.

Slowly, he got to his feet and started running. After a few hundred yards he resigned himself, catching a rhythm; the tiredness receded, and with it the sense of the unreality of the landscape. Mt. Hiei showed a rectangular bald spot, newly logged, in its lower flank. As far as you could see all of the trees had been planted and marked, every branch accounted for, all of the land parceled and dedicated to some kind of production, no space except that of the temples and shrines wasted or fallow. Gaijin could not fail to understand that everything and everyone Japanese had its correct place, because the gaijin's was outside the concentric rings of race, country, family. Just as the houses had walls around them, so was everything enclosed. When Ransom arrived he had wanted to penetrate the walls, to become intimate with whatever it was he imagined was within, behind the walls and the polite faces, something outside the conceptual frames he had inherited; he wanted to breach the appearances of the world and look into the heart of things. A discipline rigorous enough would purge and change him, he was certain.

But Ransom was no longer sure he believed in satori,

the final lightning stroke in which all is revealed. The monks stayed in the mountains, cross-legged, unmoving; and the samurai who studied Zen and landscape painting had also chopped heads at the whims of their overlords. Ransom was no samurai; at best he was a ronin, a masterless samurai, and this was a contradiction in terms. A ronin, a "man on the wave," unmoored and tossed on the waters, was an instrument without a purpose.

His legs were moving automatically, controlling their own pace and direction. As he came up on the Kitaoji Bridge he let his momentum carry him over the side of the levee, dodged a tree and came out on the edge of the river road. On Kitaoji Street a billboard showed a can of tomato juice, Japanese characters which he couldn't read and a slogan in English running horizontally across the top: RED MIX FOR CITY ACTIVES.

Otani refilled Ransom's water glass and told him that only a fool would run around in this weather. As hot as he was, the steaming towel on his face was refreshing. *Any messages,* Ransom asked.

Yesterday, Otani said, a man, gaijin, had called three times to ask for Ransom, but wouldn't leave his name.

You're sure it was a gaijin, Ransom asked.

It's not hard to tell, Otani said. *Ice coffee today?*

The phone range as Ransom was finishing his coffee.

It's him. Otani put down the receiver.

Ransom picked it up and said, "Moshi moshi."

"Hello, chickenshit."

"Who is this," Ransom asked, unnecessarily.

"You know who it is."

"DeVito."

"Are you going to give me satisfaction?"

"I don't recall ever giving offense."

"Your face is an offense."

"Complain to the authorities."

"I like to take care of these things personally."

Ransom didn't say anything.

"You can run and you can swim, but you can't hide," DeVito said. "I guess you heard about your pal Ryder."

"What about him?"

"So you didn't hear." He paused. "He came after me yesterday, got his tit caught in the wringer. He's not very smart but he's got balls, which is more than I'd say for you. Well, what do you say?"

"Not a thing," Ransom said, and hung up. He stood beside the phone, fingering the dial. For Marilyn's sake, he was glad her boyfriend hadn't done it. And if he had hoped Miles wasn't foolish enough to fight DeVito, he wasn't surprised that he had.

He picked up the phone and called A-OK to say he was sick and wouldn't be in.

"Are you out of your head?" Ransom said. Miles was sitting upright on the edge of the hospital bed, scrutinizing a go-maku board on the night table between him and the old man.

"Well, look who's here," Miles said. "The egg-sucking samurai. The strong right arm of the fucking Pope."

"Her-ro," the old man said. "How are you?"

Ransom lowered himself onto the back of a chair beside the bed and looked quizzically at Miles.

"The mule who's been kicking in my stall."

"Miles, what the hell are you talking about?"

"DeVito told me."

"Told you what? Last I heard, he beat you senseless."

"You and Marilyn."

"He told you this while he was beating you up?"

"At least you know what I'm talking about. I don't hear you denying it."

"Denying *what?* I deny sleeping with her. Who do you want to believe, me or DeVito?"

"I take my information where I can get it."

"Come on, Ryder. You're not this stupid. Why do you suppose DeVito would tell you something like that? Think he might have some motives?"

"You deny you're seeing Marilyn?"

"No."

"You deny fucking her?"

"Yes."

"I know you're pretty much of a capon, but forgive me if I don't buy it."

"You have a wife, for Christsake. Who are you to be acting injured? You've had about sixty flings since I've known you, and Marilyn was just one more."

"That doesn't mean I want my best friend screwing her."

"Marilyn came to me for advice. And for some help."

Miles rolled his eyes, one of which was blackened.

"She's under the thumb of a yakuza oyabun who wants to marry her and rent her out. She came to me because she knew you'd do something crazy. Like this DeVito thing."

"That's good, Ransom. Princeton guys like you ought to be able to come up with something a little less like a shitty movie." He turned back to the go-maku board and moved a piece. The old man nodded seriously.

Miles was right—it sounded like a shopworn melodrama. Ransom wouldn't believe the story either, but somehow he was in it.

"DeVito said I was sleeping with her? How would he know?"

"I don't know."

Suddenly Ransom thought of DeVito's call and wondered if Marilyn might be next on his list. "I think I better find her."

"She could use a little advice, is that it?"

"Miles, where does she live?"

"I thought you'd know that yourself by now. I never got that information, my own self."

Ransom was halfway down the dingy hall when Ryder shouted, "Just a few inches of advice, now, you hear?"

No one responded to his pounding on the door. The nightclub generally didn't open until seven, and it was barely past noon. He had passed a public bath down the street; he left the borrowed Scrambler at the club, and walked back. The heat and humidity were tropical. He spent an hour in the baths, finishing with a long soak in the coldest, but within a block of leaving he could feel the tingle of sweat forming under his arms and along his spine.

This time the door was opened by a heavy-set thug in a zoot suit; his expression made clear that the last thing he had expected to see was a gaijin. He waved Ransom away with his hands, pointing to his watch. "No, no," he said. He was surprised all over again when Ransom began to speak, using a much politer level of address than was required or merited.

Excuse me, but I'm looking for a friend of mine. She works here.

The man assumed a knowing frown.

A singer. It's very important that I see her. Her name is Marilyn. He couldn't imagine what the Japanese word for Vietnamese would be. *Marilyn.*

The man started to close the wide, heavy door but Ransom blocked it with a forearm. *She's not here. You can see her tonight with the other customers.*

I'm not a customer. I'm a friend.

The man pushed the door wide open and stepped out menacingly, flexing beneath his suit.

It's important.

Implacable, the man stared back at him with dark, narrowing eyes until Ransom turned away and mounted his bike.

25

When Ransom arrived for practice that night, the sensei was pacing the lot in his gi. Suzuki was sweeping. A blue Toyota sat in the center of the south edge of the lot, the area reserved for practice. The sensei sent Udo into the gym to find its owner, but no one claimed it. Ransom changed, folding his clothes and piling them on the steps beside the shower. The Monk had appeared, as he often did, already dressed in his gi. Yamada drove in and parked his car on the far side of the lot. The sensei walked over and tried the doors of the Toyota, which were locked. He called for the group to follow.

Let's move this thing, he said, directing them to the back bumper. Ransom huddled with the crew, next to Udo. Six of them on the bumper raised the car and walked it around a quarter turn. They moved around to the front and brought the wheels over into the sand. Once more from the back and the car was flush against the wall. Suzuki let out a whoop and said they could easily flip the car over on its side.

Good enough, the sensei said, seeming more than usually preoccupied and distant. Maybe it's the weather, Ransom thought. Although cooler, the air was still heavy and damp. The sensei knelt on the asphalt, the Monk knelt beside him and the rest took their places. The sensei's participation during the practice was desultory, the occasional reprimand and demonstration of a move. After an hour, he called them in to begin the sparring. Ransom sensed an edge in his manner, a sudden air of purpose, as if practice had been merely a prelude. A small void opened within his belly: fear. He was certain, somehow, that his streak of good bouts had run out, and that he was due to get hurt. As if to confirm his anxieties the sensei called his name.

The sensei examined the scar on the back of his hand. When Ransom stepped forward, the sensei looked up at Ransom as if surprised and shook his head. He called for Yamada instead.

Wa-chan, the newest and youngest member of the dojo, well under five feet tall, bowed gravely to the massive Yamada, then assumed an elegant cat-leg stance. Yamada's bearing was benign and serious. This seemed to Ransom a moment of beauty and dignity. The boy attacked with two front kicks, and Yamada scored with a front punch which he pulled just short of Wa-chan's nose. Wa-chan remained determined as they faced off again, and was clearly disappointed when he lost the match.

Yamada worked up through the ranks. After the fifth

bout, Ransom expected the sensei to call in the Monk. But the sensei called Udo, the next in the lineup, and Yamada continued.

Suzuki, his ninth opponent, gave him a very hard time, dancing nimbly in and out of range. Yamada's stance was getting sloppy; his arms were low and his crouch was high. The sensei yelled instructions and, in a lower voice, speculated that Yamada would get his balls kicked up to his chin. Yamada hit Suzuki once, then Suzuki slipped a gut-kick through his arms; although Yamada stepped out of it, the sensei called a point for Suzuki.

Yamada, frustrated, drew a series of deep breaths before facing off again. Ransom felt a trickle of sweat down the side of his own face, and he hadn't moved in ten minutes. Yamada was red-faced, the upper half of his gi splotched with sweat.

He launched himself at Suzuki, knocking him over with a wide roundhouse kick. Ransom thought Suzuki had hit his head on the asphalt, but he leaped up and bounced on his toes to show he was fine.

Three points, the sensei said, when it was Ransom's turn. Yamada had hurt him before, but now Ransom wondered how much more Yamada could take. He had not doubted that the sensei's punishment of Yamada was not over at the end of the last practice; but he didn't relish taking part in it, and he was also suspicious of the sensei's plans for himself.

They bowed. Yamada's exhaustion showed in his eyes, in the tight set of his mouth. Ransom crouched low, shifting his weight to the back foot and cocking the left leg in front of him, knee directly in front of the crotch, toes aimed at

Yamada, his forearms shaping an L across the upper body. He knew he should attack; it was the only strategy. Because it seemed too easy, not fair, he hesitated as they stood motionless, staring into each other's eyes. Then he went in, breaking Yamada's defense on the third kick, hitting the sternum solidly. *Point.*

They faced off. Ransom knew he could hit Yamada low; his knees were wide, crotch open.

Yamada attacked with his hands and slipped a kick into Ransom's gut. Facing off again, Ransom glanced over at the expressionless sensei. Standing apart from the group, the Monk held his head tipped to one side, as if he were listening to something far in the distance and hearing none of the sounds of the match.

Within minutes, both had two points and Ransom had a split lip. He could taste the blood, and his ears were still ringing from the punch. He tried not to think about how tired Yamada was; he had to fight as if Yamada were fresh, and better than the Monk. He went for the upper body, but Yamada was closing in around his chest and gut, focusing all of his energy on the area Ransom kept attacking, leaving himself vulnerable below. The sensei shouted something, uncharacteristically shrill, and Ransom knew that it was about the opening. All of Ransom's instincts rebelled against this code of the discipline, which required that he attack his opponent any way he was able.

Yamada pulled a roundhouse kick out of some astonishing reserve of energy, and Ransom ducked as the foot grazed his temple. He kicked Yamada dead center, between the legs, and he went down, gasping.

Ransom walked out of the circle to a corner of the lot.

He closed his eyes and saw the flash of agony on Yamada's face. As he stood facing the blank wall of the gym, his breath became so rapid that he felt he would faint. When he returned to the group Yamada was on his feet, hunched and pale, walking gingerly in tight circles.

The sensei clapped his hands sharply. *Ito*—he paused—*and Yamada. Four points. No restrictions.*

Ransom couldn't believe it. A dreadful silence prevailed as they bowed and faced off. Ransom glanced over at the sensei, hoping to register his indignation, but he was looking at the two fighters. It seemed to Ransom that the rest of them drew closer, implicated together in this uneven match, each sympathetic and yet profoundly glad that it was Yamada, not himself; and at the same time embarrassed by what they were about to witness.

The only sound was Yamada's labored breathing. He kicked once, but weakly; Ransom had hurt him. When he kicked again, the Monk grabbed the foot in both hands, twisted it and threw him on his back. Yamada jumped to his feet and got kicked in the gut. Ransom looked down at the ground.

Yamada lasted out the match. With the final point scored, he lay gasping on his back. All that remained was for him to bow to his opponent. The Monk waited. No one said anything. The back door of the gym opened. One of the weightlifters stuck his head out and called *Finished?,* then he saw Yamada. His smile faded and he closed the door.

Yamada raised himself to a sitting position, to his knees, and finally he was on his feet, blood dripping from his nose. He pulled himself erect and bowed, then staggered over to the group.

The Monk stood where he was, awaiting instructions. *Ransom,* the sensei said. Ransom didn't move. The sensei turned and looked at him. Ransom stared back. Even greater than his fear of the Monk was his revulsion of condoning the beating that Yamada had sustained.

Ransom walked out and stood across from the Monk; habit and training carrying him through the bow, shaping his limbs, responding to the first attack, his forearms blocking the kicks as his legs carried him backward away from the impact, detecting the rhythm of the attack and locating the point at which it ebbed, reversing the direction of the fight, Ransom himself on the attack, four kicks, four punches; then a fist coming in low, and blackness.

He wanted to stay where he was, floating in restful waters, but they were pulling him back to the place where he had been, shaking him. Even before he opened his eyes he knew he would see the sensei's face.

Get it over with.

He got to his feet by himself and walked it off. The air was almost too thick to swallow. "Okay," he said. "Okay."

Then he was facing the Monk again. He tried to buy time. When he got hit in the chest he thought, This isn't so bad.

In the center of the Monk's eyes were pinpoints of light like distant stars. You couldn't get to them, Ransom told himself, but you had to try.

He was in the air, one kick, mid-level, blocked; but he still had momentum, his body carrying high, and as he peaked he kicked again, the ball of his foot rebounding from the Monk's forehead. The Monk fell back and wobbled on his feet as Ransom touched down. He didn't fall, but the sensei called the point and allowed him time to regain his bearings.

When they faced off again, his first kick knocked Ransom flat. Being down for good was restful, and he would have stayed longer, but it remained for him to bow.

A long time passed, Ransom thought, before the sensei knelt. He looked at Yamada, who had difficulty walking the short distance to take his place beside the Monk, grimacing as he lowered himself down to his knees, as if entering a scalding bath. Ransom walked over to the steps to gather his clothes. The sensei was watching him, and the others were waiting. He wanted to say something but he did not think he could possibly express his feelings in any language. He was no longer angry. He was glad of that, because he did not want to leave on an impulse. The sensei's gaze was fierce and corrosive; Ransom tried to meet it with composure and sincerity. The sensei had always said that you could see a man's heart through his eyes.

Clothes under his arms, Ransom turned and walked away.

26

Ransom was awakened from a sleep in which he was sparring endlessly with the Monk, one hundred and eleven points, no restrictions. The clock read three-thirty. He heard the rasp of the door buzzer, a sound to which he was not accustomed. Putting on a robe as the buzzer sounded again, he descended the dark stairs, unlatched the door and slid it back.

"Marilyn?"

She was wrapped in a man's raincoat; he let her in and closed the door behind her.

"Are you all right?" he said, taking her coat at the top of the stairs.

She nodded. He could smell booze on her breath. He pulled the cord on the kitchen light and led her into the main room.

"So this is the samurai's home," she said. "It doesn't look like anyone lives here."

Ransom shrugged. "Have a seat."

"Where?"

"Anywhere, I guess. You can sit on the futon."

She stretched out on the futon, took off her scarf and shook her hair. She lay back and assumed a vampish pose. "Some men would be very excited to find me in their beds."

"I'm sure they would."

She sat up again. "I don't understand you at all, Ransom. You made it very difficult for me."

"Made what very difficult?"

"Do you mind if I smoke?"

"Actually, I do."

"But out of politeness you'll let me."

He went into the kitchen and found a saucer, which he placed in front of her. "Don't you think it's dangerous to come here?" he said. "Not to mention that it's late."

"I'm sorry," she said. "I had to tell you tonight. I had a few drinks and I had to tell you before I changed my mind."

"Tell me what?"

"You've never suspected?"

"Suspected what?"

She smiled ruefully. "If you talk to your father, tell him you never suspected. Tell him I did a good job."

"What are you talking about?"

She took a deep breath, looked him in the eye, then looked away. "Ransom, this whole thing was . . . a setup. Your father hired me."

"What whole thing? My father hired you for what?"

"He hired me to get to you. I'm an actress."

"What are you talking about?" he said, his voice sounding strange, as if he were hearing it played back on tape.

"You believed me, didn't you?" she said. It seemed like a plea. She reached over and took his hand. "I'm sorry. I'm sorry it was you, but I need to know you believed me."

"I don't understand. My father sent you here?"

"I'm an actress."

"You're American?"

She nodded.

"You're not Vietnamese?"

"My mother was Korean. She met my father during the war. I was born and raised in Oregon."

"What about the oyabun?"

"There is no oyabun."

"You made it up?"

"Your father made it up. He got the idea from a movie."

Ransom felt like he'd been gut-punched.

She reached for him again and he nearly slapped her. Seeing the look on his face she withdrew her hand.

"I'm not proud of myself. That's why I'm telling you this. I couldn't go on with it. I just felt so guilty after a while, after I got to know you. It didn't seem like such a bad thing to do at first. I met your father doing a pilot, and it just happened."

"This is fucking rich. The actress and the producer." Ransom stood up and looked around the small room for some place to go, or for something to break. He paced the perimeter of the room, clenching and unclenching his fists. "I don't believe this shit."

Marilyn sat upright, nervously observing Ransom's orbit.

When he came to a halt she said, "He sounded so sad when he talked about you. He said he had begged you to come home, but you were obsessed by this samurai trip. He was afraid you'd got involved with drugs or something in India and since you wouldn't even visit he thought you were in trouble. He wanted to get you home for treatment."

"Treatment? I love that." Ransom stalked over to the window and stared at the dark panes. A rooster called out close by. "I suppose he promised you a role in a series."

"You'd be surprised what people will do for work."

"I don't doubt it a bit."

"Listen, I don't expect you to be grateful but don't insult me. What do you know about work, anyway? I didn't have to tell you this and you might consider what I stand to lose."

Ransom glanced back at her and then he looked down into the dark garden below the terrace. "He's really lost his fucking mind over there."

"That's almost exactly what he said about you."

Feeling woozy and still enraged, he told himself to get the details straight, to learn the sequence of events. He wasn't ready to accept this version without a struggle. He turned and walked over to the futon. "Why did you come on to Miles?"

"You have a bad memory. I came on to you first but you wouldn't have me. I was quite offended, but I improvised around it. Your father told me a lot about you— your sense of duty and honor."

"I didn't know my father knew a lot about me."

"He's not so bad."

"What about the singing job?"

"That was legitimate. He arranged it through his agency. It was kind of a bonus—the pay was good and he thought it would be a good cover in case you checked up on me."

"How nice for you."

"Please, Ransom."

"Did he think I'd marry you? That's crazy."

"I'm not sure. I think that was going to be a last resort. He said if you were convinced I was in danger, you'd go back with me to the States. I was going to throw a nervous breakdown."

Ransom stood with his shoulder against the closet. He stepped back and punched the sliding paper door. The laminated layers of paper almost yielded to the impact and the wooden frame bowed and popped out of the tracks; instead of a nice clean hole he produced a crumpled mess.

"Why are you telling me now?"

"Because I like you."

"This part is real?"

"I don't blame you for being suspicious."

"What about the black eye," he demanded.

"Makeup."

He nodded.

"This may sound awful, but it's important to me that you trusted me. Maybe that's what made it so difficult to keep it up."

"Marilyn? Is that your real name?"

"Yeah. I was born in fifty-six. During the reign of Monroe." She fished another cigarette from her purse. "Christopher is a good name," she said. "You should use it."

"I don't like it," he said.

"How sad—not to like your own name."

Ransom said, "What are you going to do now?"

She shrugged and looked at the window, which was just beginning to turn gray. Birds were singing in the garden.

Ransom laughed. "You feel like the whole world is turned upside down and then the birds start talking to each other as if nothing had happened."

"There's something else," Marilyn said, "the reason I told you now instead of waiting. Your father's flying into Tokyo this morning."

"What? You're kidding."

"He had some business anyway, and he wanted to be on hand to work out our next move."

"It's not every producer," Ransom said, "who would take such a direct interest in a script. He's a hell of a guy." He tried to decide what he was going to do. "You know where he's staying?"

"You're not going to do anything violent, are you?"

"Don't worry. I'm not real to him, so I couldn't hurt him if I wanted to. Do you have a plane ticket home?"

She nodded. "I'm going to stay for another week or two. I want to finish out this singing job. Maybe you can tell me what happens."

Ransom made a pot of tea, watching his hands perform the necessary steps, wondering what was left to him beyond these basic motor skills and noticing, when he picked up the two cups, that even these were suspect: his hands were trembling. He carried the cups on a tray into the other room.

"Thanks for telling me," he said.

"I'm sorry, you know. I really am."

They sat across from each other, holding their tea cups, as the window began to glow with the first light.

"What was this stuff about a French passport," Marilyn said suddenly, as if she had just remembered something terribly important.

For a moment Ransom didn't know what she was talking about, and then he wished he didn't. "It's a long story," he said, and then to change the subject: "Who were you drinking with?"

"Just some people from work."

"Are you worried about what my father's going to do?" Ransom said.

"I don't think he's going to do much. But I doubt I'm going to get a bonus out of this. And I really don't want to see him, or even talk to him, not right now. I'm moving to a new hotel this morning, in case he tries to find me. I'm not ashamed, but I'm tired of the whole deal."

"Let me know where you're staying," Ransom said. He felt solicitous for Marilyn, almost as if he were the guilty party.

27

After Marilyn left, he shaved, changed into sweats and performed his regular workout. As he jogged he realized that for the past month his physical training had been informed by a sense of imminent crisis, that he had taken his rescue mission seriously, that it was something he had been waiting for, the chance for a partial redemption after what had happened to Ian and Annette; that he had been groping toward it even when leaving the States with a sense of purpose alloyed of escape and quest. He wondered if his father had deliberately tried to prove there is no escape, that there are no real quests.

The herons in the river were mottled red today, fishing in the crimson runoff of the silk-dyeing tanks upstream. A raptor of some kind, a hawk or falcon, cruised against the murky sky.

At the coffee shop, Otani brought him up to date on the baseball standings and complained about the heat. In the newspaper Ransom found a strange item: AMERICAN JOURNALIST PERISHES IN BOAT MISHAP. The article said that Carl Digger, special Asian correspondent for the *Berkeley Barb,* drowned off the coast of Shikoku after the boat he had hired collided with a Russian trawler during the night. For a moment Ransom couldn't recall why the name was familiar and then he remembered the conversation at Buffalo Rome.

Otani called Ransom to the phone and Miles greeted him. "Buy a cigar and charge it to me."

"You're a father?"

"Incredible, isn't it?"

"When did it happen?"

"Akiko broke water about two-thirty yesterday afternoon and the baby was delivered a couple hours later. A boy. It's amazing."

Ransom extended his congratulations and asked about the health of the mother.

"She's great. She's coming home tonight with the kid. Why don't you come over for supper tomorrow. I'm cooking steaks."

"Isn't it a little early for company?"

"She asked for you. Come on by."

The train passengers were mostly women with shopping bags and children. Overhead the ads carried strange fragments of undigested English: *"Your Beautiful Day; Let's Happy; Sexy Feeling."* The high-pitched, prerecorded android voice announced the stops: *Omiya, Takatsuki, Ibar-*

*aki-shi, Jusso, Umeda de gozaimasu. Domo arigato gozai-
masu.*

The heat of the day poured in when the doors opened
at Umeda Station; there was some relief descending to the
subways. At the office, the receptionist, Keiko, said she
was glad to see him recovered from his illness. Honda-san,
she said, was out.

"Got stuck with your Mitsubishi buggers," Desmond
Caldwell snarled, as Ransom sat down.

"Good for them to hear a new accent," Ransom said.

"Not such a bad lot, actually. They got me pissed after
class. Can't even remember 'ow I got 'ome. Went to one
of those bloody singing bars. 'Ad to get up and sing 'Yesterday.' I was so blind I dropped the bleedin' mike twice.
They're very offended, you know, that you won't go out
drinkin' with them."

Caldwell had given them a paragraph of dictation, the
results of which he dumped on Ransom's desk. *Putting
Your Best Foot Forward.*

At one o'clock and then again an hour later, Ransom
tried the Tokyo number—the Imperial Hotel, naturally—
that Marilyn had given him for his father, who by three
had checked in.

"Victor Ransom here."

When Ransom didn't say anything, his father said, "Hello,
Victor Ransom speaking."

"It's your son."

"Chris."

"Your one and only, you son of a bitch."

"Hey, what kind of talk is that?" His voice failed to
convey the accustomed confidence.

"If you want to see me, you can be in Kyoto tonight. I've booked you a suite at the Miyako Hotel."

"Why don't you come to Tokyo? My hosts here are really putting on the dog. We could—"

"—I don't know that I want to see you at all. I'll be at the Miyako tonight, or no sale." He hung up on his father, Victor Ransom, the man *Variety* called "one of the sharpest operators on the prime-time scene today."

That night he went out drinking with his class. They took him to three bars in South Osaka, each one smaller and more expensive than the last. They complimented him on his Japanese, which they had never heard him use before; he complimented them on their hospitality. He caught the eleven o'clock Limited Express, and reviewed the symptoms of intoxication. Coming up from the station at Kawaramachi Street, he surveyed the landscape of downtown Kyoto, the illuminated towers of the Hankyu and Takashimaya department stores, the tiled rooftops of Gion just across the river, the ideographic neon, and found it all strange and familiar, as if he could see it from both ends of his two-year sojourn.

He took a cab to the Miyako Hotel, arriving shortly after midnight. His father was in the bar, sitting alone at a table with his briefcase. He waved and stood up, not knowing what to do with his arms as his son approached. He settled on an outstretched hand. Ransom took the hand and shook it.

"Well," he said, indicating the chair for his son.

Ransom sat down. His father looked much as he had remembered, although smaller and a little desiccated. "When are you going to let your hair go gray," Ransom asked.

"That's a hell of a greeting."

The waiter asked Ransom what he would drink. He asked for scotch.

"You're looking skinny." Ransom's father scrutinized him with an air of professional appraisal. "I was expecting muscle-bound with all of this martial arts stuff." Ever since Ransom could remember, the old man had found something to complain about in his son's appearance. Ransom's adolescence had been especially trying. *Is that a pimple? Come over here in the light.* Now he said, "What do you eat over here?"

"Live frogs, mostly. Automobile byproducts, recycled fecal matter."

"Cute." His father was turned out in white ducks, tan raw-silk jacket, polo shirt; his style was considered Ivy League in Hollywood because he didn't wear jewelry. Sometimes he buttoned his shirt all the way to the top and knotted a piece of colorful silk, especially designed for this purpose, around his neck in such a way that it hung straight down the front of his shirt, like a trim, well-behaved scarf.

The waiter brought Ransom's drink. Ransom could see from his father's tentative manner that he was trying to decide how much his son knew about recent machinations, no doubt wondering if there was any way to cut his losses, write them off against profits, syndicate.

"I'm trying to decide," Ransom said, "if this is the worst stunt you've pulled."

"What exactly are we talking about here?"

"There was the time I brought my then-girlfriend Nancy Willard home for spring break and you offered her a part.

That was one of the sleazier moves, although in terms of sheer magnitude not quite as bad as buying my way into college."

Victor Ransom raised his hand and beckoned the waiter. "The same," he murmured.

"I'll tell you. The fact that you'd try to manipulate me this way—I wish I could say it wasn't in character. But what I can't figure out is what you hoped to accomplish. Did you really think you'd get me back to the States? Or did you just want to prove to me that I couldn't get away from you?"

"I take it you've talked to Marilyn?"

"Try not to be slick for once in your life. What exactly was in your mind when you dreamed this one up?"

"If we're talking about the same thing," he said, "I would say that from what I hear it was almost a successful venture."

"You thought I'd marry her?"

"It was an option I hoped we wouldn't have to exercise."

"Who was I going to marry her as? It wouldn't have been legal if she used phony identity and I'd find out she was American if she used her own passport."

"I had papers for her. It wouldn't have been legal, but as long as you and Immigration didn't know that, what difference? But as I say, I was hoping it wouldn't come to that."

"What the hell were you hoping for? To make me look like a fool? Prove that what I'm doing here is ridiculous since it's so easily parodied?"

"I wanted you home."

"How was that going to get me home?"

Ransom's father took a long sip of his drink and paused. He put the drink down. "I was counting on two things. First, that keen moral sense of yours, the one you like to exercise on your father. It seemed to me you saw this karate of yours as training for some grand confrontation of good and evil."

"So you thought you'd give me a fake version, show that everything's relative."

"No. I didn't intend for you to find out. But I was counting on your chivalry. I knew you wouldn't turn your back on a damsel in genuine distress."

"Genuine. That's a good one. Marilyn says you stole the plot from a movie." Ransom was trying to summon his anger, but mostly he felt numb.

"Some of it. But I had to tailor it to the situation at hand. The movie was about a naïve American girl who gets in the clutches of the yakuza. I made her Vietnamese. You can't help but stir passions with that war, and now these boat people in the news, refugees everywhere. The trick was to make it seem impossible for her to get out of the country without your help."

Ransom drained his glass. His father said, "I thought you were a teetotaler these days."

"I thought there was a limit to your deceit." Ransom shook the ice in his glass. "You're so used to manipulating people—"

"—I'm used to making things happen, not moping about how I'd like the world to be." His lips were drawn tight across his face. "You're so goddamn pure. You never had to support a family or keep twenty employees happy. What the hell was I supposed to do—watch my son piss his life away without doing anything about it? I wrote letters which you stopped answering; I begged, Chris."

He leaned back in his chair and was silent for a moment. "The second thing I counted on was that you'd turn to me. A situation like that, like the one Marilyn appeared to be in, I thought you'd finally discover that it doesn't matter how morally pure you are, how good you are with your fists. You need a certain kind of knowledge and power working for you. I thought you might get the point, trying to solve this dilemma, and I thought you might look to me as someone who had that kind of knowledge and power. I thought you might look to me for help. That's what I wanted, Chris. I didn't know if you would come home or not. But I wanted you to need my help." He was looking at the table as he said this.

"Do you think this was a good way to go about it?" Ransom said. "Forget it, don't answer that."

Ransom's father looked up, looked him in the eye. "I'm sorry."

"I'm trying to live my life here," Ransom said.

His father didn't say anything.

Ransom slammed his fist on the table. "Do you understand what I'm saying?"

"I'm sorry, Chris. I just wanted you back."

"You didn't seem to want me when I was around."

"That's not true, and you know it."

"You didn't want to be tied down. Mom died and saved you the trouble of a divorce."

"I've got a lot to answer for, a lot of regrets. I was a lousy husband, a lousy father. But I didn't kill your mother.

Maybe I lost her before she died, and that's my fault. I was trying not to lose you as well."

"You're a lunatic."

"What are you, normal?"

Ransom settled into his chair and closed his eyes. He found his thoughts slowly shifting, regrouping in apparently random configurations, then finally showing a pattern.

"I can forgive you, but who do you suppose will forgive me?"

"For what?" His father leaned forward.

"Have you ever been in a situation where you were totally helpless?"

"I'm glad you asked that question, Chris. Because you think I'm in the entertainment business, but what I'm really in—what we're all in—is the power business. Someone is going to have power and if it isn't you, then you're helpless, at the mercy of anybody who has it.

"When I was your age, a little younger, I thought being a playwright was like being God. I made the characters out of nothing. I made them do whatever I wanted them to. If I wanted to I could even kill them off. But when it came time to get it produced I found out that my power was nil. It was one thing to write the script, just the way I wanted it, but another thing altogether to get the damn thing on-stage. That's when I found out it's the director and the producers and the actors and the critics who have the real power. I screamed and shouted about artistic integrity; I threatened to withdraw the play. But I wanted it produced so I finally went along. And you know what they did to my play?"

"What?"

"Not much. The changes weren't earth-shattering. I see that now. In fact, they might've made it better. The point is, I realized my plays weren't going to change the world. As a playwright my power, my talent, was very limited. But that experience taught me about power, that I wanted to have it. I want you to understand this, Chris."

"What good is power if you use it just like everybody else does?"

His father looked frustrated. "The point is, *you* have it. Not someone else."

"It's good in itself, is that it?"

"What are you, Socrates?"

"What are you, Attila the Hun? You're a fucking TV producer. You don't even run that little corner of the world—it runs you. The shit you crank out has your name on it, but it's still shit."

"I ought to belt you."

"I wouldn't if I were you. That's my power sphere. Not that I'm particularly proud of it."

His father reached across the table and grabbed his hand. "Haven't you heard a word I've said? I run that game, too. Do you know what happens to freelance tough guys in this world? You don't think I can pick up a phone and hire as much muscle as I need?" He let go of his son's hand and slumped back in his chair. "I'm trying to teach you what I know. I might not know the big answers to the big questions, Chris, but you live in the same world I do, and I don't want to see you get hurt." He picked up his glass, swirled the ice in his drink. "Let's call a truce here, okay?"

Ransom ran his finger around the edge of his glass and

looked into the wood-grain pattern of the table. When he looked up he saw that his father, too, was running his finger around the edge of his glass.

After a minute or so Ransom's father asked if he wanted another drink.

"None for me. Are you tired?"

"I couldn't sleep right now."

"How's your suite?"

"Probably very expensive."

"I was hoping it would be ridiculously expensive." Ransom paused. "You want to go for a walk?"

They took a cab to Okazaki. The moon was nearly full. They walked up the hill and then north on the ancient cobbles of the Tetsugaku no Michi, the Philosopher's Path, which Buddhist sages had trodden hundreds of years ago, although father and son talked of things which had only parochial significance: friends, family and home.

28

When he arrived at the coffee shop, Otani said there had been a phone call for him—a very rude gaijin who refused to leave his name—quickly adding that most of Ransom's friends were very polite. Setting a coffee in front of Ransom, he predicted the rain would start any day, then the phone rang. Otani picked it up. *It's for you,* he said. *It's him.*

"Seen your girlfriend lately, samurai?"

"What are you talking about?"

"I'm talking about the chick you snaked from your cowboy friend—Marilyn."

"She's not my girlfriend," Ransom said.

"Right. That's what you tell the cowboy. But, hey, I've *seen* you two lovebirds."

"What do you want, asshole?"

"Whoa! The zombie awakes."

Ransom hung up the phone.

Shortly after he had resumed his seat it rang again. He asked Otani not to answer. Otani stared nervously at the red phone as it continued to ring, and finally Ransom picked it up.

"What do you want?" he said.

"Same thing I've always wanted," DeVito answered.

"You want to fight?"

"You're catching on."

"Give me a reason."

"I'll give you any number of reasons. First—your girlfriend. You don't want to see anything happen to her, do you?"

"You're sick, DeVito." Three uniformed schoolgirls entered the coffee shop, giggling, modestly covering their mouths.

"I'll write that remark down in my little black book. Meantime, I know where your girlfriend is. She suddenly picked up and moved yesterday, am I right?"

Ransom didn't say anything.

"I keep tabs on these things. I can find her if she moves again, too. You know I can. Now, what I figure is that you guys had a little lovers' quarrel and that's why she decided on a change of address. You probably don't even know where she is."

"What if I don't care?"

"So, I was right, was I? I bet you'd start to care all over again if you thought she might come to harm. You wouldn't like that a bit, would you? Shit, you should be grateful to old Frank. I'm kind of a matchmaker here, reviving tender

feelings for your old squeeze. Anyway, there's one reason—the health and well-being of a loved one."

"What if I still don't care?" Ransom said, uncertain if he
was bluffing DeVito or himself.

"We'll find out, won't we. If Marilyn doesn't get you
going, there's always Ryder and his little family. They're
next. Maybe I had you wrong. I thought you were the
sensitive type who cared about his friends."

"You're not this fucking crazy, are you?"

"The problem from the very start is that you haven't
taken me seriously. I'm a serious person, very serious."

Ransom felt a sickening dread, a feeling of having already lived this dream. He suddenly knew DeVito was
serious, that he would keep coming after him through his
friends, that he wasn't going to go away. No reasonable
strategy could answer this kind of fanaticism. Ransom wanted
to bust the phone against the wall. He wanted to pound
this bastard into oblivion, and for reasons that DeVito
could never imagine.

"You're a disease, DeVito."

"Sticks and stones, Ransom. Are you going to fight me,
or do we try plan B?"

"I'll fight you, you sick fuck." The schoolgirls, who had
taken a table, broke into fresh rounds of stifled laughter
every time Ransom spoke.

"Now you're talking. You could've got this thing over
a long time ago, but no. You thought you could ignore
me. You thought I wasn't a serious person. You tried to
pretend that I didn't exist. That's what we're talking about
here—existence."

"You're a real philosopher, DeVito, a fucking idiot savant."

"Let's not get snotty. This isn't the Harvard Club or whatever."

"When do we do this?" Ransom said.

"When I say so. You made me wait, now you can wait. Be at Buffalo Rome tonight at midnight and I'll give you your instructions."

He hung up. The dial tone was absorbed into the buzz of traffic from Kitaoji Street as Ransom laid the receiver back in its cradle. The bells on the door sounded as a young man entered, stopped and stared. Ransom instinctively wondered if he looked peculiar, but the man recovered his composure and took a seat, having seen nothing more than a gaijin, the everyday strange. Ransom saw that he was wearing cowboy boots. *Are You Ready for Boots?*

Okay? Otani asked him.

Ransom nodded, trying to remember if Marilyn had mentioned the name of her old hotel. But even if he could come up with it, she probably hadn't left a forwarding number. For more than an hour he waited for her to call, time enough to realize that he didn't even know how to use the phone book. He wanted to get her out of DeVito's way, although he wasn't convinced that this would solve the problem. Some things wouldn't go away unless you faced them head-on.

29

Ransom met his father for lunch at the hotel. The senior Ransom, sitting at the bar with a Bloody Mary, appraised his son as he walked over to the bar. "You could have put on a decent pair of pants and a jacket."

Ransom let the remark pass.

"Want a drink?"

"No thanks. Out of practice."

In the dining room they sat among Caucasians in bright colors and Japanese men in dark blue suits. "I hear the tempura chef is first-rate," Victor Ransom said, putting the menu aside.

After they had ordered, Ransom said, "You haven't talked to Marilyn yet, have you?"

"I called her hotel this morning and they said she'd moved out. I thought you'd know where she is."

"Promise me you won't give her a hard time."

"I don't even know if I'll see her."

"I want you to make a point of giving her a hand."

"Did she spill the beans, or what?"

Seeing every reason not to tell the truth, Ransom said, "I found her passport in her purse one day when I was getting her a cigarette. She didn't have much choice but to tell me what was going on."

Ransom's father nodded. "She's a nice girl," he said. "I was hoping you two would hit it off." The waiter arrived with a tray of sashimi. "What *are* your plans, Chris?"

"I'm not sure."

"Come home."

"I'll think about it. What about you?"

"I have to be in Tokyo for a few days. Maybe you could come out and join me."

"Maybe." Until now flight had not occurred to Ransom as an option, and for a moment he let himself pretend to consider it.

"Are you feeling okay? You seem out of it."

"I'm fine," Ransom said, as two trays of tempura arrived at the table, piled high with shrimp whose shells had been replaced with spiny crusts of batter.

After lunch, they stood in the lobby and awkwardly traded information, Ransom's father repeating his itinerary and Ransom giving him the phone numbers at the coffee shop and at Miles's house. Finally, they shook hands.

"Think hard about the long term," his father said, clasping Ransom's hand firmly.

"I will," Ransom answered.

· · ·

After lunch Ransom made a sweep of the major hotels, asking unsuccessfully after Marilyn. The city air was dense and smoggy. Late in the afternoon he took a bath, and from the bath he wandered into a nearby covered market, wondering why he felt so restless and finally realizing that what he was missing was karate, which had structured his life for the past two years. The market was a chaos of sensations and individual missions of procurement. He paused at a fish stand, where ocean creatures reclined on shaved ice: green shrimp, hoary oysters, a bonito with a woeful eye. At a fruit stand he admired a rack of perfect strawberries, then bought an apple. Women with babies on their backs and baskets under their arms shouted questions at the shopkeepers. Ransom admired the confidence with which they proceeded, and thought how good it would be to belong in this simple procession, to be the man for whom the broad-cheeked woman in the blue scarf was buying food, whom she would sleep with that night, moan for, quietly, so as not to wake the baby or the neighbors. He watched her point toward a sea bass and felt a surge of tender, erotic emotion. Looking up, she met his eyes and registered alarm at the interest of his gaze. She nervously completed her transaction and hurried away. Ransom observed her retreat and walked back toward his bike, which Udo had finally repaired, realizing along the way that, for the moment, he had nothing to do and no place to go.

With a black eye and stitches in one cheek, Miles answered the door wearing an apron that said *Prime Texas Ribs* and pictured a ribcage across the chest. "Welcome to the Ryder nursery and grill."

"How are you?"

"Great."

"Akiko?"

"She's good. She's real good. So's the kid. Of course, who wouldn't be with a faceful of warm nipple? Those were the days. Did I tell you he weighed in at eight-and-a-half pounds? I freaked when they first told me it was three something, but then I realized they were talking kilos."

Ransom handed him a bottle of Australian champagne with a blue bow. "It was either this or Rumanian."

"Baby-san will never know the difference."

Ransom left his shoes among the collection of boots in the entryway and followed Ryder inside to the kitchen. "Does the kid have a name yet?"

"We're working on it." Miles picked up a bowl in which three steaks were marinating. "Consider the short happy life of a Kobe beef cow. They feed you beer and massage you every day to keep the fat from bunching up."

"You haven't named the young master?"

"Well, Miles junior has a certain ring to it, but it just won't play in old Nippon. It doesn't seem fair to give the kid a name nobody could pronounce. Which raises the question, do we stay here for the rest of our lives, or what? This fatherhood number is no cinch. It makes you think."

"So you might repatriate?"

"Thinking about it. You hear about Mojo Domo? They've got an offer to go to Chicago to work on some documentary about the blues. Hit the rice cooker, will you?"

Ransom flipped the switch on the appliance while Miles broke apart a head of lettuce.

"Akiko's parents came to the hospital, all smiles. Big breakthrough in East-West relations."

Ransom heard the shuffling of slippers in the next room, and Akiko appeared in the doorway with the baby in her arms. Ransom approached carefully, feeling awkward and bulky in the presence of mother and child. Akiko smiled and looked down at the round face within the blankets; she bounced the bundle gently in her arms and the baby made a faint birdlike noise. Akiko turned her back to Ransom, allowing him to see the tiny face. For a moment the dark eyes seemed to focus on Ransom's, registering this new presence, then were lost in a blur of light, shape and color.

"Would you like to hold him," Akiko asked.

"I don't know."

"It's not hard, Christopher."

Ransom put out his arms to take the baby. It was heavier than he expected, and from this new vantage point he could see the mist of auburn hair on the baby's head and smell its milky breath. The skin of his hands looked incredibly worn and wrinkled beside the baby's face. He gingerly returned him to Akiko, who said she would take him upstairs.

"What do you think?" Miles said.

"Good-looking kid," Ransom said, uncertainly.

"You liar. You think he looks like every other baby you've seen."

"I haven't seen too many. What do you think?"

"I think he's a good-looking kid."

They went out to the garden, where Ryder filled a hi-bachi with wood chips. "Mesquite," he said. "I shipped in twenty pounds." He spit into the fish pond, and several orange-and-yellow carp came up to investigate.

"I've never even heard you joke about going back before," Ransom said.

"Time for a change, maybe. Akiko's always wanted to go to the States, and opening a business over there will be like falling off a log after what I had to go through to set up here. I'd have a nice piece of capital if I sold out my interests." Ryder stirred the fire and put the grill in place. "I'm sorry about all that at the hospital the other day. You were right, what you said."

"I already forgot it."

"Say hi to Marilyn for me if you see her. Tell her my news." His tone was casual, vaguely solicitous.

"If I see her," Ransom said. He had thought about telling Miles about DeVito's phone call, and about who Marilyn really was, but he didn't see what that would accomplish. He certainly didn't want to disrupt this new family scene, nor would he allow DeVito to. For a couple of months he had kept Marilyn's bogus dilemma a secret from Ryder and now there were better reasons for withholding the truth.

The three of them ate supper together in the tatami room off the kitchen. Decorated with Remington repro-ductions and mounted steer horns, this was the room in which Ransom had slept during his first months in Japan. They listened to Hank Williams, Akiko frequently slipping upstairs to check on the baby while Miles and Ransom debated names. Ransom was distracted, but Miles didn't

seem to notice. At eleven o'clock Ransom said it was time
he pushed off.

"I think I'll stop in at Buffalo Rome," he added. "Any
messages?

"Tell my minions to salt the food and water the drinks."

"Business as usual."

"Right."

Ransom kissed Akiko, shook Ryder's hand, and said
goodnight. As he was putting on his shoes in the entryway,
Miles said, "Let me know when you're ready for boots."

Ransom stopped by Marilyn's club, where he learned that
she was off for the next two nights. He wasn't really sure
what he would have said to her, anyway. Presumably she
was safe enough unless he chose not to fight.

At the bar Ransom ordered a beer and told the bartender
he was expecting a call. A new narc had taken up the post
near the door, the old one having blown his cover on
DeVito. Mojo Domo was playing and he was glad for the
music—blues falling down like hail, songs of exile from
love, home, self—and relieved that for a moment he didn't
have to talk to anyone.

Ten minutes after he arrived, the phone rang at the bar.
The bartender told him he could take it in the back office.
Ransom went back, closing the door behind him, and picked
up the receiver. "Yeah?"

"Are you ready to deal?"

"I'm ready." Ransom held the receiver and stared at the
map of Texas on the wall.

"The stakes are higher now," DeVito said. "You insisted on escalating hostilities."

"How did I do that?"

"By turning up your nose. By pretending I wasn't worthy of your attention. You could have gotten it over with a long—"

"Spare me your attempts to reason, will you?" Ransom said, but DeVito wanted to finish his speech.

"—a long time ago. But I had to convince you, which took a certain amount of time and effort on my part, Ransom. And you owe me for that. Which brings up the question of weapons."

"Weapons?"

"Swords."

Ransom had vaguely expected something like this, although he hadn't thought DeVito would spell it out in advance. "I don't have a sword," Ransom said.

"I can provide one."

He could refuse; it was up to him, not DeVito. Marilyn should turn up by tomorrow, somehow, and he wouldn't have to fight. They could both leave Kyoto. As the alternatives to fighting DeVito with swords flashed plausibly across his mind he found himself unconvinced, or perhaps just uninterested. He tried to imagine himself on a plane to the States. "All right," he said.

"Sunrise tomorrow. The top of Mt. Hiei, in front of the main temple."

Showdown at sunrise. Ransom wondered which movie DeVito was living out. All of them, maybe. But this, Ransom thought, was his own movie now.

"I don't think so," he said. "I'll meet you on the west bank of the river. The wide stretch halfway between the Kitaoji and Imadegawa bridges."

Ransom waited for a response.

"Are you backing out on me?" DeVito said finally.

"I'm just telling you where I'll be."

"You'll be at the temple, Ransom."

"I'll be at the river at sunrise," Ransom said and hung up.

Ransom returned to the bar, the buzz of conversation and laughter rising and fading rhythmically, even as he was in the midst of it. He saw Kano sitting alone at the bar and walked over. Kano put out his palm, and Ransom gave him five.

"What's happening," Kano said.

"Nothing much."

"You feeling okay? You look weird, man."

"I'm fine, really," Ransom answered. "I hear you're going to Chicago."

Kano took a seat and nodded gravely. "Maybe."

"Not definite?"

Kano shrugged. "I don't know if I want to go."

"You're kidding, right?"

"It's difficult to explain. You want a drink?"

"Sure," Ransom said. "Whatever you're having."

Kano ordered two bourbons. As Ransom waited for him to speak, he wondered how he should feel, wondered why he felt fine. He felt free to devote his attention to Kano or to anything that he liked.

He and Kano lifted glasses in unison, tapping them lightly. Kano drank and lowered his glass, his face registering the

attempt to gather his thoughts. "For ten years I play blues.
I listen to records, I make an image in my head. The place
where the music comes from, for me maybe it's like the
place that black folks sing about, the place they can't go
back to. It's a place in my head. I don't know if I want to
go there." Kano shook a cigarette from his pack and lit it
up. "You think I'm crazy?"

"You may be very smart."

"Everyone thinks I'm crazy, man."

"Don't worry about that," Ransom said.

"You know what I mean," Kano asked hopefully.

"I think so."

When Kano returned to the stage, Ransom thought about
the morning. In a few hours he would meet DeVito, something he had decided to do not for DeVito's reasons but
for reasons of his own. He was very much awake, but he
would go home to lie down for a few hours, getting up in
time to wash and dress and walk down to the river. He
left his unfinished drink on the bar and waved to Kano on
his way out.

30

The sun had just dropped behind the mountains into Afghanistan. Ransom had no idea how long the Pathan had been gone. The bazaar was closing down. Ransom was sitting at a table in front of a tea shop. The old man who had served him came out of the shop to look at him, then went slowly back inside.

Someone was addressing him. At first Ransom didn't hear what was being said. The man who was speaking had bushy hair tied back in a ponytail and wore a gold ring through his left nostril. He was waving his hand in front of Ransom's face.

"Hey, man. Do you read me? Anybody home in there?" He unstrapped his backpack and took a seat across from Ransom. He put his finger to his ear and said "Bang!" then patted his shirtpockets. "Got a smoke?"

Ransom shook his head.

"Got a voice? Speak to me, man. I'm going crazy. Five fucking hours at the border. They tear my pack down. They strip me. Check my asshole. Under my toenails. Behind my ears. But I'm clean. Jesus, I'd kill for a toke right now. Swallowed my last half gram on the bus. Once that hit I thought the Khyber Pass was going to swallow me. What a place. Journey into Hades. So tell me. What's the scene here? These dudes toting guns, they got a war going on or what?"

Ransom saw the Pathan approaching. He stopped a few yards short of the tea shop, took a pistol from his holster and pointed it at Ransom, whose companion stopped talking. He followed Ransom's gaze and when he saw the Pathan he dropped to the ground and rolled under the table.

The Pathan said, "We had an agreement." His voice was strange.

Ransom nodded.

"Perhaps you think to make a joke."

Ransom opened his mouth to speak, but he could not catch his breath. The pistol followed the back-and-forth motion of his head.

"My offer was more than generous," the Pathan said.

"Where is Annette?" Ransom said, although he was not sure if his voice could be heard.

"Where? Do not worry about where. She is just where you left her." The Pathan stepped forward and examined Ransom's face. "You do not know, then?" He shook his head in apparent disgust. Then he spit on the ground between them. Stepping forward, he went through Ransom's pockets with one hand. He found the envelope and put it in the sleeve of his shirt. Then he left.

The man with the ponytail crawled out from under the table. Ransom looked at the ring through his nose. He wondered if it had hurt when the ring was put in.

"Jesus Christ," the man said. "That was close, man. Somebody could've got killed."

It was almost dark. Ransom looked up at the huge gray sky. He could see the first faint stars. He could feel the planet turning and moving through space. He could feel the tug of gravity in his arms and legs, and he could hear the roar of darkness sweeping toward him like a fist.

31

The alarm was unnecessary; DeVito was awake when it went off at a quarter to four. Sunrise was 5:09. Last night, after talking to Ransom, he had laid out the weapons and a kimono and then lay down, allowing himself to float just beneath the surface of consciousness, half dreaming of battle.

DeVito filled a basin with cold water and washed his entire body. Then he prepared a bowl, shaved his face and his forehead up to the point where the hair of the topknot started, and the top of his head on both sides of the inch-wide stripe beneath the topknot. When he was finished he brushed out his hair and tied the topknot in place. He put on a pair of sweats and jogged once around the temple compound to get his blood moving. The air was dense and saturated. The rainy season would set in any day. Back in the house he filled a blender with a pint of orange juice, a pint of milk, three bananas and three eggs.

He took up his katana in its polished lacquer scabbard, the weapon made by the great swordsmith Yasukuni of the Soshu Branch of the Sagami School. From sitting position, holding the scabbard in his right hand, he drew the sword in a single continuous motion. Last night he had polished it. Along the graceful curve of the temper line, the cutting edge showed the wavy pattern of its layers; the ancient swordsmith pounded the steel into sword shape, folded it in half and hammered it out again, doubling each time the layers of steel: four, eight, sixteen, thirty-two, sixty-four . . . the method of the Sagami swordsmiths calling for fifteen folds, which gave the finished blade more than thirty-two thousand layers, each a molecule or two thick. DeVito had worked it out, many times, on a calculator, amazed in the face of this simple mathematical progression.

He could have handed Ransom the sword he had picked up in Okinawa, the prewar, mass-produced item turned out for flunky officers of the Imperial Army to carry into the jungles of the South Pacific. But he wanted a fight, not a fix. He had stolen another sword from the temple's cache, a seventeenth-century weapon nearly as good as his own. For their purposes, the technology was about equal. Although DeVito was confident of the outcome, he'd been briefly rattled when Ransom switched the location and hung up the phone. He had felt his authority diminished. But it didn't make a damn bit of difference, he told himself, where Ransom wanted to buy the farm. In two weeks DeVito could finally join the kendo dojo, but this way he could give himself the most important lesson first.

At four-fifteen he changed from his sweats into the kimono, put both swords in a big fishing-rod case and set out.

When he reached the Kitaoji Bridge, light was beginning to show over the ridge of the eastern mountains. He left his motorcycle in a bicycle-park area and walked down along the deserted riverbank, the rod case slung over his shoulder by the strap. When he was halfway between the two bridges he sat down on the ground to wait. As the sky grew brighter he began to be certain that Ransom wouldn't show.

DeVito did not hear Ransom until he was standing directly behind him.

"Either you're a very trusting soul," Ransom said, "or very unobservant."

DeVito leapt to his feet. Ransom was in his white karate gi. "Are you ready to fight?"

Ransom didn't answer. He turned and looked over his shoulder at the eastern mountains. DeVito looked too, thinking that it was stupid of Ransom to expose himself; as they watched, a yellow glow seemed to spread among the thick clouds spilling over the ridge.

"Do you have a weapon for me?" Ransom said, turning back to face DeVito.

DeVito unslung the rod case and unscrewed the cap, removing the two katana. Cautiously, watching for sudden moves, he extended one sword. Ransom took it, examined the hilt and scabbard, and then unlaced the ties that fastened the guard to the scabbard. DeVito stepped back as he partially unsheathed the blade.

"It's a good sword," DeVito said.

Ransom looked again to the east. "I don't think we're going to see the sun today, but I believe it's dawn."

"I'm ready when you are." DeVito took another step back, and slid the scabbard of the Sagami sword into the obi fastening his kimono.

Ransom unfastened his obi and retied it, then drew his sword and threw the scabbard into the river. DeVito set the balls of his feet in the sand and drew his sword in a smooth arc which Ransom leaped back to avoid. DeVito held his sword aloft, two-handed, above his right shoulder; Ransom raised his to a similar position. He parried DeVito's first cut and slashed low. The two blades rang like chimes, each with its distinct tone, as DeVito blocked and threw aside Ransom's blade. Ransom was open for a moment but he managed to raise his blade in time to stop DeVito's just short of his neck. They stood face to face, so close that DeVito could see the pores on Ransom's nose, and for a moment the assurance of Ransom's gaze robbed DeVito of his own.

Ransom pushed off from DeVito's blade. He thrust low. DeVito slashed, deflecting Ransom's blade into the sand at his feet. Ransom raised his sword just in time to parry the following slash. He threw DeVito's blade back and came in from the side, cutting the sleeve of DeVito's kimono and slicing the flesh over his ribcage. DeVito gasped— the wound seeming to burn deeper into him even after he had slipped away from the blade, burning with all the heat that had gone into the forging of the steel. Ransom paused, his sword in the air showing blood.

DeVito inhaled deeply and tried to suck all the pain into his lungs. He let out a yell and attacked. As Ransom's blade met his own, DeVito kicked him in the gut, and when he doubled over DeVito drew his arms back and struck with what the sixteenth-century master, Miyamoto Musashi, called the Flowing Water Cut. The blade entered diagonally between neck and shoulder, severing Ransom's spine.

Standing over the body, DeVito watched the blood spilling from the open neck onto the white sand of the flood plain. So this is what it's like, he thought, as the rain began to fall and the rainy season commenced.

ABOUT THE AUTHOR

Jay McInerney is the author of two novels, *Bright Lights, Big City* and *Ransom*. His work has appeared in such publications as *Esquire, The New York Times, The Paris Review, Granta, Vanity Fair, Playboy, Vogue* and *The New Republic*. He lives in upstate New York with his wife, Merry.